HEAVEN GOT A GHETTO 2

Renta

Lock Down Publications and Ca$h
Presents
HEAVEN GOT A GHETTO 2
A Novel by *Renta*

Renta

Lock Down Publications
P.O. Box 944
Stockbridge, Ga 30281

Visit our website @
www.lockdownpublications.com

Lock Down Publications
Like our page on Facebook: Lock Down Publications @
www.facebook.com/lockdownpublications.ldp

Cover design and layout by: **Dynasty Cover Me**
Book interior design by: **Shawn Walker**
Edited by: **Nuel Uyi**

Stay Connected with Us!

Text **LOCKDOWN** to 22828 to stay up-to-date with new releases, sneak peaks, contests and more…
Thank you.

Submission Guideline.

Submit the first three chapters of your completed manuscript to ldpsubmissions@gmail.com, subject line: Your book's title. The manuscript must be in a .doc file and sent as an attachment. Document should be in Times New Roman, double spaced and in size 12 font. Also, provide your synopsis and full contact information. If sending multiple submissions, they must each be in a separate email.

Have a story but no way to send it electronically? You can still submit to LDP/Ca$h Presents. Send in the first three chapters, written or typed, of your completed manuscript to:

LDP: Submissions Dept
P.O. Box 944
Stockbridge, Ga 30281

DO NOT send original manuscript. Must be a duplicate.

Provide your synopsis and a cover letter containing your full contact information.

Thanks for considering LDP and Ca$h Presents.

Note from Author

NOTICE- (*This book does not start where part one ended! At the time of creating this, my mental had become an animal, so I allowed it to run wild.! Vibe with me!*)

Peace, world. Please listen, fam, the way in which I inscribed Heaven Got A Ghetto 2, is (*not)* a mockery of Christianity nor God! I respect both !I'm merely being creative and doing something (*different)*. I respect the legacy of Jesus and *(all the messengers)* of the ages. I salute (*all)* Gods ,whomever you may praise. This is merely urban *(literature)* at its finest! LOL! Besides, name one other urban author that's taking you (*beyond)* the slums like this? I love yall! All my readers, and my intent is *(never)* to offend, but to create and entertain, me and my earth enjoy the art of doing something new, and please believe this lady critiques my work in depth! Laughs, and fusses as she changes (*what she wants to!)* LOL! So, here it is, family, y'all tell me what you think. We're open for it all! If you're not too familiar with the books of Job or the Gospel of Jesus in the bible, you may not understand my vibe, but fuck with me, I'm applying pressure! We're gonna hurt 'em with this one! LOL! Pressure season! If you haven't read any of my other works, check me out, fam, I'm the Jeweler! Son of a Dopefiend 1-2, Heaven Got a Ghetto, Who shot Ya 1-3 and Ski Mask Money 1-2. I'm up and do it for the culture! Carla Thomas, Talisha Z Mallory, Shirley McQueen, Shaquanna Bibbings, and all y'all who fucks with my work. Leave reviews, and rate me! Listen, (*my heart is y'alls, fam!)*I'm fighting for my life with this shit…17 years tight behind these bricks and I'm…Almost….there! Don't bend, stay on all ten! B.I.T.S Lifestyle! Wud up Cash! (*You know!)*LDP, we're up! If you need a bit of advice? Just wanna chop game? Speaking of choppin game, look fam, y'all bear with me and my wife, Red. The units giving us a little resistance about a few things with B.I.T.S, but as soon as we're on deck properly, we're gonna bless the ones that's thuggin with us. On ME! Red gonna keep it a kilo tho, so if it's something that's not too exotic, hit the spot. Wud up Heidi Kalous in Florida! Y'Quan

Holloman and David Porter in the Carolinas! We up! Appreciate the love, respect and support. To all those that hit the box, it's all love.

You can reach me at:
Delarenta Ridge #1304586 (*J-pay me!*)
Or
B.I.T.S
P.O. Box 2387
Baytown, TX 77521

Dedication

Dear Mama...*(Eddie Ruth-Black-Ridge August 21,1968-February 15,2002)*
It's been twenty years since your life was stolen from me and, mama, I *(still)* can't feel my heart. For sooo long I was fucked up...Lost! You're Black Diamond, Moose...You weren't supposed to go so soon! It hurts, baby, raw pain! Yet, hey...I never forgot your lessons, the love you gave me even while the rain fell upon us! I remember it all, mama. I love you, baby. Desmond and Jasmine are grown now, and though I haven't heard from them in almost twenty years...I still remember, mama. It's just hard to see forgotten love. Today is the 15th of February 2022 , exactly 20 years since I kissed your cheek for the last time...Nothing's the same, Queen, *(but)* even as my tears splash against this paper, I can still feel your arms around me. Nothing compares to what I lost in you, but maybe that's the greatest lesson you've ever given me. The Law of Appreciation! Appreciating what I can never get back. I love you, and wanna let you know that though it may be too late to tell....I appreciate you, Lady, there will never be another (Black: with the???? Shiiish! *Wink!)*

Renta

CHOPPIN GAME *(Ghetto)*

I hail from the middle of nowhere, a small piece of "somewhere" that was stolen from the Indians. I was bred upon this land, where my people were brought to against their will, and now it's the land we rob, steal, and kill for. It's the ghetto, where boulevards are named after activists like Malcolm X or Martin L. King but owned by the same people that had them killed. I'm from a land where even gorillas are hunted, tigers get ate, and the snakes out lurking. And though you may not be able to slay one of these beasts with your bare hands, if your mind is sharp, you'll not only have a good meal, but also be able to show up to the playa's ball sporting one of their skins. It's the law of the jungle: You eat what you kill! A mu'fucka needs a lot of game, forty percent observation, and sixty percent of swift decision-making to survive my Nightmare on Elm Street, 'cause the darkness on these corners is scary enough to give even Freddy Krueger nightmares. It's wicked, and a no-flex zone where the demons play and a miscalculated step can lead a stranger head long into the spider's web, where the black widow is famished. This place is a jungle with few trees, a place where the Chucky doll is as real as life, but the only difference between the buddy doll and the adolescent killers I know, is the doll murdered with a knife, whereas the child soldiers from my tribe slay with guns that are taller than they are. By default, I'm a product of my environment. The struggle turned us all into Trayvon Martin, Sandra Bland, OG Puddin, Peabody, Tookie Williams, Wayne Perry, and Larry Hoover. Shid! With these two eyes I've witnessed the lion eat the zebra, the anaconda squeeze the spirit from a crocodile, and the fox outfox a predator only to make prey of the rabbit. Let's cry for each other. Family, we're bred from the street code of honor, within streets that have lost their honor. It's a game of life that loses its rules when a pistol is trained at one's thinking cap, or when a mu'fucka facing calendars while standing before a judge. They say only God can judge us. But the judge judges before banging his gavel, leaving behind a fatherless tribe and broken promise of happily- ever-afters. What you know about it? Cold nights, no love within a city gone mad. A dope fiend for a mother, but she's still a queen, just a queen with an addiction that tarnishes the shine of her crown. A queen that is faced with the responsibility of showing her sons how to become kings 'cause our fathers were stolen by the streets. The same crooked bitch that seduces us into her many bedrooms, and now me and my father have fallen in love with the same bitch. Though me and pops have never met, I'm familiar with him 'cause the streets create replicas of the sucka every day. The streets! Our mistress! A seductress that opens her legs to many, and somehow still convinces me that we're in love. She spreads her legs wide for me and allows me to penetrate her essence in every position, and I ride her every curve with passion before her climax becomes destructive. It's a black matrimony where many pledge forever. It's a game of life where jail or death is the only promise, and the next one up watches, rooting for your downfall from the bleachers. When the Bush administration was helping Noriega push work across the gulf from the 80's into the 90's, it was swept under the rug, but Meech and Hoover got sent up the river for doing them. Now every hood across the world has become part of the Juggernaut, and in the hood there's no difference between poverty and famine. Hunger pains got us living crooked. The game is cut-throat. So you gotta wear a turtleneck to hide your jugular from the cut-throats. Makes me wanna holler, and throw up both my hands, but I guess even a wolf will eat her own pups if her stomach blindfolds the love. It's the ghetto. It's where I've seen a shark eat a shark when it bled too much. I've learned that merely because a child meant no harm in reaching out to pet the crocodile, doesn't mean that the crocodile meant any harm when it eats that child! Cold reality, but it's taught me that when throwing stones, you have to make sure your arm is strong 'cause niggas out here facing football numbers for aiming for the stars but coming up short when the stone lands too close to the penitentiary. So when asked if I believe in God? Shid, I don't know! I've been calling on dude my entire life, and still ain't heard from that boy. Or have I?

***

12

God and the Devil

The sun blazed high above the Caribbean Sea, its reflection dancing over the turquoise water as waves lapped into one another. A flock of tropical birds flew overhead, their wings flapping lazily as they formed a strange shape in the sky. Without warning, one disengaged and became a colorful blur against the baby blue heaven as it dived head first toward the deep waters. With barely a splash, the coastal bird cut through the surface as gracefully as an Olympic diver. Nature was beautiful. In seconds, the bird exploded from the water and returned to the air with a wriggling fish clutched in its beak. At that very moment, the waves of the sea began to viciously toss as if the water itself was offended by the act of nature, and it was there in that very moment that God appeared in the center of the Caribbean. His skin was sun kissed, and the locks of his hair were freshly oiled. Standing on top of the turbulent water, the deity was casket-fresh. The heaven white, celine inspired three-piece suit he wore breathed life into the honey hued Canali loafers on his feet and as if the waters of the sea were afraid to offend the shoes, the waves raged around them. "Be still!" he demanded, and the water became as placid as a sheet of glass. He smiled before gazing up toward the heavens and allowing the rays of sunlight to massage his chocolate tanned face.

"That was a nice little trick you just did with the water and all, OG, but I thought you were beyond child's play?" A baritone voice disturbed his peace, and God exhaled a breath of frustration. Yet, before he could respond, the baritone voice added: "You may want to watch out." It was the warning in his visitor's tone that God noted and with a suspicious glance, he fixed his vision on dude. The creature smirked mischievously before nodding for God to look to his right, and with a flicker of his eyes, God spotted a violent surge streaking across the water heading straight for him. The sharp fin of the great white cut through the tropical water like a sharp blade through skin, and just a few feet away from its intended snack, the shark launched up out of the water. Its jaws opened wide with its razor-sharp teeth gleaming in the sunlight, and just before the beast's jaws clamped down, God's spirit overtook it. Their eyes met, and fear was born in the eyes of the predator fish. The shark twisted at the last moment and splashed into the water at a weird angle. Watching as it disappeared below the surface, God's eyes slowly lifted to take in the beast that had just twisted his vibe. The devil stood upon the now tranquil water with a crooked smile on his handsome face. His skin was ivory-white, and his eyes were pure red. He was an albino! Neat, blond dreadlocks swung from his head and rested perfectly over the wickedly shaped ram's horns that sprouted from his skull. Shirtless, the *666* tattoo that was scrawled across his abdomen was on display in wicked design. God took it all in before his eyes appreciated the pressed pair of black, tailored slacks that was a companion to the suede Ferragamo boots on the creature's feet.

"Where have you come from, Satan?" God asked. The beast chuckled as his eyes fell to the group of seven shark fins that appeared suddenly and began to encircle him in a dangerous game of *Ring Around the Rosie.*

"Aww," he said in a mock woman's voice while nodding toward the sharks. "Another trick, huh? A'ight, a'ight, pimp, I get the message! I send *one* at you and you send *seven* at me." The devil threw his head back and laughed, revealing two rows of pointed, gold-plated teeth.

After a moment, he composed himself and squatted down onto his hunches. God was watching as Satan placed a sharp finger into the water and began to stir in a slow motion. In an instant, the sun dimmed in the heavens. A strong gust of wind blew across the tropics, and the creature's hand became a blur, causing the water below their feet to whirl as waves crashed against one another. "This hurricane, they'll call *Ida*," Satan prophesied.

God's eyes narrowed. "Where have you come from, Devil?" His question became a demand as a light rain began to drizzle from the sky. A streak of lightning cut across the heavens as the wind picked up speed, causing the dreadlocks of both deity and demon to whip in the breeze. The once beautiful day took on a dreary appearance as the devil's red gaze lifted to find God's piercing observation. The demon gave a crooked smile to reveal his golden slugs.

"I've stomped the land of the earth, going to and fro, visiting and dismissing. Egypt, Italy, France, H-Town, the "A", the crooked Triple "D"." He paused with an indifferent shrug of his chiseled shoulders. "Jamaica, Trinidad and Tobago, Cuba. Say, God, have you ever fucked an island gal?" He exclaimed with an appreciative whistle. "Pussy juicy like mango, man!" He mimicked a Jamaican dialect. God's eyes became slits.

"Stop being disrespectful!" He spat through clenched teeth. The devil chuckled.

"Yea." He paused to erect himself, never taking his eyes away from the omniscient being before him. "Yea, I forgot, you're too righteous to get you some pussy, huh, OG?" The Devil smirked before cupping his hands as if he were attempting to catch the raindrops, and extending them toward his polar opposite. God's vision fell to the gesture and watched disinterestedly as a black rose sprouted from the palm of the creature's right hand. Before their eyes, the flower blossomed, raindrops falling softly upon its charcoal petals, and strangely the thorny stem of the flower began to bleed.

"Stop your silly tricks, Satan. I have a question for you!" God spat impatiently. The devil merely smirked as the rose began to melt, and just when things couldn't get any stranger, they did. The flower transformed into a hissing snake.

The oil black cobra moved back, the flaps behind its head spread wide in all its beauty as the serpent uncoiled itself, and without warning, struck at the almighty. Its jaws were opened just as wide as the shark's were only moments ago, but its curved fangs were poisonous. It made it to an inch of God's throat when—*Poof!* In midair, and with only a mere glance from the deity, it exploded, spraying the devil with a thick mist of dark blood and pieces of flesh.

"Nigga!" Satan spat before lifting his hands in the air as if he were a praiser at church. His red eyes fell to his suede footwear.

"These are five hunnid dollar shoes, fool, you *almost* pissed me off!" he declared before snapping his fingers, and in the blink of an eye, his attire changed. Glancing down at the fire-red, two-piece, Louis Vuitton suit, complete with a black silk Vuitton button down that had the first three buttons undone, the devil began brushing invisible lint from his lapels. Glancing up, he allowed his vision to appraise God's attire before sucking his teeth. "Yea, you fresh, but you ain't this freaky with it." He chuckled before wiping himself down. "Not a damn stain on me!" Smirking, he nodded, as if to say: *Wud up! What you wanted to ask me, G?"*

God's vision fell to the swirling ocean beneath their feet. It had become a vicious dance and when his eyes shifted toward the distance, he noted the storm had become exactly what the demon had predicted, *a hurricane!* The devil laughed. God frowned. The wind in the eye of the storm was still, and the gray clouds above had darkened the sky. Lightning danced across heaven's floors like a pit of giant snakes as God's vision captured the being before him. "What do you think of my servant—Ghetto? He's a righteous man that I believe can leave his past behind. He just needs a different perspective. What do you think of him?" He asked. Satan chuckled before waving his hand in a sweeping motion, and there, in the eye of the storm, a table appeared with a crystal chess set positioned in the center of it. After two chairs appeared on opposite sides of the table, the devil nodded toward the arrangement.

"I like dude. I just don't appreciate how he gives you all the credit, when it's your punk ass that let him struggle his whole life! Shid, it was *you* that fucked over him, but *I'm* the one that fucked with the homie and put food on his table!"

"You led him to murder!"

"You kill what you eat!" Satan shrugged.

"Thou shall not murder."

"Thou shall not starve either, *that* should've been somewhere up in that mu'fucka." The devil was on a roll as he counted off on his fingers.

"Thou shall not snitch! Thou shall not fuck yo' homeboy's bitch." He paused on that one and gave a thoughtful expression.

"Well, unless the bitch fine and throw that pussy at you! Shid, *then* you fuck on that slut and tell ya potna on her punk ass! Know what I'm talking 'bout?" He exclaimed before extending his fist for God to bump. The deity merely studied the gesture before the devil pulled his hand back. "Fuck you too, play boy, come on, bro, you be *acting* all stiff and shit, but *it's you* that creates bad bitches! Nigga, *I* know you be fuckin' on somethin', dick hard like Rottweiler!

Again, he mimicked the Jamaican dialect. God didn't respond.

"Hoe ass dude!" Satan spat.

"Excuse me?" God's tone was deadly.

"Huh!" The devil jumped in surprise; he didn't think he said it aloud.

"Naw, I was just saying, *Ghetto* is a hoe ass dude for—"

God raised a hand, cutting Satan's lie off. "Ghetto is a good dude, but he's just like most men. He believes that since he's had to struggle, the streets are his only option."

"Let me have him for a weekend. I bet you wouldn't have the same perspective of our boy."

"No, you'll twist his mind deeper. I believe in him, but I must help him see the truth of life. *I want* him to *live* and be fruitful. I believe this man can be my atonement and . . ." God's words trailed off as he gazed out into the storm, lost in thought.

"Man, ole sensitive ass nigga, atonement for what?" the Devil spat with a smirk on his unusually pale face. His fire-red eyes studied his long-time enemy before realization dawned on him. "Ohhh!" He jabbed a pointed finger at God. "You still regret creating the hearts and minds of men! You knew free will would bring madness to your precious earth." He spoke as if he were reading the great's mental, but paused; head tilted slightly to the left as he gave God a thoughtful appraisement. "Or did you, almighty God?" He spoke as if he were onto something. "Maybe you don't know everything that's gonna happen before it happens? Maybe that's why you be so fucked up 'bout the crookedness of the world?" He snapped his fingers as if he'd just had a eureka moment before wagging an accusing one. "Or, is all this merely a science project? Is that why you placed good and evil in one place and watched and kept record of mu'fuckas behavior? Then the good you'll keep, and the rest you send to me? Matter of fact, who the fuck came up with that bullshit ass conclusion of a lake of fire?" He chuckled. "You're really a BS dude, man. You try it all to alienate a real nigga! You make *me* evil when *you're* the one doing *the most*!" The creature laughed when God eyed him. The devil sneered. "Wish you had a heart when you and that pussy boy Michael, the arch *fuck him* angel, jumped me and kicked me and my folks out of heaven."

"Do you think Ghetto deserves to live? A second chance?" God ignored his *extras*.

Satan chuckled. "Depends."

"On?"

"On which of us he feels is the realist, because after this, he'll no doubt sell his soul to one of us, just for another go at it." The devil nodded toward the table. "Let's play for it. Winner takes all! Mind, body, and soul!" He challenged. God studied him as the rain began to fall a bit harder. Thunder rolled across the heavens like the roar of a thousand lions, as a flash of lightning illuminated both being and monster. Within that brief moment of light, God nodded his agreement, accepting the challenge. Deity and Demon took their seats, and there, as the rain poured down, God made the first move. He pushed his thirteenth pawn up to the twenty-ninth square on the board and watched as a wisp of smoke became a vision trapped inside the glass piece.

***

Ghetto

Nothingness: that's the best way to describe what I was seeing. What I felt! It was as if someone turned off all the lights and left me to roam within the triple stages of darkness. Yet, I walked, blinded but with ample time to think of my every flaw, error, and my every weakness! I walked with no destination. I walked because standing still would drive me mad. I walked because I wanted to find light

and life, but the craziest thought seems to be the most logical. The
more I walked, the more I was convinced that this darkness had no
ending. Like the hearts of men. Like the fuck boy that whacked me!
I walked and walked until—"Ghetto! Ghetto! Where are you?"
Someone called from deep within the darkness. I paused and lis-
tened. "Ghetto!"
  "What's the business, man, who are you? Where are you?" I
shot off inquisitions. "Where am I? Fuck that, just turn on some
lights in this mu'fu—" my voice trailed off when the darkness began
to slowly melt away and before my eyes, an orange sunset appeared,
falling against a pale purple horizon. I blinked in confusion before
glancing down at my tattered attire. "Fuck!" I whispered at the
sight of the sack cloth shirt and pants. When my eyes fell to my bare
feet, I noticed I was standing upon a red dirt road, and as my vision
followed it, it seemed to twist so far into the distance that it faded
into the scenery. On both sides of this was barren land. Lifeless!
Red dirt stretched as far as the eye could see, and the only other
fixture to disturb the sun-baked land was the lifeless and black skel-
etal trees. As my vision swept throughout the land, I wondered
where the hell I was. As I stood there pondering, a strange feeling
crept into my gut; a feeling I'd learned never to ignore—the feeling
of being watched! I slowly pivoted, bracing myself for an attack, but
all around was endless land. "I'm trippin, fam," I told myself.
Yet—just as I returned my attention to the road ahead, they attacked! *Squawwwk! Squawwwwk!* They screeched viciously. They
rushed me, cutting me with razor-sharp knives. I fought hard, but
there were just too many of them. "Fuck!" I growled as a blade
sliced into my face. Their screaming was deafening and scary.
Though I blocked their onslaught, my attackers bit more fero-
ciously, and cut my arms severely until they were bloody and raw.
Even after I fought the good fight, swinging with all my might; falling, rolling about in the dust, and kicking out with brute force, they
still came! Thirsty! Their blood lust was pure evil as I caught
glimpses of vicious, bloodshot eyes that held no love or pretense.
They wanted my blood! Yet—just as quick as it began, it ended. My
attackers seemed to have vanished! Simply disappearing into thin

air. *Or,* I wondered, *maybe it's merely a play?* Many thoughts flowed through my mind as I lay there; curled into the fetal position, head and face tucked into the protection of my bloody arms. I moaned in pain as I awaited death, but when seconds turned into minutes and the reaper hadn't snatched my soul, I risked a peek from between my forearms. *Squawwwwwk!* The vicious sound made me flinch, but still there was no attack. *Get to your feet, bruh, don't die on your back like a coward. Fight!* My nature spoke to my thoughts, and with encouragement, I fought to my feet. Staggering slightly, I fought for the control of my equilibrium. Blood leaked from my wounds as I glanced around. *Squawwwk!* The shrill sound caused me to dodge before my eyes shot to where it came from. A tall, withering tree jutted out of the earth at a vertical angle, giving an illusion that at any moment it would fall the rest of the way to the ground. But its trunk was strong, the roots running deep into the earth. It wasn't the aged tree that froze my blood in my veins; it was more of the swinging body that hung from one of its thick branches. From the mop of curly hair, and the tanned portion of his face that hadn't been eaten away, I placed him as Middle Eastern. The moth-eaten robe he wore was made of the same cloth material as my own attire. As the man's corpse gently swayed from the noose that held him suspended from the thick branch, a putrid odor wafted in the wind. The sickening funk of decomposition turned my stomach.

Squawwwwwk! Squawwwwwk! The irritating screech drew my vision to the six birds of prey that were perched on various branches of that strange tree. *Vultures!* They were perched on the tree and had blood dripping from their hooked beaks as they watched me. *I'd found my attackers!* "Ghetto! Ghetto!" There was that voice again. Bloody from my wounds, and eyes wild, I spun on my heels to confront the dude.

"Look, fam, what kinda games are you playing? Show yourself!" I demanded while glancing over my shoulder to ensure those heartless birds weren't trying to snake me. *Squawwk!* One perched on a low branch screeched before lowering its bald head and plunging its sharp beak into the cheek of the dead man. The rotting flesh stretched as the bird wrung it free and swallowed it.

20

"Why do the sons of men defy the father so?" the voice asked as if I hadn't just posed my own demand. The sun chose that moment to drop a little lower, and stars made their appearance in the night sky when the speaker stepped from behind the leaning tree. Turning back to the tree, I was just in time to see the birds of prey screech simultaneously before spreading their large wings in all their glory, and in formation, they took flight. My mouth was agape as I watched, eyes fixated on their talons; the sharp claws I'd earlier mistook for blades. I watched until they were merely silhouettes against the purple canvas of the sky before I allowed my vision to reclaim the man that stood about ten feet away. His hair was long, and the color of wheat. Dressed in a pure white robe and a pair of weaved sandals, there was no mistaking the man I'd seen so many portraits of. *Jesus!* I studied dude, his skin was latte brown, nothing like the white man with blue eyes Christianity depicts him as. Jesus was just as Middle Eastern as the man that hung from that tree, and for reasons unknown, he seemed lost in thought as he stared up at the swinging man. When he spoke, his voice was soft; almost sad. *"There was once two men; one deaf and the other blind. Both fellows lived on opposite sides of a vast stretch of land that they'd both tilled their entire lives. One day, as the sun beamed down upon the earth, a king and his loyal subjects appeared upon the deaf man's side of land. But lack of hearing left him oblivious until they were already upon him. Lost within the labor of tilling the earth, the deaf man jumped in surprise before regaining his composure when realizing he was in the presence of royalty. The king studied him with keen eyes before leaning to whisper something to his scribe. The secretary hurriedly inscribed his Majesty's message upon a piece of parchment before extending it to the deaf man.*

I am King Maximus, and I am a man dying inside from the dark spirit of cancer. I never found a queen to bear my seed, and so there's no heir to my vast riches. So I've taken the liberty of filling a raging river with my most valued possessions. With merely just a taste of the water of this river, it will give the sightless sight, give hearing to the deaf, and heal the lame. I've searched the kingdom for a worthy man, and in my search, I've only found two. You, of

course, and the blind man that tills the earth on the other side of this land. In two nights, you and he will set off to find this prosperous river that's flowing with treasures. The first to find it will prosper beyond their wildest imagination. I wish you luck, deaf man.
   Sincerely,
   King Maximus

   The deaf man glanced up from the parchment to capture the King's studious eyes— "And where can one find this precious river that flows so greatly with treasures, your greatness?" he inquired. Instantly, the King whispered to his scribe, and again, the secretary inscribed the man's words before extending the sheep-skinned paper to the deaf man.
   'The river flows wherever the heart leads, deaf man, so listen to yours,' it read, and so the journey of the deaf and blind man began. The deaf man was an arrogant one that got by mostly on his trickery, and figuring that beginning his search for the river of prosperity a day earlier than suggested couldn't hurt, he set out a night before the second moon.
   "The blind man is at an disadvantage anyway; he can't see! I will use my eyes to find this river and declare myself the heir to the King's treasures!" he told himself. All the while, on the other side of the expanse of land, the blind man sat humbly beneath the stars. As he listened to the earth, time ran fast, and the sun and moon exchanged places for the second time since he'd been approached by the King, and before he knew it, the appointed time had arrived. On the night of the second moon, he set off to find what he knew would already be claimed, but—
   "Maybe the deaf man will allow me merely a sip of this magical water so that my sight may be restored?" he mumbled hopefully. And so he set off with a hope in his heart." Jesus paused his tale, and with steps as silent as a cool breeze, he made his way over to me. Eye to eye, we faced off. The sun had fallen asleep and the moon sat upon its throne in the night sky. "Whom do you think found the river first, Ghetto?" Jesus asked. I shrugged indifferently.

I didn't give a damn 'bout no blind man or deaf man; I wanted to know where *my* people were! Kiest? Mo3? Lil Juicy? *My* niggas!

"Look, bruh, fuck what you're talking 'bout, is this heaven or—"

"Humor me, Ghetto, answer me and all your questions will be answered." His cutting me off was a riddle. I glowered in frustration.

"Look, homeboy, I don't have time to—"

"Nonsense!" the Nazarene declared before waving his hand in a sweeping motion.

"You have all the time in the world." His eyes fell to the perpetually long road that shined like an oily snake under the luminous glow of the moon. "All roads lead *somewhere*, Ghetto, but a road can never determine where you *should be*. Only your *choices* can decide that."

Exhaling a frustrated breath, I did what he asked—humored him!

"The deaf man found the river first," I answered. Jesus' gaze lifted to the moon before falling back down to capture the hanging man.

"But *why* do you place your faith in the deaf man?"

"Hell 'cause he can *see* where he's going, so he can navigate to his destination, and 'cause a man with no destination tends to find himself down bad; lost somewhere another mu'fucka led him to be. Besides—" I used two fingers to point toward my eyes. "If a man can't trust his own eyes, he'll never be able to lead or find success."

Jesus chuckled. "What about Stevie Wonder? Ray Charles? They are and were successful. Ghetto, that's what's wrong with most men. Think of Shaka Zulu, Napoleon Bonaparte, Genghis Khan, and every other great ruler. Yes, their eyes allowed them to see, but if they couldn't *listen*, how would they have heard or known the weaknesses and mistakes of their enemy?" Jesus jeweled me and when his eyes took me in, there was a strange scene playing within his pupils. A vision depicting the man that swung from a branch not even ten feet away from where we stood. Within the vision, the man stood before a group of elders, frowning with murder in his eyes. I watched him toss a cloth sack to the ground, and out spilled thirty silver pieces—*the cost of his treason!* Jesus blinked and the vision vanished.

"It took the blind man precisely seven hours to *feel* his way to the river of prosperity, Ghetto, and upon reaching the land in which it ran through, he paused to *listen*, and it was the sound of rushing water that led him to his find. So, yes, son, you're correct! The eyes help lead you to your destination and in many ways to success. What the eyes can't do is tell you how to think, to find what can't be seen. *See, it was with respect that the blind man had to think his way to that river bank, and falling to his knees with reverence, he cupped his hands before dipping them into the cool waters. His heart pounded against his chest as he brought his hands to his trembling lips and drank, and it was there in that instant that he obtained sight. With sight came wisdom. His mouth agape in awe, the once blind man glanced down into the miracle water. Amongst all the precious stones, wisdom, and other riches, he also discovered the bloated corpse of the deaf man!"* Jesus chuckled before allowing his vision to drift to the hanging man that seemed aglow beneath the light of the stars in the night sky. "You see, Ghetto, in his arrogance of finding the river before the blind man, all the deaf man relied on was his sight. Unbeknownst to him, the river had been hidden to protect its vast treasures from the heart of greedy men. The king knew all the while that the deaf man's heart was crooked, so he pointedly mentioned the two day wait period, *knowing* the man's confidence in *sight alone* would *blindfold* him to *thought!* The king needed those two nights so his men could clear the moss, enchantments, dirt, small stones, and cloth he'd used to conceal the part of the river he'd hidden his wealth, but the deaf man's greed led him blindly until he stumbled head long into the raging water that sucked him beneath its currents. To add insult to injury, legend has it that the blind man, upon obtaining sight, came to realize that the deaf man had the advantage the entire time. For the river of prosperity was only a mere sixty yards to the east of his home—*his own land!"* When Jesus concluded his tale, he studied me, and with a sad smile, he shrugged.

"For he who has ears, let him listen. For he who has eyes, let him be studious, and for he who has a brain, woe to him who knows not how to *think!* Maybe that's why you're here, my friend, because you saw with the eyes, but not with the mind."

"Friend?" I chuckled before allowing my eyes to drift from dude's head down to his feet, before shaking my head in disbelief. "If this is how you and God almighty treat your friends, I'd rather be your enemy. If truth be told, homeboy, I'm here 'cause I was crossed and stepped on by a snake I trusted."

Jesus' laughter was mocking as he pointed to the hanging man. "And what would lead a man to place trust within the serpent; the very creature that led the first woman to betray the first man?" His question was also mocking. "And no, my boy, you're not just here because you trusted a snake, but more because you trusted with your heart. When the heart can't *think*, it can only *feel*. You're here, Ghetto, because–" he paused to ensure he had my full attention, "a snake should never be able to strike the heel of an observant man." He seemed to spit the words before tilting his head toward the man that hung from that tree. "Judas!" He whispered the name, and it seemed to echo within my mind like a gunshot in an empty room. Glancing at the dead man as his story played out in slow motion in my mind, I was snapped out of my reverie by a sudden, strong gust of wind. My vision snapped to the Nazarene as he began to laugh, and without warning, he took me by the wrist.

"Come, Ghetto, walk with me through betrayal; to the place I was murdered by people I loved," he declared. I attempted to snatch away, and that's when shit got crazy.

***

33 A.D—Pilate

Ghetto

It took a moment for my mind to catch up with what I was see-ing. We'd somehow been transported to some kind of palace or court, and we were surrounded by a group of angry men. It was as if we'd wound up in another era, two thousand years backward! "Are you the King of Jews?" The man speaking seemed more curi-ous than accusative. He was a slightly muscular, pale-skinned man that possessed a piercing gaze that seemed soul-searching. The white tunic he wore was of Roman influence, and the off-the-shoul-der attire seemed only to add to the man's air of superiority. My vision took it all in: the massive room we stood in was majestic. Authentic marble statues of Roman gods were everywhere, and the ivory and gold decor only added flavor to the setting. My eyes found Jesus who'd somehow wound up bound at the wrists and sur-rounded by men in strange robes. Some of the robes were fashioned from rough sack cloth and others were made from fine silk, but in spite of the differences in clothing, the group of men surrounding him all shared one commonality—they all hated Jesus. "Dammit, man, I've asked you, are you the King of the Jews?" the pale-skinned man repeated. His eyes were steel gray; yet, somehow, the eyes reflected a darkness that was reserved for killers. The man in-troduced himself: "I'm Pontius Pilate, the fifth governor of the Ro-man province of Judaea, serving under Emperor Tiberius. I have the authority to free you from your accusers." There was a grum-bling from the chief priest and elders that I now understood were plotting against Jesus. Jesus' eyes bore into the ones of Pilate, stud-ying him.

"It is as you say—" His voice was sure, and seemed to outrage his accusers.

"See! This man has committed blasphemy. He not only claims to be the Christ, but also says he's able to destroy the temple of God and rebuild it in three days!" the chief priest shouted before tearing his robe. The elders and others took sharp intakes of breath at the claims.

"Blasphemy!" one declared.

"Punishable by death!" another condemned. Pilate held up a hand for silence. Slowly, order was restored. Jesus said nothing. He

merely stood there, eyes on Pilate as those suckas spat on his name.
I found it annoying because I hate bullies, but Pilate was more
stunned than anything.
"By the gods, Jew, do you not hear what they're saying of you,
man? Do you see how many testify against you?" Pilate asked in
disbelief. Jesus held his tongue, surprising the Governor.
"C'mon, fam!" I stepped forward. All eyes shot to me in
outrage, and I almost regretted speaking up. Fuck it! I thought, as
my vision bounced from Jesus to Pilate. "This cat,"I nodded to-
wards Jesus, "hasn't done shit wrong. These pussy boys just hating.
I'm Ghetto, and I've read—"
"Blasphemer!" someone screamed. "He's one of them!"
"He's a demon—he even refers to Jesus as a cat!" another
shouted in shock. Before I could react, they rushed me!

***

God and the Devil

"Give me this shit, dude!" the Devil exclaimed as he snatched
the third pawn from God's chess formation. God didn't blink, flinch,
nor show any indication of being disturbed. He merely studied the
board in silence. "You know what, my G—" the devil began with a
wicked chuckle. Leaning back in his seat until the chair was balanced on only its hind legs, the creature crossed his arms over his
chest. The storm surrounding them was ferocious and had hit the
island of Jamaica at full force. Nevertheless, in the eye of the storm
where he and God sat, it was as peaceful as an infant sleeping.

"I've always wondered what type of sick mu'fucka would send
his only begotten son to a crooked land to get whacked by a bunch
of mu'fuckas that doesn't give a damn about his sacrifice. I mean—
" he smirked before lifting his arms as if he were a referee signaling
that a field goal was good. "Look at the church! The pope is a pe-
dophile and most preachers are pimps!" Satan smiled. God frowned.
"Tell me though, God, and keep it solid with an old devil." The
creature's face wore a golden, mischievous smile. "Mary *had* to

27

have had some *fire* pussy for you to have gotten her pregnant with Jesus. I mean, be for real, family, you really a hoe ass dude!" The evil one laughed while slapping his palm against his knee. "You knew that woman was married and still put that—" he used his fingers to make quotation marks—"*Holy Spirit* up in her. Me personally, *I* think Joseph was a true sucka to have stayed with the lady after she had another nigga's baby." His mocking tone was spoken to get beneath God's skin, but the deity held tight to his divinity. Placing his knight piece on the thirty-fourth square of the chess board, his gaze finally lifted to the creature across from him. Lingering for a moment, his eyes slipped away and fell to the three pawns Satan had captured before allowing a wistful smile to touch his lips.

"You've always been a greedy creature, Satan. Even after you were given dominion in the heavens, you wanted more and more." He chuckled as the devil's red glare fell to the chess board. The man creature leaned forward and touched the queen piece; it glowed neon as it came to life, and he smirked evilly as a vision took shape.

"Naw, OG, it was never *greed* that motivated me, but worth!"

Satan paused as his red vision lifted to capture his company.

"I've always believed that a mu'fucka should get what they deserve, but you—" The devil chuckled as he lifted the piece from the board, and gazed deep into God's eyes. "You're not only a jealous God, but a controlling son of a bitch as well. Yet, *everyone* reaps what they sow, God, isn't that the way of life, G?" His laughter became manic as the vision within the glass chess piece sucked him in. "My move."

***

Agg Town, Texas—

After Ghetto's Death

"Noooo, not my chile! Somebody killed my babies, lawd have mercy!" The cry rose as the woman rocked back and forth on the front pew of the church. She was a dark-skinned, well-fed woman with eyes that poured a thousand heartaches.

The black heels and dress she wore were ideal for the occasion of paying her respects for the dead, but it was the African Violet hued, pill box hat that sat fashionably askew atop her freshly done hair that brought life to the color of death. The pink veil that attached to it hung down just below her nose, but not long enough to conceal the streaks of salty tears that raced down her dark cheeks. She blew her nose on a Kleenex as her sister sat beside her, fanning her with an obituary card.

"Let it out, sista, let it out," she encouraged, but the grieving Queen paid her no mind as she hugged herself, and rocked back and forth in her seat. From behind the netted veil, her eyes had captured YB, someone her heart detested, and as the preacher preached, YB stood over the casket of the woman he was supposed to have loved and protected. His lady, but her daughter. The church was packed that morning as the pastor spoke over the twin, snow-white caskets that were trimmed in gold, but the differences lay within size. One was fit for an adult's body, whereas the other was created for a child. Mourners began to line up to pay their respects as Reverend Davis spoke.

"Cry your tears, but cry knowing that the good lawd, I say—I say, the good lawwwd—" He sang, pausing to wipe sweat from his forehead. *"Makes no mistakes! He knew this evil would happen. He knew the time and date of the devil's hate, and it was written that these two beautiful souls would have a place in paradise!"* He shouted to the Amens of the congregation. There wasn't a dry eye in the church as the two slain were observed for the last time. As the grieving grandmother rose from her seat, she seethed, watching the man that caused her daughter's and grandson's death. YB's eyes were bloodshot from letting his pain go, and ever since his woman and son's souls had been snatched, that's all he seemed able to do: drown the pain in liquor, and allow the tears to fall. Dressed in all

black, the color matched his temper as he made his way to the smallest casket. His son, his legacy—the child lay peaceful within a cushioned box. YB ran a sleeved arm over his eyes to clear them of their salty baptism.

"Sup, lil' man," he whispered, the tears invading his vision once more.

"I know I—I fucked up, man, I–I, mannnn!" He broke as a powerful sob wrecked his body.

"Damn, homie, this shit crazy!" The voice belonged to a six foot fat man known to the streets as Fat Dawg. YB didn't respond as the man slid up beside him to view the child he loved like his own. Tears baptized the fat man's eyes as he gazed down at the little boy lying lifeless in the casket.

"I'm gonna kill every one of them RNO niggas, I swear on my son's soul!" YB's voice was low, but deadly. Fat Dawg nodded his agreement, though he didn't understand why the RNO family would start the war in the first place. They'd always had enmity between them, but not to the point of this.

"You really think RNO did this? You know I wouldn't question you, bruh, but I have to be sure," Fat Dawg treaded softly, knowing that an emotional man's actions are irrational. His eyes fell to the bulge on his man's hip, and knew homie was strapped in God's house. Being the founder of the BGM (Been Getting Money) Movement, he knew he had to be the thinker. YB's bloodshot eyes shot to him with a murderous glint dancing within his irises. Before he could respond to Fat Dawg's comment, he was interrupted by an angry voice:

"You have no business here, you had my daughter and grandbaby murdered! Get out!" The woman's tone was shrill and drew the attention of the church. YB turned to face off with the woman who stared knives into him.

"Ms. Taylor, I—I—"

Smack! The slap stung as the impact forced his words back down his throat. He glared at her while massaging his jaw.

"How dare you show your face here! It's your fault that they're—they—God, noooo!" The woman's strength betrayed her as she crumbled to her knees. "I hate you. I hate you, I—I—"

Blam! The sound of the church doors crashing in sliced her words in half. Though the room was filled with BGM affiliates, and most went for the metal on their hips, the sight of the jungle pouring into the room was a dangerous spectacle that froze them on the spot. Apes flooded the room, brandishing army artillery, every weapon either had a banana clip or were equipped with the double drums known to the streets as monkey nuts. Taking up their positions, those animals glared from the eye holes of angry apes' masks. Some wore faces of angry orangutans and others, the face of roaring gorillas, but no matter the species of ape, one could tell that each of those men had showed up on their monkey business—RNO shit!

"Oh my god!" someone shouted in fear.

"This is a funeral, we don't want any trouble," another began. It was hysteria within the place of worship. Old women cried out to God, children cried, and gangsters glared.

"Ohh, Lord!" an old man cried as he held his hands in the air as if it were a stick up. "I just lost my bowels. It's a shitty situation, don't shoot!" he cried.

"Now, brotha, this"—the preacher shouted while stabbing his finger down against the pulpit for emphasis, "is the house of the lawd! The devil ain't welcome here!" He glared with the words. At that moment, one of the shooters spun on him and aimed the business end of his banana shooter at the ordained man. The pastor's hands shot in the air in alarm. "As I walk through the valley of the shadow of death, I fear no evil, but don't kill me, brotha. Man, if this about the little some'n some'n I take from the collection plate every now and then, it wasn't much, brotha. I have a beautiful wife and she's pregnant, and I got grandkids"

"Negro, I ain't pregnant!" a woman declared. The gunman's eyes shot to the beautiful woman that wore her Sunday's best, before his vision recaptured the pastor who'd just fibbed in God's house. The man smiled meekly before cutting his eyes to his wife.

"Shut ya trap, Vern!" he demanded before his vision reverted to the gunman. "She's pregnant with the *Holy Spirit*. The Lord is good, amen?" he said with a sneaky smirk. Luckily, he noted the mischief dancing in the apes eyes and dove for cover before the burst of gunfire vomited from the barrel. The pulpit was cut to shreds as the 5.56 mm bullets knocked chunks of wood into the air and added to the fear in the atmosphere. Meanwhile, Fat Dawg stood frozen in place, hands in the air in surrender as YB clutched the butt of the tool on his waist. Yet, even as he glared murderously at the animals that had the nuts to disrespect his peoples' going away ceremony, he tamed his impulses. "Ohh, Lord, the devil is a liar!" Fay, the mother and grandmother of the deceased cried as she crawled on her knees to the casket of her grandbaby.

"See," she cried as she hefted herself to her feet and leaned over the small casket to shield the dead boy. "You've caused all this! You killed your own family!" She wailed as anguish liquefied and seeped from her eyes. "It's been enough! Enough killing, enough black-on-black killing, pleeeeeease!" She sounded tired as her tears bathed the stiff face of the child as she gazed upon him. "Please just—just leave this place, and let me bury my babies." The southern accent in her tone ran as deep as the Nile.

"You niggas for real?" YB gritted, his clutch tightening on the iron on his waist, but he knew to completely up the burna would be suicide! He and his squad would take some of the op with them, but there was just too much innocence in the church that day. Children clung to their mothers and the elderly made their peace with God. YB's eyes swept the room, tempted, but allowing resolution to set in. The shooter standing before him and Fat Dawg waved a black assault rifle that was guaranteed to snatch the souls of enough casualties to ensure the East side of Arlington Texas would run red in blood for weeks. YB exhaled a frustrated breath at the same time that the fragrance of Chanel wafted through the room. All eyes drifted to the three newcomers that stepped into the equation. Red Diamond was fashionable in a silk, skin-tight, silver slip-on dress with a pair of silver, sling back heels to compliment her pedicured feet. Her shock of fire-red hair was a devious contrast to the feminine projection, but the big .40 she clutched in her manicured hand was testament to the evil dancing in her blood red contacts. Sharp intakes of breath could be heard throughout the room as she made her way down the aisle. Nukkey and Thugga were both clad in black Brunello Cucinelli jackets and trousers, but rather than the black ostrich on Thugga's feet, Nukkey opted for a blackish green pair of lizard-skinned ankle boots.

"Of course, bruh, have you ever met an ape that ain't for real?" Nukkey chuckled before pulling the dark pair of Dolce eyewear from over his eyes. As he and Thugga made their way to the front of the church, all eyes fell to the gallon cans they each carried. YB frowned.

"Who are you niggas? I don't even know who—"

"Yea, you may not know them, but you surely know who *I* am; RNO shit, don't play, nigga." Red Diamond smirked, but her tone was deadly. YB seethed as his heated gaze swallowed her, but it was Fat Dawg that spoke.

"Wud up, Red, what's all this 'bout, fam? I thought we agreed family was off limits?" He nodded toward the two coffins. Red Diamond's snicker was cruel as her eyes swept over the casket containing the body of the woman who was to be laid to rest. Almost immediately, her bloody gaze drifted to that of the smaller casket, where the woman sporting the pillbox hat prayed over her grandson. A flicker of sympathy flashed in Red Diamond's bloodshot eyes, but just the thought of how they'd slain Ghetto; the man revered as a teacher, lover, and real nigga, strangled her heart and let the devil in.

"I ain't your fam, fat boy, and y'all made this personal when y'all touched one of ours!" she spat as her gaze crawled to capture Fat Dawg and YB. When she smiled, the two rubies on her canine teeth glistened. "That elevated us from raw beef to sworn enemies, and in war, an enemy's entire liege must be eradicated!" She hissed. Nukkey tapped her shoulder before handing her the gallon can.

"Let me and Flesh properly introduce ourselves, sis," he prompted before taking the .40 from her hand. With eyes as dark as ink, Nukkey stepped forward and without warning, extended the burner until it planted a cold kiss against YB's forehead. *Boom!* The explosion echoed as the man's head jerked backward, blood splashing from the back of his cranium before his body crumbled to the floor.

"We're here on RNO bidness, homie, one of you pussy boys spilt the blood of my fellas, and turned my squad into vampires!" He paused to gauge the shocked expression on Fat Dawg's face. Nukkey smiled evilly.

"Now we're all thirsty for blood," he whispered. And at that moment, one of the BGM goons decided to get active.

"Mane, fuck RNO, let's get—" *Bttttah!* The short burst of gunfire not only sliced through his act of defiance, but almost sliced through the man's chest and stomach. All eyes shot to him just in time to see the pistol he'd snatched off his waist slip from his grasp. With eyes wide open, his body fell crookedly and his soul escaped his body. The church exploded into pandemonium as some of the mourners dived to the floor, and others ran for the exit. The risk cost them; automatic gunfire played a dark melody that only the dead could dance to. Sharp bullets cut through those bodies so powerfully that as one of the apes let his weapon breathe, the woman he'd chosen for target practice appeared to be possessed by the holy ghost as her body convulsed in a crooked dance. Bullets penetrated her at such a rapid succession that even after her soul had separated from her body, she was still twitching. Blood sprayed as innocent people were cut down, and by the time the deed was done, the church floor ran red with stolen lives. Bodies littered the ground in a gruesome bloodbath, and the smell of gun smoke rode the air as Nukkey studied the carnage. "Now we see panic isn't the best path to tread—" He paused as his vision beheld Fat Dawg, whose hand was paused down by the bulge on his waist as if he were frozen on the thought of whether to pull his gun or not. Sensing his indecision, Nukkey chuckled.

"It's not always the most "intelligent" decision." He concluded as the smell of gasoline tainted the air. All eyes traveled to its source and the heartlessness of the unfolding scene stole gasps from its observers.

"Oh lawd, I—I think I'm hav-ing-huuuu—" a woman from the crowd cried as her hand flew to her chest in panic. Nukkey watched the lady as her body betrayed her. The heart attack was vicious as she fell to the floor, back arching in agony. Oblivious to it all, Red Diamond had just finished emptying her gas can upon and into the casket of the deceased woman that was about to be buried. Curiously, Red Diamond turned her vision to Thugga. He stood behind the older woman who knelt beside her grandchild's coffin, head bowed in prayer.

"If I shall die, good Lord, lay me down in green pastures, or lead me beside still waters. I won't fight your will, God, 'cause I know your will is best," she prayed softly as Thugga bowed his head in respect. Red Diamond's face balled up, giving him a stank look. "Flesh, we ain't here to praise no mu'fucking God. We doing the devil's dance today, nigga!" she spat before making her way over to him. "Wasn't nobody crying and praying over my baby when these weak ass niggas were filling him with lead."

"Say, Red, I swear to God that—" Fat Dawg tried to explain.

"Nigga, fuck God!" She wasn't trying to hear it. Red Diamond's glare captured the fat man as the whites of her eyes began to match the red contacts she wore. Liquid pain saturated her orbs before a diamond fell from her left eye. The tear fell, resembling a gem as it tumbled down her cheek, before splashing against the floor. "Word on the streets is, Ghetto's blood is on BGM's hands, and that's a sin that can't go unpunished!" She spoke through gritted teeth before her vision returned to Thugga. As their eyes tangoed, he overstood inflicting pain was Red Diamond's outlet. "And even if it's not true, being Ghetto's enemy, that alone is punishable by death!" she spat as she reached down and aggressively pried the can of gas from the man's hand. His eyes became suspicious slits as they drifted to the direction of the woman whose prayer didn't waiver, as Red Diamond began to drench her and the small casket in the flammable liquid.

"Diamond, you're trippin, ma, let the lady live."

"Fuck her and that dead ass boy! This shit is bigger than their pathetic little lives! They—they killed our–my–my—" She paused, unable to formulate the notion of death that had been cast into her world. "Fuck em!" She hissed, eyes daring him to refute. A moment passed with their eyes conveying lines drawn in the sand. Thugga was a killer with a heart; Red Diamond was a killer that couldn't feel hers. With a quick nod, Thugga placed his hand in the pockets of his coat and came out with a Zippo lighter and a pre-rolled Backwoods blunt. Placing the stick between his lips, he took a step back before lighting the purple filled cigar wrap. Nukkey had taken in the exchange with indifference before nodding to Fat Dawg, and turning to make his exit, but paused with a thoughtful expression on his face. Gazing out at the church, he shook his head, dismayed. Out of the many apes of the RNO faction, he was a player and had lost the taste for bloodshed, but even as he gazed out at the destruction about him, he knew that within the jungle, death was a necessary evil. *The animal knows not the consciousness of good or evil, only survival.* Exhaling, he stuffed the pistol down into the waist of his trousers

"There's a hundred bands on the table for the one who leads us to the killer. We're hungry for the mu'fucka that stood behind the trigger of that gun. You have two weeks, two weeks." He paused to hold up two fingers. "And after that, we're gonna fuck shit up in this city." His vision drifted to Fat Dawg. "Let's be gentlemen, don't make us mask up again. One life isn't worth what's gonna fall upon these city streets." He nodded before making his exit. The BGM affiliates knew the message was meant for anyone of them, and most glanced at one another; the lack of trust evident within their gazes. Fat Dawg noticed it and spat on the floor in disgust. Most times, when building gangs and squads, niggas never consider the morale of who they lock in with because they're more focused on the numbers. At that moment, the fat man realized his mistake. The clicking sound could be heard just over the cries and silent prayers of the church, and drew Fat Dawg's curious eyes to Thugga. The man had struck the lighter before placing the flame to the tip of the Backwoods, the exotic aroma of purple wafting through the air as he took a deep pull from the gut. Exhaling a thick mushroom of smoke, he handed the lighter to Red Diamond. She glanced down at the still burning flame, its shadow dancing within her irises as her orbs lifted to capture the praying woman. At that moment, Thugga smiled a sinister smile. Things took on a slow motion effect as she tossed the lighter into the small casket and—*Whoosh!* Combustion! The fire was instantaneous as the flames greedily licked up the flammable fluids. Red Diamond stared in awe as the flames raced over the praying woman's body. No matter how hard the woman prayed, when the flames began to eat her flesh, pain overrode the Holy Spirit. Her screams were soul-shaking as she slapped at them in a futile attempt of extinguishing the burn.

"No! Lord, no! Noooo! Not—Not my sister, Help!" the burning woman's sister cried desperately, and within a moment of insanity, she hurriedly scrambled to her hands and knees, screaming as she attempted to reach the woman who'd been born from the same womb as her. Luckily, the man that rested on his stomach beside her intervened.

"No, sister, Jaqueline, you'll only hurt yourself!" he cried before tackling her to the floor, and as he held her close to his chest, his gaze lifted to the burning inferno just fifteen feet away from them. During the commotion, Fay had fought to her feet, she was a walking torch as the starving flames gluttonously fed on everything in its path. Fay was crazed in agony as she swatted at the flames, and within her useless fight for life, she stumbled into her daughter's casket. *Whoosh!* It went up in a blazing glory of fire, and before long, the entire front half of the church had become a crematorium. The floor-to-ceiling sized cross, with the depiction of a crucified Jesus, held Red Diamond's attention. Flames rushed up its length, pausing at the horned crown atop the savior's head. Red Diamond smirked wickedly before casting one word into the scene of destruction. "Amen," she whispered.

***

God and the Devil

The devil laughed haughtily before placing the queen's piece down on the thirty-second square of the chess board.

"Check, playboy," he declared. God's eyes fell to the piece, frowning disdainfully at the wisp of Ghetto's soul trapped inside the crystal. The devil was turnt as he jabbed a finger down against the table. "Now, *that,*" he growled before chuckling, "is how you sacrifice some shit!"

The wind around them was harsh as the violent water beneath their feet swirled in a vicious circle. Though the slanted rain poured from Heaven's floors as if God had broken his vow to never again destroy the world with water, not a drop touched either deity or demon. God's vision lifted to behold the creature he'd banished from heaven, and Satan sneered his crooked smile, revealing his gold capped teeth. "Ohh," he dragged the word mockingly, "so *you* can sacrifice as many mu'fuckas as you please, and it's deemed righteous just 'cause you're God; the big Kahuna, but it's evil when another mu'fucka does it, 'cause we're beneath you, huh? Get the fuck outta here, clown!" He spat in disbelief. Wagging a finger at God, he tsked. "See, *that's* why I can't fuck wit' you, dude, ain't you the same cat that sent your only begotten son to get whacked by his own folks? Matter of fact, Pimp—" He paused while rising from his seat. Placing his palms on the table, he leaned toward the omnipotent being across from him. "Why is your bitch ass the only one that has the authority to judge?" he spat, as he glared with a diabolical blackness clouding his eyes. And it was then that God had had enough! His eyes became deadly and with merely a stare, a powerful wind began to swirl around them. Satan's eyes widened in surprise as the wind lifted him into midair, and fighting against the unseen, he cursed God. The energy forced his arms out wide into a crucifixion's pose as his eyes revealed his fear of the unknown. Yet—unbeknownst to him; just behind his airborne form, a seven foot, weathered wood cross materialized in thin air. The cross was wickedly designed, with needle-sharp, eight-inch nails protruding from its surface. Satan's back slammed into the structure with an unearthly impact, the sharp spikes impaling him through the chest, stomach, and thighs. Before he could recover, God waved his hand with flourish. The devil's eyes grew wide in alarm as two sharp nails shot swiftly toward him "Arrrugh!" His growl shook heaven and earth as the first sharpened piece of metal drove through his left palm, nailing him to the cross. The second followed almost instantaneously, driving through his right wrist, and knocking a strong spray of blood into the air. "Mu-tha-fuck-ahhh!" he screamed before thrusting his head back in agony. Glancing up at the heavens, the rain finally rebelled against him; a thousand drops pelted his skin and soaked through the designer suit he wore. The devil began to weep, the melody of his pain creating the hissing sound of a hundred snakes as tears of black blood ran down his ivory cheeks.

"No more disrespect, Devil, I will tolerate it no longer!" God's tone balanced between control and finality. After a brief moment, his expression of resolution melted into a pitying assessment. "I am God, Satan, the designer of all things. I judge only the conclusions, while man judge out of spite." He spoke sadly before returning his attention to the chess board, and fiddling with the diamond cufflinks about his suit jacket. "I judge for my judgment is fair after granting humanity the power of free will," he whispered before lifting his eyes to the creature impaled upon the cross. "Have you not noticed that *every* religion has *a man* they praise, follow, and proclaim that *I* sent a message by?"

The devil bled as he wept; his body trembled as he cried out in pain. "Godddd!" he cried, but in an instant, his weep began to sound demonic. God watched the demon as his head lowered and his blood-red orbs settled on him with a mischief within his glare. As the rain bathed the devil, he smirked crookedly. God watched as the bloody tears that ran down the creature's face began to change course and retract back up toward his eye lids as if they were guzzling his life's sustenance. The black blood pouring from his wounds did the same and with mischief dancing in his gaze, the devil took in the deepest breath. It was as if he were sucking the powerful winds of the storm into his lungs, and his stomach bulged with effort. God's eyes were suspicious, and just as the demon's belly swelled to the size of a whale's, the devil's smile widened into a golden Joker's grin. *Splash!* He exploded into a million pieces, brain matter, black blood, exploded heart, and guts splashing the chair he'd just sat within moments earlier. God ignored the bloody mess as he glanced down at the chess set, and it was there that he found a pair of blood-red eye balls gazing up at him. One winked, and before God lost all patience, the devil materialized across from him, back in his seat, butt ass naked in all his glory. He stared, eyeless

"Oh, pardon my manners." He smirked before reaching over and scooping up his eyes. Popping them back into their sockets, the devil laughed at the perturbed expression on God's face. "Now, where were we?" he probed mockingly. God shook his head disapprovingly before his vision reclaimed the crystal chess set. Reaching down, he moved his sixteenth pawn to the twenty-fourth square and gazed down into its internal, where the wisp of Ghetto's spirit began to form a scene.

"See, Satan, what if religion becomes bigger than I? Man praises the men I've sent more than they praise me, but each of those men must return to the dust from which they came. Sacrifice, you ask?" God's tone became solemn as he gazed down into the pawn he'd just moved.

"Sacrifice can be pure or evil, just depends on what's being sacrificed and for what reason."

***

Peter, The Denier

The day was humid as a mass of people gathered out in the courtyard of the court. As the sun beamed down upon the people, a man in a flowing robe stood with a sadness in his eyes. He was so lost in thought that he never registered the dirty servant girl until she was upon him, grasping the sleeve of his robe. "Who are you? Fore I say you're one of them, you were with Jesus in Galilee, correct?" She accused with an angry expression on her bronze hued face. Peter flinched in shock before feigning innocence. "Me?" He pointed to himself. "No, I've never met the man!" he cried as others turned to assess him. His eyes were alert while taking in the mob, knowing this could go very bad for him if the truth was revealed. Fuck it, Jesus has to ride this out by himself! His thoughts were serpentine as the girl pulled on his sleeve, glaring at him suspiciously. At that moment, the girl stepped closer, and this was when Peter's gut screamed for him to tear his ass, and that he did! This mob cursed him as he fled, but he was already beyond earshot. Moments later, as he strode through the dirt paved streets, another girl approached, stepping directly in the path of the disciple and scrutinizing him suspiciously, she spoke. "I say ye are a follower of the supposed Christ!" The masses' attention was captured. "It is one of those who follows the Nazarene!" she spat with menace in her glare. Peter frowned. "Damn you all! I've told you, I've never met the man! Don't bother me again!" he spat before hurriedly making his way down the road. Head down as he strode, his frustration was paramount. "Damn, Jesus, what do we do now? Why did you lead us this far only to let us down here?" he mumbled.

"Look, it is he, one of the fellows that follows Jesus!" another girl exclaimed as she stepped closer, eyes digesting him.

"I know 'cause your speech betrays you!" she declared surely. Peter noted the dangerous gaze of the crowd and feared for his life.

"I have said it twice, and now for the third, I am not he! I know nothing of the man Jesus, you are mista—" He paused as a rooster crowed somewhere in the distance. At that moment, he recalled the foretelling of Jesus prophesying that before the rooster crowed, he'd deny him three times. He fled, weeping, fore it was then that he realized that he was a hoe-ass dude!

***

Golgotha—The Place of a Skull

Ghetto

To say I was mad would be an understatement. I was truly fucked up about how those crooked ass Pharisees and the chief priests had fed that boy Jesus to the sharks. I was twisted off of how that dick sucker Pilate had known that the man was innocent of the blasphemies they spoke of, and still, to keep order, he ordered the man's blood to be spilled. At that moment, the burning sun scorched the whole of Jerusalem as hundreds of people shoved, elbowed and cursed at one another. The whole thing was horrible as I trudged, struggling to bear my own cross. For my speaking against their lies, I was sentenced along with the Nazarene to a horrible death.

"It is the King of Jews, how mighty you are, King, I praise you!" a dinghy man in a tattered robe shouted before stepping from the crowd and hawking a thick globe of phlegm onto the man that struggled before me. Jesus was so weak from his earlier berating that he could barely turn his head to set his eyes upon his mocker, yet, even with the man in sight, Jesus' eyes were forgiving "You shall be forgiven by my father, who reigns over all." He spoke in a Hebrew dialect. The man that had just spat stood stiff, frozen in place with fear. It was something about those words that rocked dude's foundation. He and Jesus' eyes danced until one of the Roman legionnaires stepped over and cracked him over the head with the butt of his sword.

"Be gone, Jew!" he demanded as the wounded man ran, bleeding, back into the rowdy crowd of people. They lined up along the paved road as if watching a presidential motorcade, shouting curses at us as we were led to our deaths. Jesus stumbled from exhaustion, falling to a knee, and as I watched, two of the Roman soldiers accosted a man that stood in the crowd, and they demanded he bear the cross of the weakened man. I could hear the name Simon of Cyrene drift upon the wind just before the man shook his head vigorously, refusing the command. He was slapped viciously, and just as the second soldier unsheathe his sword; malice dancing within his glare, the man known as Simon relented. His frustration was evident as he eyed Jesus. Nevertheless, after a few words were exchanged between he and the condemned man, Simon the Cyre-

nian hoisted the heavy cross upon his shoulder. "Move on," the soldier beside me demanded. I glared at him, dreads wild on my head
as I contemplated spitting in his ugly face, but when his hand drifted
down to the handle of his sword, I was reminded how defenseless I
was. I walked, as the riotous crowd shouted.

"Hail the King of the Jews!" someone declared.

"Save yourself, son of God, hey!" another cheered. My eyes
found a bronze-skinned woman pointing an accusing finger towards
us.

"If he is who he say he is, why can't he save himself?" she
mocked before spitting at the ground.

"Punk bitch!" I hissed through clenched teeth. When I glanced
about, I noticed we were exiting the red dirt-baked walls of Jerusalem and I knew we'd soon arrive at the place known as Calvary—
Golgotha—the place of a skull! For some reason, the closer we got,
the slower I dragged my feet. Damn! I wasn't feeling walking to my
own death, but the more I considered trying my luck, the more I
realized that I'd never been fortunate enough in life to have any at
all. Up ahead I could hear a tortured scream that caused me to
pause, sweat ran down my face as I stared straight ahead. The le-
gionary beside me chuckled menacingly, drawing my attention to
him. The rotten tooth smile he gave me confirmed my suspicions
even before his words did.

"They always cry like pigs led to the slaughter when the nails
are driven into their palms, eh?" Dude's indifference to death made
me wonder if I'd ever been that heartless. "Move on, we're not too
far away now, and we'll see if you will scream as well." He chuckled before pushing me.

"Move, now!"

"Fuck you!" I spat, struggling to balance the heavy cross and
to keep my footing, while praying for God to save Jesus. I wanted
to tell them that even though I'd learned that God is real, dude is
just as heartless as any other ruler that realizes that it's too much
evil in the world to give a fuck about every transgression beneath
the sun. I wanted to tell them God so loved the world that he not
only destroyed this mu'fucka, but now the nigga has sent his only

begotten son to be betrayed just to fulfill a prophecy! Shaking my head, I was beginning to think the bible is a mu'fuckin' lie! I think people 'assume that since God created the world, he has to know everything that's gonna happen before it happens, but I beg to differ. If the bible is used as a reference, then in the scripture of Genesis 6:7 God proves that he hadn't expected shit to spin the way it did when he spoke of being sorry he created life. A mu'fucka can't be sorry or fucked up 'bout what they already expected to happen!

"Nooo, Yeshua, it's not true," a woman wept behind us. The group of women were heavily robed as they mourned, and though a great multitude of people followed, it was the small group that Jesus paused his execution for. He turned to face the women and gave a gentle smile before speaking the heart of a condemned man, "Daughters of Jerusalem, do not weep for me, but weep for yourselves and for your children. For indeed the days are coming in which they will say blessed are the barren women that never bore, and the breast which never nursed!" When he said these things, a sudden gust of wind blew through the land, kicking up a light sheen of fried dust. My eyes roved suspiciously as he spoke. "Then they will begin to say to the mountains, fall on us! And to the hills, cover us! For if they do this to the son of man, what will they not do to his followers?"

***

Heaven

Current Time

The hospital room was dark, save for the glowing buttons and parts of the many machines Ghetto was hooked up to. Those machines were the only things retaining life in my baby's shriveling body. Since I'd learned that Ghetto had been laid up in that cold room, I hadn't left his side; save for a shower and a quick snack my girls had forced upon me, I hadn't had reason to move, think, or do anything else besides pray that he woke up. I sat in that chair beside his bed, watching him as I reflected on the conversation I'd had with the doctor, who'd been surprised Ghetto'd made it this far.

"Is there any chance he may make it, Doc? I mean—" I paused with a shrug, words failing me. The doctor's eyes told a tale all of its own, but he gave a weak smile before squeezing my shoulder in encouragement.

"Do you believe in God, Ms. Domingo?" The question rattled me and I shrugged again.

"I don't know anymore," I admitted, my eyes falling to my man.

"If there is a God, he's cruel," I whispered before my vision lifted to capture him. The man smiled ruefully.

"Cruel or not, he's the only one that can save him now. This man's chances of survival is one percent in a hundred, and I would recommend that you consider pulling the—"

"No!" My answer was fierce as I glared at him, contemplating blowing his brains out just for the suggestion. The physician paled from the intensity of my gaze. "I'll never cut off his air. Ever!" I remember declaring with a vigorous shake of my head to emphasize how deathly serious I was.

Even if I have to spend the rest of my life giving him CPR; breathing my own breath into his lungs, I'd do just that and more! I vowed just before a lone tear dropped from my left eye. I had become so lost within the memory that I didn't realize that my emotions had followed me back into the present until the roof began to leak. I glanced up with a frown on my face, staring in confusion at the *dry* ceiling, and that's when I realized it wasn't the roof leaking, but my eyes! Another tear fell, zig-zagging down my face in a warm trail as the ventilator's low hum drew my eyes to my man. I wondered if he could feel me or hear me? Did he know I was trooping for him frontline like a soldier? The vision of how weak he appeared stole a sob from me. Ghetto's dreads seemed to have grown, but his once powerful body had rotted into a small, frail thing. Unconsciously, my eyes fell to the stack of cards in my lap; *the cards of providence!* Wiping the salty water from my face, I smiled despite my heartache.

"Baby," I whispered while taking the cards into my hands and shuffling them. "You don't miss me, Ghetto? Don't you want to see and hold our love child?" I sniffled as another drizzle cascaded down my face. Flipping the first card from the deck, through blurry vision I studied the depiction: *The tale of deep searching.* The same prediction his reading had revealed since the first day we'd met. "His name is Khalief "Ghetto" Bousard, and he looks so—" I paused to compose myself, using my wrist to wipe my tears away and trying to be a big girl. "He looks so much like you, daddy, you'd be proud," I whispered as I flipped the second card. *The card of conflicting hearts.* "You know, Ghetto, men like you are so rare," I mumbled as my eyes lifted to him. "But it's merely because of your expiration date. Niggas like you, for all your gangsterisms and toughness, are so dumb where it counts the most." I talked to my baby before leaning forward and gently patting my hand against his chest, "Your heart, baby, creatures of the streets, especially men that hail from the slums, y'all have a sick addiction; a tendency to give your hearts to shit that comes with a *guarantee* of cracking it. No warranty, bae, you get no warranty when the things you give your heart to consumes you in the streets. I-I just don't understand *why* you, or any black man, would invest so much into something with such a crooked return." I wept, salt water dripping down my face like hot wax down the candle it melted from. I'd unconsciously flipped the next card, and glancing down at the image of the man staring out at the long, snaking road, I smiled. *The wandering man!* I smiled at the thought before leaning forward and resting the card on Ghetto's stomach.

"You have a journey, bae, but only you can decide the direction you should go. Every man has to be the navigator of his own journey. He must lead his tribe to fertile land that he can rule over, but, King—" I paused, eyes drifting to the ceiling as if I wanted God to count my tears. "But how, King, can a mere man rule not only *his* empire, but also the empire of the streets! An empire that can *never* be ruled by one king alone?" As the words slipped from my lips, it felt as if my tears were forming a lake in my lap. My eyes fell to the man that I'd relinquished my heart to, the man that I'd fought tooth and nail during the tug of war for my heart. "Who did this to you, baby? Who tried to body you? Just—just give me a sign of—" I paused mid-sentence. The hospital room had always been cold, but the arctic breeze that had suddenly stole through its confines was swift and threatening to steal the breath from my lungs. I crossed my arms over my chest as I frowned. Just as suddenly as it had come, it had gone. I found it *weird, but* returned my attention to Ghetto. "You have to tell me who," I began, but something froze me still. My eyes shot up, searching the darkness and that's when I noticed him—her—*somebody*, hidden in the shadows of the room. On impulse, I reached down for my purse where I usually kept my protection, but paused when I remembered I no longer lived that life. "Who are you?" I treaded lightly, not knowing if Ghetto's attempted killer had returned to finish him off. My blood turned black in my veins as I studied the intruder. I knew I'd die that night, but for him, I was a lioness. The stranger was merely a silhouette against the darkness, and by the shape, I could tell that they were small. Then it dawned on me. *How the hell did they get in here, I didn't see them enter the room and it's no way I'm slipping like that?*

"What do you want? If you're here to—"

"I warned you against the union, Jea?" Her voice was old-southerly raspy, and I knew exactly whom it belonged to. *Genevieve!* Her name echoed through my mind like a clap of thunder during a storm.

"Now look what cha done caused my boy, gal, I told ya you was de devil!" she hissed before stepping from the darkness. The gloom in the room cast strange shadows across her face, and I didn't know if it was just the way she was moving, or if my mind was playing tricks on me, but I could've sworn that woman was *floating* on air! There was something in her hands—a teddy bear.

"Wha-what? What are you talking about, lady? How-how did you get in here?" I sputtered with a confused expression on my face. Maybe it was merely the lighting of the room, but Genevieve's skin seemed to glow against the darkness—almost white. Ignoring me completely, the woman's eyes fell to her son's supine form, studying him with a tenderness that tugged at my heart. Exhaling, my vision followed hers, falling to the man that the cards told a cracked tale of. "I—I tried to warn him, I had—" My words faltered as I shook my head sadly. "I had a bad feeling that night. I tried to tell him. I—I—the cards never lie," I whispered, tears converging in my eyes again. Her eyes lifted sharply, hate radiating from her glare in waves as she studied me.

"*You* should've heeded the cards long ago, gal, I warned you that de union was cursed by de spirits, Jea, but you let de heart bring devil to ya home!" She seemed to breathe the words, her chest heaving rapidly as if she were on the verge of a panic attack. I eyed her suspiciously, taking in for the first time; the charcoal black dress she wore, before my vision fell to the doll sized teddy bear she clutched in her shaking hands. *Fuck!* I wondered as I studied it. No. Not a teddy bear, but a rag doll with wild hair. *A voodoo doll!* The revelation swam through my mind like a diver exploring the tranquil waters of the Caribbean. Though I didn't know too much about dark magic, it pissed me off that she'd even brought such darkness into an already dark moment. *What was her purpose of bringing it anyway? A ritual?* I shook my head against her words. "No, it wasn't my love that brought Ghetto here; it was people's hate that did— did—this." I fought for the right words as I nodded toward his prostrate body. Anyone with eyes could see that Ghetto hadn't flatlined completely, although there was no life in him. What prevented the plug from being pulled was only *my* love for that Gangsta, *my* need to believe that being a soldier for him was a sign of loyalty. "Love doesn't kill, Genevieve, hate does."

"Love *can* kill!" she spat, eyes returning to the man she'd raised. "Love is the greatest killer of all because it kills the soul." Her Louisiana accent was strong, the words sounding cryptic, as if she were speaking of something particular, but being evasive. I shook my head in disagreement.

"No, love *feeds* the soul, and mine feeds this man's just as his— "

"Enough, she-devil!" Genevieve spat, spittle flying from her mouth with the demand. I frowned, tempted to take it there with the old hag, but out of respect for my baby's peace, I held my tongue. The woman's laughter began low before rising to an offensive cackle. We glared at each other and within that moment, evil appeared. I blinked repeatedly to make sure my eyes weren't deceiving me. Yet—no matter how hard I tried to convince myself that what had just happened was unreal, the proof just couldn't be refuted. A small, but sharp dagger-like blade had appeared in the woman's hand, and clutching the sack-clothed doll tight, she began to carve into its chest.

"Ahh!" I exclaimed a painful breath as my hand shot to the left side of my chest. Shocked, I took a step toward the evil bitch, clamping her wrinkled fingers down around the legs of that doll, Genevieve had somehow stolen my control of walking. My eyes grew wide as she began to chant in a Latin tongue, and with each slice of that knife, my chest ached; burning deep inside. Whatever the hell she was speaking in that weird language was no doubt as dark as her heart, for at that moment, the temperature dropped in that room. The darkness seemed darker. Though barely audible, what seemed to be thousands of small voices began to speak in different languages. Some seemed to be praying, some sang praise to the darkness, and others cried tortured screams.

"I call upon the power of the dark that intertwines the serpents within the dark well. Cometh unto aid of the weakened body where de soul needs the taste of blood to revive." Genevieve hissed before piercing the doll in the stomach and slowly dragging the blade down its length, and the pain inflicted upon *me* was unbearable. I cried out, hands clutching my stomach as tears began to pour from my eyes.

"Pl-please!" I whimpered, but the woman's eyes had rolled to the back of her head, leaving only the whites of her orbs to be seen. In the darkness, the sight was demonic, and as I watched the woman make her way over to stand above Ghetto, I wondered: *How could this moment be real? Am I dreaming?* I pondered as Genevieve held the doll just above my baby's mouth before pulling the breathing mask down.

"From de well of your spirit, I offer the sacrifice of enemies' blood, the sustenance of mortal life that's sinned against thee. I ask, light bringer, what must be done to free de soul of my child, to break the chains of Hades and allow him to pass your gatekeeper; speak!" The woman seemed to beg as darker shadows formed against the blackness. My heart pounded in my chest as I tried to cry out, but my scream escaped in a whimper and a splatter of blood stained my lips. I wanted to just ball up and die, but my body was frozen in place, forcing me to watch the evil unfold. The whites of her eyes still showing, Genevieve's fingers began to tighten around the doll like the hug of an anaconda, and just as more blood poured from the corner of my mouth; to my horror, blood escaped the doll in drips as it spattered against Ghetto's lips. In seconds the dripping became a steady steam, and to my shock, Ghetto's lips parted to accept the thick liquid.

"*More blood!*"

"*More!*"

"*Kill thy enemies!*

"*Murder.*"

"*Kill the one with the tattoo.*"

"*Murder them!*" The multitude of voices spoke simultaneously. The black shadows began to take form at the same time that the machines Ghetto was hooked up to began to go haywire. If my eyes had grown any wider, they'd popped out of their sockets! *Oh my God!* I thought as Ghetto's eyes shot open and as if an invisible hand had just driven into his chest and was attempting to yank his soul free, my baby's back arched in pain. He gulped as if fighting for breath as his hands balled the sheets in a death grip. And then—

"Heaven!" The door to the room flew open. Catrina, my sister, flicked on the lights and when her eyes beheld me, she screamed at the top of her lungs. Before I could blink, the room was filled with medical personnel, but I was so weak that I just stood, eyes focused on my sister. Her hands were cupped over her mouth as if she were holding her scream in a jail cell.

"Oh my God, Honey, what happened?" the nurse that was in charge of checking Ghetto's vitals cried as she rushed over to me. She was an older black woman that I had gotten close to over the past few weeks, and when she wrestled something out of my hand, I allowed her to. "What has gotten into you, child?" she asked in disbelief as the rest of the staff rushed over to tend to Ghetto's now still form. I blinked as if snapping from a deep trance before studying the woman with a confused expression. That's when her eyes fell on the object she'd just pried from my hands. My eyes followed hers, and my mouth fell open in shock. The small blade she held glistened with blood, *my* blood!

"I—it wasn't me, it was her." I pointed to where Genevieve stood, but she had vanished! I shook my head in confusion.

"She was jus—I—I swear, she was just there!" I fought to make them understand. My voice was filled with disbelief as my eyes scanned the room, taking in all the sympathizing glances. Genevieve was gone! "Man, I swear!" I declared before my eyes shot to my sister. Her eyes studied me as if I'd lost my marbles. "Catrina?" I begged.

"Baby, we need to get you checked out, you're bleeding all over the place," Nurse Daniels proposed, drawing my attention down to my chest. Mouth agape, I stared down at my body. Blood saturated the middle of the tee shirt and sweatpants I wore, and remembering what Genevieve had done to the doll, I hurriedly pulled the shirt over my head. In nothing but sweat pants and a bra, I stared down at the long cut running down my stomach; it wasn't deep, but it bled as if it were a gorge. That's when I saw it! Just above my left breast, *Red Rum-666* had been carved into my flesh! *Murder* spelled backward along with the sign of the devil!

"Heaven," Catrina's voice was shaky and when my eyes lifted to hers, I saw the fear as her vision fell to my feet. Frowning, my eyes followed hers, and my world tilted. At my feet was the smiling voodoo doll with the same slice running down its stomach, and the words sliced across its chest. I screamed at the top of my lungs before everything went black!

***

Ghetto—33A.D

The Place of the Skull

"Seven eleven!" the brute exclaimed when the dice landed on eleven. The group of men that knelt below Jesus' cross cast lots and

gambled for the man's personal possessions as if him watching from where he hung nailed to that cross meant nothing! The brute of a man that had just won the gamble for Jesus' sandals quickly shuffled out of his own and slipped on the Nazarene's. Though in much better condition than his old pair, anyone with eyes could see that the straps of his new kicks were cutting off the circulation in his big ass feet. His eyes lifted to capture those of Jesus., with a shrug he said,. "You're not gonna need them where you're going." He laughed. That's when another man that at that moment was being nailed to his own cross for a crime I knew nothing of cried out, his agonized plea making my skin crawl. The sun had dropped low against the horizon, and the burning ball of reddish-pink fire appeared so low to the earth that one could throw a rock and hit it. I lay prostrate on top of my own cross, arms stretched out like a scarecrow and tied to the cross beam. Sweat poured from my body, and though I'd never been a quitter, I'd become one with fate. As I lay there, gazing up at the heavens, I'd never felt more alone in my life! For the first time in a long time, fear resided within me, and it made me come face to face with the differences between reality and realism. The reality was that everyone has an expiration date. Every living creature has a death date and no matter how well we tend to our bodies, or what we feed our souls, the reaper was waiting on our destined time. The realism is—immortality is merely the opposite of its definition if one breaks it down into two words—"I'm mortal". No matter how many riches, depth of fame, or type of reputation a mu'fucka has, all that shit can't fit inside the mere six feet of earth the body will be buried within! So, I wondered what the meaning of life is! I considered this as Jesus cried out in pain.

"Father! Fa-father, forgive them, for they know not what they do!" he pled. A flock of birds flew overhead as I studied the sky, wondering what kind of dude pled for the forgiveness of his killers. I turned my head so I'd be able to see him. One of the legionaries stared up at the inscription above the man's cross that read: "This is the king of the Jews". Holding a long spear with a dirty sponge-like material skewered on the end of it, the man poured sour wine

onto it. Lifting it toward Jesus' lips, he laughed when the man turned his face, refusing to partake.

"If you are the King of the Jews, save yourself, King!" he shouted in jest and mockery of his fellow people.

"What about him?" Someone shouted over the laughter. All eyes fell on me and I smirked with tears in my eyes as mine and Jesus' eyes met. "Finish him!" the speaker roared and they fell upon me. Someone splayed my fingers out wide so that my palm would be flat against the beam. I instinctively tried to ball my fist, but it was no use, someone hit me with something hard—metal. Dazed, I lay back, watching the birds disappear into the distance.

"Be still, thief!" someone demanded before—Bam! The first nail was driven into my palm with brute force, "FUUUCK!" I cried, back arching away from the beam. I gritted my teeth against the pain as blood gushed out of my hand. The pain shot through my entire body as my mind stole me away.

***

Ghetto

Reflections

I opened my eyes in confusion when I heard the voice.

"Why you leave the door open, bae?" The familiar voice trailed off. I'd somehow transported myself into Empress and Stick Talk's apartment. Fuck? I wondered as I glanced around. Empress paused in the middle of their living room, eyes moving slowly around the room in suspicion as she slipped her feet out of her heels. The tan, mini she wore showed off her thick thighs, ass on rotund. I watched the snake slip a burner from her purse before tossing it on the couch and training the gun ahead of her as she made her way toward their room. I followed, lost as to what the fuck was going on. "Baby? You okay?" she asked as she took slow steps past the point of no return. The room was dark, save for the light that spilled from the opened closet door. The scene was eerie from my view, a ghost, invisibly lurking through the home of my murderers. Empress' eyes swept

*slowly around the room; gun hand steady as she moved. "Baby?"
she whispered as she spun toward the closet with deadly intent in
her stare. Her body visibly relaxed when she found the room empty,
but I sneered with a crooked smirk when I saw the devil slip from
behind the bedroom door and slide behind his lioness as silently as
a shadow following its possessor. She froze when the barrel kissed
the back of her skull, and as elated as I was to see enmity between
the two serpents, I was clueless as to what had created it. So, I
watched, listened, and what I heard fucked my world up! Stick Talk
gripped his tool with one hand, and the neck of a bottle of V.S.O.P
in the other.*

"Stick Talk," Empress whispered cautiously.

*"Bitch, you're dead! Dead—Biiiitch!" Stick Talk growled, a
trail of salt water rushing down the left side of his face. He clenched
his teeth so tight that they could shatter from the pressure. As I studied the mask of menace his face had become, one thing was certain:
Stick Talk was as high as the big dipper! His eyes were bloodshot,
and snot was running from his nostrils from crying, I could tell that
whatever the snake bitch had done had cut as deep as a ravine. I
chuckled while shaking my head in disgust. A snake has no arms or
legs, so all it could do is bite or hug, and I've never heard of a
snake's squeeze being compassionate!*

*"Bitch, you—" He gritted before digging the steel into the back
of her dome. His jaw muscles were prominent as spittle flew from
his mouth. "I—I whacked my br-brother over you, and you—you—
" he spat before literally spitting on the floor. Wiping his mouth
with the back of his hand, he glared.*

*"You played the game raw; you fucked over me, mane, and be-
cause of my love for your bitch ass, my flesh wants my head." Stick
Talk snorted before nodding as if he'd made an unspoken decision.
"It's okay though 'cause you'll be my blood payment to the gatekeeper." He chuckled before guzzling from the bottle.*

*"Bae, what—are—you—talking about! What's wrong with
you?" Empress' eyes had already found the answer to her question,
but verbalizing it, she was merely buying time to get her ups on
dude. Her eyes never lifted from the crinkled papers that littered the*

floor of the closet. The evidence of her sins lay at her feet, the only trail that lead to who she used to be. "Are you high? Naw, it has to be the liquor." She shook her head as a serpentine smirk curved her lips. I could tell she'd realized what I had already overstood. A drunk man could be manipulated, and any man that clouded his mind with shit that could knock him off balance was merely food to a thinker.

"Stick Talk, I'm turning around, Papi, at least look me in the eyes before you do the deed," she whispered, adding some fake-ass sadness to her tone.

"Mane, you better not fall for this weak ass shit. The bitch has a gun, goofy!" I warned him, knowing he couldn't hear me. I watched with a shake of my head as Empress slowly turned to face her man, and as soon as she felt secure in her shot, the evil bitch wasted no time getting to her business. Boca! She squeezed one off but missed by inches. That slug must've shaken his stupid ass out of the drunken stupor, 'cause as soon as the bullet tore through his shirt, he stumbled back in shock but wasted no time hurling the bottle of liquor at her face. Empress dove into the closet, but not before her "scary bitch" instincts kicked in. Eyes squeezed shut, instinctively aiming the gun backward, she fired once more. Boca! Blood shot from Stick Talk's shoulder. "Ahhh, bitch!" He growled. Empress didn't want a bullet to the back of the head, so with a feral scream, she hurriedly rolled onto her back, and with the face of a mad woman, she aimed with murderous intent. Stick Talk slammed the door shut on her just as shots rang out—Boca! Boca! Boca! She squeezed off, but Stick was back in his element! He'd dove to the side just as the slugs tore through the door.

"It don't matter, fuck nigga, if she don't body your stupid ass, RNO will! You've been sentenced to death, lil' daddy, and I'm thirsty to see about you in the afterlife!" I growled. Stick Talk scrambled to his feet and stood with his back to the far wall, silent as he waited, clutching that banger as if it were the key to his heart and he didn't want anyone to have it. Sweat trickled down his face as he panted, waiting for more shots to ring out.

"Baby?" Empress whimpered. "I'm—I'm sorry, baby, I was just—just, so scared!" she cried. I chuckled as Stick Talk's eyes became slits as he listened.

"I know you're not that lame, you're a fake, sucka for love ass dude, but I taught you better than that! I know you're not gonna fall for this shit!" I spat, shaking my head at the weenie ass sucka, but his next words caused my mouth to fall open.

"Bitch, you finished, you're—you, you're a fucking man!" He growled before spitting on the floor, as if that could purge his mouth of all the times he'd locked lips with—A man! What the fuck is dude talking about? I wondered. Silence held court for a moment, but I'm assuming Stick's mind was stuck in homicide mode. He took a deep breath before exhaling a rush of profanities while spinning toward the closet, about his business. "I loved yo, fuck ass, you crossed me, fag, but you won't live to tell about it!" Boom! Boom! Boom! Boom! The .40 barked in his hands. I stared as the slugs knocked chunks from the closet door. Stick Talk wasn't in his right mind, and if the sounds of police sirens added to the equation, it would be too late for him to realize the stupidity of firing shots inside an apartment building. "FUCKKKK!" His anguished growl drew my attention just in time to see his thigh explode into a bloody mess. Confused, my eyes shot back toward the closet door and I frowned. Empress must've been tired of being target practice; the bottom of the door was being punched through by bullets.

"She's shooting from the floor, clown, aim down!" I schooled even though we resided in two different realms, but as if he could hear me, Stick Talk's aimed lowered. The scream of pain that emitted from the small confines told the tale at the same time Empress' gun stopped firing. She was hit! Stick Talk was leaking everywhere, but even a wounded lion could still be aroused by the smell of its prey's blood. He turned, putting his back to the wall.

"You—you can kill me, but it won't change the fact that we have history." Empress's voice was strained as if she were speaking through clenched teeth, and the sound of pain in her tone brought a smirk to Stick Talk's lips. He clutched the steel with his right hand and his thigh with his left.

"Fuck you, Preston. We ain't got no mu'fuckin history. I'm 'bout to erase that tonight. Either you 'bout to be stretched out on flat line, or you're gonna body me. Either both or, one of us 'bout to—"

"It don't matter, nigga!" Empress cut him off with a wicked giggle. *"If you kill me, we still go viral"* She put emphasis on the last word. *"All our texts, videos of us fucking, screenshots of my sex change, all of it! All of it is documented and ready to be posted on social media, so even if you dead me in this bitch, them RNO niggas will whack you just off principle alone. Not to mention the recording of the night your own flesh begged you for his life."* Her words made me remember the moment. Gritting my teeth, I was ready to turn my devil up, but was hurting inside because I couldn't.

"Bitch, quit lying, ain't no way," Stick Talk chuckled with a shake of his head. *"Mu'fuckas will say anything to keep breathing."*

"Oh, you think it's a game?" Empress asked before doing the unthinkable to prove her point. There was movement behind the ruined closet door before portions of her body could be seen through the holes the bullets had punched through it. When she pushed it open, it creaked before falling completely off its hinges. The punk bitch stumbled out, manicured hand clutching his-her side. I shook my head in confusion at the beauty the she-thing possessed. There's no way that could be a man, no mu'fucking way. Blood oozed from a wound; Stick Talk's poisonous ass had got him one in. Empress tossed the still-warm metal toward Stick Talk's shadow that stood off from the side of the wall he had his back to. It landed with a soft clunk. *"My phone is in my purse on the couch, log into my iCloud account and you'll find all you need to see. I sent copies to my sisters just for this occasion! What? You thought you had a dumb bitch?"* She laughed bitterly as Stick Talk's eyes fell on her discarded tool. I saw him studying with a skeptical expression; she had him in think mode! Shid, the snake hoe had me in think mode too. This was some real Jerry Springer back in the '90s, whoop-yo-ass-on-stage type shit. Stick spun away from the wall, tool aimed and ready to spit.

"Bitch, you cappin, ain't no way you recorded that shit."

"Nigga, fuck all that, the proof is on my phone, go get it!" she spat with a roll of her eyes. Indecision was written all over dude's face, but curiosity is stronger than intelligence in most people. Stick Talk smirked before reaching down to snatch up her gun, and turning to hobble to the living room. Empress exhaled before placing her back against the wall and gritting her teeth against the pain.

"Please don't let me die, Pleeeease!" she prayed. Stick Talk returned, aiming his tool with one hand, and working the phone with the other. His eyes grew big at whatever he was witnessing on the screen, and when his thumb touched something on its surface, my eyes watered. My voice, the night the sucka whacked me filled the room, then-gunshots. Even now I could feel the burn of those bullets.

"Pussy!" I gritted as Stick Talk's eyes shot up to capture Empress within his shocked gaze.

"How—wha—what the—"

"You remember that night when I was partially in the car? I was going for my other phone, remember while you and Ghetto's bitch ass had it out?" she asked as he reflected on that tonight. "I didn't know if you'd side with me or him, so—" She paused to shrug indifferently. "If things wouldn't have been the way I needed, I'd be able to shoot back from the grave!" She waved a dismissive hand towards the phone. Stick Talk's knees almost buckled as his eyes fell back to the screen.

"So," he nodded, the pain of his sins cutting deep, "it was all a lie. I D.O.A'd my dude for nothing."

"For soning you!" Empress spat, suddenly energized as she glared at him. "You did right to dirt that man, and if you would just listen to me, you can rule RNO with an iron fist!" The lady spoke passionately but was obviously blindfolded by the DNA of that RNO business. Nothing—and I mean nothing— can rule the table of RNO without the brains of the table as a whole, and the flesh of the body is birthed from a rare creed! My blows would close casket, Stick Talk, and every man like him before they bled, killed, or followed a traitor. Empress exhaled a long breath. "Even if you still spill my blood, Stick Talk, you're an outcast to your family. Behind all the

greetings and love, they suspect you! I suggest you wise up and let's do "us". We can spread the word in the streets that Ghetto's blood was spilled by the other side, BGM, them Ski Mask Cats, the North Side, KNO—anybody other than us! Then boys will never know our secret. Come on, baby, you have to trust me, we're all we got!" she pleaded.

"Bitch, you're a-a man!"

"No," Empress said. "Damn, I'm getting weak, sick. I need to get to the hospital." She paused as her eyes fell on his bloodied leg. "So do you, Papi." Empress was in her mode.

"You're a fuckin' mannnn!" Stick repeated as if to convince himself. I couldn't blame the fuck boy. The creature before him was a true yella bone that appeared all woman! Gots to be more careful! I thought. Empress rolled her eyes again before fuckin' both of our heads up. She cocked her right leg out in a sassy manner. Though on impulse, I wanted to turn my head, shid—I had to know the truth! He-she, whichever one classifies Empress, reached down and pulled her skirt up until it bunched around her waist, the champagne-colored thong she wore bulging in the crotch area! Aww, mannnn! My mind cried as I finally turned my head. That had to be dingoling, fam!

"See, bae, I'm all woman!" Empress' words struck me.

"Wha—what? I—the papers said you—"

"Yes," Empress cut his sputtering short. Curious as to why he hadn't smoked that fool yet, I snuck a peek, and—what the hell—I didn't know what to think. Empress stood, holding her thong to the side, and there was a bare vagina on display. "I may have been born a man, but I'm all woman." Her words rocked me, but not as much as the sound of police sirens fast approaching. Their eyes locked; they knew they were going to jail.

***

Golgotha—33 A.D.

"Ahhhh! Fuuuuck!" I cried when the second nail was punched into my other hand and snapped me back into the present. The pain rolled over me in waves as my back arched once more. They used ropes to lift the cross upright, and as soon as it fell into the braces that held it in place, I found myself nailed seven feet above the ground. Tears welled up in my eyes as I gazed out at the masses of people that had shown up just for this moment. Three of us were crucified as criminals. Three, the same number of days Jesus said he'd rebuild the temple within. Three of us, the number of the trinity, three—the number of the mind, heart, and spirit! A man to Jesus' right whimpered as he bled. Jesus's head hung downward, blood dripping from the places the thorned crown cut into his scalp. His blood-drenched hair hung about his face as I glared at him. Suddenly, he roared—

"Eloi, Eloi, lama, sabachthani!" I'd read the bible enough to know he'd just spoken in Aramaic, to say: My God, My God, why have you forsaken me? I was truly fucked up with dude as the hundreds of sun-burned Middle Easterners taunted us. Though the sun barely shone now, I could see.

"Save yourself, King of the Jews!" Someone laughed. "If he is the King of Israel, let him now come down from the cross and we will believe him."

"He trusted God, let God deliver him now if he will have him, for he said: I am the Son of God," another shouted before spitting at Jesus' feet. Yet, there were a few that were skeptical.

"Listen, listen, the man is calling for Elijah!" one shouted.

"Let him be, let's see if Elijah will save him," another spoke his peace, but I had to speak my own mind.

"Say, fam, I've never understood this shit!" I spat as my eyes drifted to the falling sun. "I'm not saying you're not who you say you are, but my question is, why the fuck God letting you—us—die by the hands of the unrighteous if he's so mu'fucking righteous! Furthermore, J, I don't get this. Why the fuck are you saying God has forsaken you if this is the reason he sent you here out of the gate? To be forsaken!" I spat as hot tears dripped from my eyes. Then, the other condemned sucka stuck his long ass nose in my mix.

"Do you not fear God? Seeing that you are under the same condemnation? We are indeed treated justly, for we receive the due reward of our deeds, but this man has done nothing wrong!" He scolded me before his vision shifted to Jesus. *"Lord, remember me when you come into your kingdom."* Jesus glanced at him from beneath a spider web of bloodied hair.

"Assuredly, I say to you, today you will be with me in paradise."

"First off, dusty ass dude," I spat at the cornball to the right of Jesus, *"I wasn't talking to you. I'm talking to you!"* My eyes were guns aimed at Christ. His vision connected with mine as we bled, hanging from crosses beneath a purpling sky.

"Ghetto, have you ever had anything you'd die for?"

"Yea, what that gotta do with—"

"Everything!" Jesus cut me off. *"See, people claim to have things they'd die for, and most of those things have no worth. Gangs? Money? A woman? If one told you they heard of a man that traded his life for a pair of Jordans, would you believe that, Ghetto?"*

"Shit like that happens in the streets every day."

"So people die for the things they love, am I right?"

"Yea."

"So, I must ask, Ghetto, what's so hard to believe that I, God's son, would die for my cause? A man that knows not his own destiny is merely a man living for nothing! He's merely a man living just to be a name within a greater man's story. So when I tell the world who I am, why I've come, and why I must die, why does man knock my destiny?" His words left me at a standstill, silent, as I peeped at things from his lenses.

"But I think it's more that people believe that you are a prophet more than they believe that you are the son of God," I spoke as my body began to numb. Jesus coughed a wide spray of blood as his head fell, chin to chest.

"Or, it's more of the color of the flesh that causes them to doubt? If my skin was darker, would blacks believe my claim? Wouldn't that make Caucasians unbelievers? They depict me with

61

fairer skin to fit their beliefs, and blacks give me dreadlocks to make me less like the ones that enslaved them, but we're all sons of God, Ghetto, haven't you read Genesis 6:1-2? Psalms 82:6?"

"I don't know too much about the scriptures, but can I ask you something?" I inquired. But at that moment, the sun was completely stolen from the heavens, and the earth began to shake. A loud tearing sound could be heard in the distance and people in the crowd gasped.

"The veil of the temple has torn!" someone cried in fear. My eyes shot to the man known as Jesus at the same time that a full moon winked awake; its illumination gave the man's skin a waxy pallor.

"Father, into your hands I commit my spirit," he whispered. As soon as the words slipped from his lips, he exhaled a powerful breath, casting a thick white mist into the air. I watched it snake from between his parted lips just as the strangest thing happened. I couldn't take my eyes away. I stared slack-jawed as the man's skin began to melt away from his body. It peeled away until there was nothing left but a bleeding skeleton with a crown of thorns on its skull.

"It is done," the man to the right of Jesus cried. All around us, it was pandemonium, people shouted, people ran; it was madness. Remembering the thick mist that had escaped from Jesus' mouth only moments ago, I glanced up. I was just in time to see it become absorbed by the moon. The earth quaked viciously as the moon became a deep shade of red as if someone had just filled it with blood. I cried out from the pain of the long nails in my hands, and that's when the sound of demonic laughter overrode my cry of agony. Head heavy from weakness, my chin fell to my chest just as Jesus's had only moments earlier. Death was sweetly beckoning me into its inviting arms. My eyelids were heavy; it became a struggle to keep them open, but I was a fighter. Fight! I encouraged myself, but that's when the earth could take no more and it split open at my feet. The crazed chuckling became more pronounced, drawing my attention to the split ground beneath me, and that's where I found my mocker! He stared up at me from deep within the recesses of the gorged

earth; eyes fiery red. And the beast smiled a crooked smile, reveal-
ing wickedly sharp, golden teeth that twinkled beneath the kiss of
the blood-red moon. With all my strength, I tossed my head back.
"Where you at, God? See why I don't fuck with you? Huh? Why are
you always turning your back? You ain't ever had love for the
ghetto nigga! When I need you, you're silent when you should be
talking! Talk to me, mu'fucka!" I growled until my throat was raw.
The night was evil as I hung from that cross. "Why you can't just be
a real nig—" I began, but my words died in my throat as my vision
was drawn to the moon. My mouth fell open in shock, for there—
just across the surface of that moon, it looked as if someone had
taken a very sharp knife and carved a blood-dripping message. My
breath left my lungs as the beast I now knew to be the devil laughed
demonically at my plight. Tears rolled down my face, and I knew
shit was about to get more wicked, 'cause right there, carved into
that red moon were the words:

Heaven Got a Ghetto 2
666

Renta

Chapter One

RNO Bidness

Heaven

Three Weeks Later

What's blessin', Flesh? The fruit I bare before you is "INSUR-ANCE!" Now that I think about it, creatures of the street rarely have insurance! A plan! Surely not a will! Nine times out of ten, we stomp the earth as if our footprints will forever be engraved to show who we were and the section of land we made our names upon. Unconsciously, most brothas from the slums adapt the misbelief of immortality, as if we'll thug forever! So, we leave the ones we loved with nothing, just broken memories trapped within warm tears. Shit crazy! When my curtains are closed, one of my grandest hopes is that I don't get whacked by a traitor. One I gave my love and trust to. If I have to go, I hope my blood is spilled by a righteous nigga, for a righteous 'cause, and, Flesh, if I ain't fuck with 'em while I'm here, don't let nobody stand over my casket, fronting like we were locked in. Real niggas and bitches only, Famo! Bury me a "G". No shirt, so I can show all my tattoos, and don't forget my RNO Cuban, so I can drip on them boys wherever I'm headed. Chunk an FN in my casket with two extra clips just in case I don't like where I'm going and don't forget an ounce of exotic so me and Kiest can blow our brains back while we chilling. Nigga, you know if there's really a heaven or hell, I know there's a lake of fire awaiting cats that walk, talk, and act like us! Crazy! Why do real niggas gotta fry, and blow? Just two requests—one: All my shit, the house, cars, and dogs go to my Nubian and our seed, they deserve it, Nukkey, Baby's a rida, and the little world she'll bear is bred from the DNA of RNO! Lastly, my nigga, I don't give a damn 'bout what kind of casket I'm laid down in. All I ask is, don't bury me beneath the earth where mu'fuckas can walk over a real nigga like I'm some kind of rug. Fuck naw, Flesh, like the days of old, the days of Kings and great warriors—the days of our people, I wanna be placed on a pyre and set aflame! Boss shit! When it's all over, spread my ashes over the pond in my backyard so I can be one with the place I once found peace. All in all, my nigga, know my love is pure, and I'll be waiting on our reunion. Nukkey, be sure to whack the nigga that stole my breath.

PS: Play me some M03, I don't wanna hear all that sad organ shit. I ain't goin' to see Jesus, nigga, I'm going straight for the boss of all bosses—God! Me and that boy got some straightening to get to!

A slow tear dripped down my face as I reflected on the letter I'd found outside my door after I'd returned home from Millwood, *the crazy hospital.* The letter was left anonymously, concealed within a black envelope, and had a single black rose resting on top of it. After the episode at the hospital, I'd been forced to spend two weeks in the nut house, and it took me every day to convince those people I hadn't lost my marbles. Since they were not trying to hear the truth, I took the blame and pleaded temporary insanity! The cysts were now an inkless tattoo, and I'd blamed it all on the pain of my baby's condition. These same cuts that I now wonder if were self-inflicted drove me crazy in thought!

Had I momentarily lost my mind? Naw! Hell naw! How else can a voodoo doll I've never possessed or seen just appear? A knife I'd never owned just wound up in my possession? Fuck! How'd Genevieve got into that room undetected? How'd she leave? My mind was a maze that the sound of MO3's Lyrics entered as the pastor spoke over my baby's casket. *A closed casket that was filled with ashes, but no body. Yet—me and Catrina were the only two in the know.*

From behind the white netted material of the veil that hung from the fashionable hat atop my head, my eyes swept over the hundred and fifty or so people who'd shown up to pay their respect to Ghetto. Most were RNO officials, and many I'd never laid eyes on before that morning. The casket filled with ashes was a beautiful, solid gold-painted box that was soon to become a torch. A gentle breeze blew through the crowd; its chill was a sure sign that winter was near. Gazing aimlessly as the pastor spoke his piece, my vision settled upon the Brazos River that flowed powerfully through the land. As I watched its rippling waters, I could feel a strange sensation come to life within my stomach. It was my senses. *The feeling of being watched!* The streets always were watching! I kept my vision focused on the water in the distance, never allowing my enemy to see the predator in me. I wanted them to see me as prey so that by the time they pounced, there would be no time to save themselves from their mistakes. One of those sneaky sons of bitches had attempted to dirt Ghetto, and though I'd promised him I'd lay my guns down, the taste of sweet revenge played over my taste buds. "I'm gonna get you, and when I do, it's rock-a-bye baby," I whispered as my vision changed direction and locked into the dark lenses of a pair of designer glasses.

***

Nukkey

"And ashes must return to ashes, brothas and sistas! Now, I can see that this man was loved by many, and through that love, he shall live on—"

The pastor continued to speak his bullshit about Ghetto's spirit dwelling in heaven and all that bullshit, but I tuned his dumb ass out. I mean, I *know* the dude could see from the assemblage of Gangstas that the way my dude lived wasn't ideal for the qualifications of heaven. My vision drifted to the strange platform that we'd rested my man's casket upon. The golden casket was surrounded by black and white roses and a pile of numerous, flammable items. I smiled at the thought of big bruh's last rites. Ghetto was a real nigga, and he prepared for all eventualities. *Even death!* I was truly fucked up. Heaven opted against having a final viewing; yet, somewhere deep within the recesses of my mind, I knew it was probably for the best, it would've killed me slowly to see a hole in my guy's dome—

The evidence of treachery! I knew my flesh too deeply to believe that he'd allowed a stranger that close! Executions are granted to mu'fuckas that've been tied up and, on their knees, a person that's caught sleeping on the job, or the coup de grace served on a cold platter to accept their fate from the hands of someone they'd betrayed. Ghetto was a gangsta from his dreads to the tips of his feet, hand-tied, gagged, or at gun point, he knows *we* were built to die on our knees! Never that! I shook my head at the thought, that shit wasn't in our DNA! So, as the ordained man did what he did, I stood observing the faces of the gathering, all black, designer *every thang*—I peeped the world from behind a pair of wood grain framed Prada glasses. Behind the champagne-tinted lenses, my bloodshot eyes revealed a pain my body language didn't expose. I was in pieces on the inside. Ghetto was my brother, my teacher. Though everybody dies, some people should live forever! At that moment, the sun was hidden behind the clouds, and the block of its light cast a shadow upon us just as a streak of salty eye water raced down my face. I wanted to wipe it away, but as I fixed my vision upon that golden casket, I came to a raw conclusion—*My boy was worthy of letting the world see my diamonds falling.*

"Hold ya pain for when you're alone, Flesh, our Blow's murderer is amongst us, and whomever it is, they don't deserve to see your diamonds," Thugga leaned and whispered just low enough for me to hear. I nodded before glancing at him, and when I noted the wet river that dripped from beneath his Dolce glasses, he shrugged with a guilty smirk.

"The shit sounded cool, and I think I was trying to convince more of myself than you." He chuckled sadly, his heart was cracked too. I smiled, sharing the small escape from the pain before my vision lifted towards the center of the wide circle of gatherers where a group of women stood. Heaven and other women wanted to make a statement, a loud and clear statement: *We're not the same and we're not friends!* I smiled at their attire, the soft white fashion statements were the complete opposites of our all-black mourning clothes, and for the millionth time since me and *The Squad* had shown up in that crooked city, I wondered if those beautiful women had bodied my man. I'd done some digging and found some strange intel on that small circle of ladies, and just to keep it a buck, as I studied them that morning, I just couldn't see it! Killers? The shit I'd heard of those four females was too heinous for their pretty faces. *Or was it?* I wondered as I watched Heaven kiss my god son's forehead. Again, I smiled. *Damn, Flesh, you left too early, mane, your son is a replica of you!* I mentally vibed with Ghetto as my vision drifted to Empress. She seemed not so bothered by it all, the look on her face revealing she'd rather be anywhere else but there. My eyelids dropped to slits as I watched the bitch glare down at the golden casket. *Strange!* I thought, but even with that indication of something being sour with the lady, the other thing that fed my curiosity was the walker she used to help her stand.

She's wounded? I wondered what had transpired just as Red Diamond nudged me with her elbow. My eyes diverted to find her nodding behind us. Glancing over my shoulder, I spotted the lone figure standing a short distance away with a dozen black roses, (*one of RNO's signatures, signifying a different type of love),* in his hand. Stick Talk nodded before making his way toward us *using a crutch!* "Fuck?" The word slipped from my lips as I remembered Empress' use of the walker. *Maybe they had a wreck?* My curiosity was at the stage beyond the one that killed the cat.

"What's blessings, Flesh?" he greeted once he reached us, but his tone held a tinge of meekness; skepticism even. Studying him, I recalled a portion of RNO's creed: *If man, woman, or child was solid enough to be accepted by the table, they are deserving of a fair trial before being banished from it. No man, woman, or child can be found guilty by way of assumption or hearsay of a civilian. With the thought, I turned and embraced our flesh.*

"Flesh of my flesh, what's the fruit, Blow?" We clasped hands with an RNO greeting before I pulled him into the brotherly embrace. After we'd separated, bruh extended his hand to Thugga, who studied him from behind the tint of the glasses before clasping hands and locking up in a brotherly hug; Thugga spoke low.

"You've been a stranger, Blow, you know the table's creed holds tight to that 12:30 business." His words were loaded: *Your behavior was suspect, a guilty man's actions tell the tale!* When they separated, Stick Talk turned his attention to Red Diamond who sneered at him with a stank face.

"2:21, Flesh, I've just been twisted behind our loss. It ain't a secret that me and Ghetto were as close as Siamese twins. So, me and baby just got low for a while," he said while his eyes danced with Red Diamond's, but it was clear that he was addressing the poeticized slugs Thugga had shot. Extending the purchase of black roses to the queen of our family, Stick Talk offered her a confident smile. "What's the fruits, Nubian?" His greeting was met by a blood-red glare.

"The fruits, huh?" Red spat as if the words left a vile taste in her mouth. Rolling her eyes before shaking her head sadly, Queen looked him up and down; disgust evident within her features. She allowed her vision to trail to the golden casket just as six of our shooters hefted the makeshift lift it rested upon. MO3's lyrics were aggressive but real, and when someone changed the song to the slain rapper's song titled, *'Everybody'*, Red Diamond allowed the hook to play out before she spoke *again. Everybody ain't yo friend / Everybody ain't yo potna/ Everybody ain't no real nigga, if I say I got you, I got you/ When it gets fucked up, it gets fucked up/ just hold it down and keep it solid / and when you not around, I protect your name / I won't let a nigga talk about ya / Everybody ain't yo friend.* Nodding as if the lyrics were an omen sent from Ghetto himself, Red Diamond set her reds on Stick Talk.

"*Your* fruits are rotten, dude, and spoiled fruit has never been appealing to a real bitch. I'm not built to do any faking, Stick Talk. I don't know how, so I won't even attempt to. You have the smell of the serpent on you and *I* think you had a hand in Ghetto's soul getting snatched and when it's confirmed," she paused to cup her hands before making a rocking motion, "its rock-a-bye, baby." Her words were laced with venom as we watched our brother's casket get lowered by the edge of the river bank. *Everybody ain't yo friend / Everybody ain't yo patna,* MO3 spat as we all took in sis' words. Stick Talk's shocked expression was priceless as he studied her. The black Givenchy jumpsuit accentuated her curves, but the black bandanna she had tied around the bottom half of her face gave the feminine ensemble a gangstress appeal, and added flavor to the black, *heeled* Jordan boots on her feet. Stick Talk stared at her as if he couldn't believe her realism, but typical of the young killer, the surprise didn't last long. Smirking, as their eyes wrestled, bruh switched his game to southpaw. Withdrawing his offer of the roses, he pulled a single flower from the bunch, and without taking his eyes from hers, Blow placed the black rose at her feet. "For the blood of my flesh, I'll turn my devil up, and isn't our creed never to speak such blasphemies against the table without proof? Doesn't it say that before I betray my flesh, I'll slice my own neck?" He smirked after reciting RNO's bylaws.

"Yea, Blow, that's law, but my question is—" Red Diamond paused before using the toe of her Jordan boot to ground the black petals of the flower into the earth. Smirking almost seductively, the lady fixed our estranged brother with a bloodied glare. "Why haven't you sliced *your* throat, Gangsta? Judas was a perfect example of the guilty."

"Red, you're being disrespectful," Thugga began, but Nubian buried that.

"He spoke to *me,* Thugga, so how 'bout your *friendly* ass let a real bitch be a real bitch! You spoke your piece already." She sliced the throat of his words before returning her gaze to her target. Thugga chuckled while giving Stick Talk a shrug. We both knew that Red Diamond always got her way. She was the gangsta ass little sister that we all catered to; Ghetto had written that in stone. She closed the distance between her and Stick Talk. Me and Thugga exchanged quick glances once more; we both knew how unpredictable our sister could be. She smiled at her prey before reaching down and gently wrapped her fingers around his hand; the one holding the eleven roses. Eye-fucking dude, Red Diamond brought the flowers to her nose and inhaled deeply. Stick Talk was so lost in the sauce that he never noticed her free hand move until it was too late. Stick Talk froze as he felt the barrel of the baby Glock press against his groin.

"They should bring the guillotine back for people like you, see," she began while soul-searching his eyes. "A woman knows when a man wants to fuck her, even if he never verbalizes it. Yea, you're the type of dude that can know a female belongs to your potna, and if she's a weak bitch, you'll get that pussy. Stick, you're the type of *sucka* that a female with some wet wet between her legs can lead, mislead, or simply turn you against your morals," she whispered just loud enough for us to hear. Stick Talk's' vision became murderous, and we knew he was a natural shooter. "Ya girl Empress comes off as a boss bitch, the type that knows how to use her sex to get what she wants." Red Diamond gave him a sneaky smirk.

"You gonna pull the trigger, Nubian, or keep speaking your heart? This how we share the fruits, Flesh?" Stick Talk's eyes trailed to me. The wind hugged us, blowing a bit harder. I took a step toward Red; she was speaking out of emotions.

"RD, this ain't the place."

"Who shot you in your head a few months ago, Stick Talk? Word on the wire is that Hurk used *females* to take you and Ghetto down that night. Did you know that your girl has some skeletons in her closet?"

"Shisshh," she blew through her teeth when she noticed the surprised expressions not only on me and Thugga's faces, but also Stick Talk's. The man's jaw hung loose as his eyes became unfocused.

***

Stick Talk

"Say, Flesh, I got someone I want you to meet," Hurk offered before stepping back, but that's where I tripped out! See, we all knew not to bring civilians to the bando, so when the words left his lips, I should've slammed the door in his face. Yet, hindsight is only relevant in regrets, and even regrets are useless when the past is already the past. I remembered the pink ski-masked face as the shooter attempted to stick the burna through the crack of the door. I remembered it all, up until the head shot. Red Diamond's giggle

snapped me back to the present just in time for her to lean forward and place a gentle kiss on my cheek. I wanted to slap fire from her, but she had me by the balls; literally! The devilish bitch placed her lips next to my ear and whispered: "If you didn't kill Ghetto, your bitch had a hand in it, and that makes you just as guilty! I just don't get it though, how you laid up with the same bitch that put a bullet in you?" Her words rocked me, and I pushed her away from me with all I had. Stumbling, Red Diamond barely regained her balance, and as soon as she did, I witnessed a demon staring out from within her gaze. Yet, my mind had taken me too far outta my mind to give a fuck. I could still feel the recoil of the gun blast from when I'd squeezed the trigger. I could still see the shocked expression on Ghetto's face when he spun to face me, clutching his side where the lead had knocked his blood loose. *"Nigga, fuck! What you doin', Stick?" He growled in anguish. My heart pounded in my chest, but even before I stepped on that boy and closed his curtains, my heart was already black. I was gonna kill him anyway, I was tired of being the shadow! At the time, the punk bitch Empress had made sense in saying the dude was trying to son me, so it was only a matter of time before I Alpo'd bro, but thinking back to that night was fucking with me! I remember the hurt in bro's eyes as he saw the uncertainty in my glare, but even more, I know he saw that it was something crooked inside me.*

"What the fuck is up, flesh? You—you were 'bout to do my gal?" I asked before my eyes drifted to Empress.

"Nigga, you shot me? Bruh, this hoe is the one that stuck us that night, she—"

"Don't believe him, bae, the nigga followed me out here and tried to push up on me! I told him I had a man and even asked him why he'd had you set up."

"Shut the fuck up!" I'd shouted then and unconsciously in the present. I didn't know my eyes had drifted shut with the reflection until they flew back open; wild and searching as I stumbled backward a few steps.

"What the—" Thugga mumbled as I continued to back away. Red Diamond's eyes had a twinkle in them as she smirked at me.

She knew her words were effective. *Were they deceptive? But why? Why would Empress cross not only me, but—* My mind had become a wicked spider's web as I frowned in confusion.

"Sucka ass, nigga!" Red Diamond hissed before spitting on the ground. Taking a glance at the two men that would no doubt expire me if they knew the truth, I knew that they were just as perplexed as I was. Diamond hadn't pulled their coat tails, *why?* I wondered, but I'd figure that out soon enough. At that moment I needed some mu'fuckin answers, and it was only one person who could give 'em to me. My eyes drifted beyond our small circle. I spotted Empress leaning on the walker the hospital had given her, and even from that distance, as MO3 rapped about trust and betrayal, I could feel her eyes on me.

***

Heaven

"You see this shit, girl, who are the people over there with Stick Talk? Egypt leaned toward me and whispered. Of course, I'd seen the confrontation between the RNO heads, and of course, I was just as curious as my girl as to the cause. *What could cause a circle of people that's built their name from stiff principles to go for each other's throat?* I wondered as the strangest thing happened. Stick Talk seemed to offer the red-haired girl a dozen black roses, but rather than accepting the gesture, I watched the lady lean to inhale the fragrance of the strange-colored flowers before leaning to plant a kiss on his cheek. I frowned as six eyes shot to Empress—mine, Catrina's, and Egypt's! Our girl's eyes were slits as she observed the exchange and just as I returned my eyes to the craziness, Stick Talk pushed the girl. I was so caught up in the madness that I hadn't registered the stranger to make his way to me and my girls until he was close enough to kill if that was his intention.

"It's time, Nubian, we're just waiting on you." The man couldn't be any older than seventeen, but his dark eyes reflected the troubled waters of a man twenty years his senior. My eyes fell to the golden butane lighter he held and as if he'd just remembered his reason for approaching me, dude kinda jumped in surprise before extending it to me.

"Nubian? first off, who the hell is Nu—"

"Egypt!" I cut her off with a roll of my eyes before recapturing the handsome young brotha with my gaze. Though the veil hid the searching of my eyes, I gave dude an apologetic smile before waving a flippant hand toward sis. "Never mind her. She isn't up on your family's lingo, but—" I paused as my eyes briefly fell to the lighter before reclaiming its possessor. "How about *you* do the honors?" I suggested. His expression went through stages; first, a frown, then shock, and finally—pride! It made me proud to see how much respect Ghetto held amongst his team. Most bitches are good with just being loved by a stepper, but not many knew the feeling of being loved by the Boss, and I loved it.

"*Me?* Naw, Nubian, I'm just one of the—"

"Yes, *you*, and you're just the man *I*, Ghetto's Nubian, chose to do the honors." I killed all excuses. Dude seemed to weigh my words as his vision fell to the sleeping infant I held against my bosom.

"Man, is that Flesh's lil world?" he asked with such excitement I almost felt uncomfortable, but my nod confirmed his curiosities. Playboy nodded before using the fingers of his left hand to form a capital *R* and the ones of his right to create an *O*, I'm assuming to mean *real only!*

"Like a man!" he vibed before taking my hand and touching it to his forehead.

These niggas! The thought was in remembrance of the day I learned of the meaning of the gesture. *Nukkey touched my hand to his forehead on that night me and Ghetto frequented his establishment. "Why'd you do that, the head thing, I mean?* I was curious. The look he gave Ghetto was one of shock mixed with a bit of disdain.

"Nigga, you mean to tell me you're brought a woman to the table without Jweelin her?" I remembered Nukkey's reprimand. Ghetto's chuckle was just as powerful as it was that night as he slipped my hand away from his brothers.

"Nukkey, this is Heaven, my Nubian Queen. Flesh, since you're dry talking table talk in front of her, allow me to help you." Ghetto shook his head with a smirk before jeweling me, as they say. *"Heaven, my god brother touched your hand to his forehead because it's against our laws to put our lips on another brother's lady, and so we touch the lady's hand to our head because the mind is the strongest portion of a man and the deepest thing he can give a woman."* The smile I gave was forlorn; the thought brought a flood to my eyes. *Ghetto, you have to make it back, daddy, please? Fight for us!* I cried inside my heart. Little Ghetto stirred, and I knew he'd cause hell in a moment. I watched dude turn and make his way back over to the large group of men and women surrounding the golden-hued casket. Some touched it as if it were some type of spiritual relic. Some cried, many placed personal tokens of love upon the platform holding it, and others rested blunts and black roses beside the coffin. In fact, the long-stemmed black roses were plentiful and caused me to fall into an ocean of curiosity. *What's their meaning?* I wondered as I studied the faces of each man and woman present. I looked beyond the fake tears and make-believe love. One of those snakes had committed treason; my heart was sure of it.

"You feel it too, don't you?" Egypt leaned and whispered. I kept my eyes fixated on the group but gave my sister-in- arms a morose smile before kissing the top of my son's head. Nodding, I confirmed her suspicions.

"Ghetto's killer is here *now!* Yes, I can *feel* it, sis." And as if the gods agreed, a few drops began to softly fall from heaven. Glancing up, I watched the clouds roll in. A storm was coming *in more ways than one.*

"Heaven," Egypt's tone was strange, and when my vision went to her, I frowned when I followed her gaze to the mass of people surrounding the casket. Simultaneously, all eyes drifted back to where me and my girls stood. "What the fuck," Egypt murmured as men and women—a hundred plus—in all-black attire, saluted us. Mo3 played as I smiled wickedly, knowing the dead rapper's lyrics were gospel.

Everybody ain't yo friend / Everybody ain't yo potna / Everybody ain't no real nigga, if I say I got you, I got you / When it's fucked up, it gets fucked up / just hold it down and keep it solid / and when you not around, I protect yo name / I won't let a nigga talk about you / I woulda kill for you niggas / Now I can't deal with you niggas / Talking to the grim reaper / Finna get rid of you niggas—

As he told the truth, the whole truth, so help me God, my eyes caught movement from my peripheral; he was as silent as the wind. Egypt's eyes cut to him, and her lust was instant.

"What's blessings, Nubian?" RNO Nukkey greeted me, sliding up beside me.

"It was you!" I said without taking my eyes off the crowd. "The one who left the letter and the roses?" My question was more of a statement.

"Yea, Ghetto gave it to me months ago. Everyone in the RNO familia has to submit *a death wish.* A will, for when the time comes. Feel me?" He fixed his eyes on the men and women surrounding the casket. The Prada lenses were a nice touch for his attire. "How have you been?"

"Someone *close* killed Ghetto." I ignored his question.

"Close?"

"Family."

"You sound *too* sure." His statement was a borderline accusation. My eyes shot to him. I prayed that he wouldn't allow my beauty or the fact that I was his boy's girl to lead him to tempt fate.

"Meaning?" I snapped. RNO Nukkey was a gangsta through and through; He chuckled before turning his head so that he could see me. The raindrops fell; one here, another there, like the clouds above were fighting their cries. Pulling the wood-grained specs from his face, the man tried to study my eyes from the other side of the veil.

"Meaning, I know that you're not afraid to get your hands dirty" He paused to nod toward my girls. "And neither are they; the streets talk, and now I know why it's said that beauty can kill." He smirked, nodding knowingly.

"Never heard the expression before, but *any* intelligent man should *already* know the cost of beauty. Yes, beauty can kill, but jealous niggas seem to be closer to the reaper's touch than a beautiful woman who's just given a man a child. Right?" I gave him a knowing smirk. "Jealousy, Nukkey, is more potent in men *that are close,* but feel they deserve the seat at the head of the table." My eyes told the tale. Nukkey smirked before sliding the glasses back onto his face and returning his attention to his people.

"Who is she?" I asked after following suit and spotting the red-haired woman. She and the other stranger joined the mass of people surrounding Ghetto's casket, and the crowd of people seemed to part around sista girl. *Who is this bitch? Queen Elizabeth or something?* I thought as she stood before Ghetto's casket. Even from that distance, and with her back to us, I could see the tremble in her shoulders; she was crying. I frowned, for some strange reason, a speak of dislike bloomed inside me for that woman.

"That's a she-demon, Heaven, the shit nightmares are made of."

"Is that a threat?" I spat as my eyes shot to him, that *other me* clawing its way up to peek at him. RNO Nukkey lifted his hands in surrender, smiling.

"You're *family,* Heaven, you're more protected than Uncle Joe is. You're Ghetto's rib, and the respect he demanded is inherited by you and his little world," he nodded to my son who began to whine. "It's automatic that RNO protects, provides, kills, and reps for you. Shit just ugly right now and when someone as solid as Ghetto gets touched, by default *everybody* becomes a suspect." He exhaled a breath filled with grief.

"Even you?" I said. He chuckled but nodded his confirmation.

"Even me." Waving a hand out to the redhead, he gave an introduction.

"That's Red Diamond, our sister, the Boss bitch of RBO."

"Real bitches only, right?" I recalled what they told me about the female sect of RNO. Nukkey nodded in confirmation.

"Yea, yea."

"But who is she *to Ghetto?*" I got to the point. Though he hid it well, I noticed the slight rigidness in him.

"That's a question you should only ask your dude or the woman you're inquiring about. Never"—he paused to watch Red Diamond made her way over to the dude that held the golden lighter. I slick admired her fashion as words were exchanged between her and dude. Whatever was said, Red Diamond's red gaze trailed to me. I kept it gangstress to gangstress with her as I held the stare off. *Bitch, I'll give you all the smoke!* My thoughts were on go as I willed her to see the side of me I was trying to bury. I smiled wickedly as I rocked Khalief. Though the bottom half of her face was hidden behind the black bandanna, from the glint in her red eyes, I could tell she was smiling. Waving with her fingers, the little bitch turned her attention back to the man-child, before extending her hand for the lighter. More words were exchanged and from his posture, I could tell he wasn't feeling whatever was said. His reluctance was evident, but her words must've been some type of order, because grudgingly, youngin handed over the lighter.

"Who the hell is this bitch?" Egypt spat in contempt.

"Looks like a bitch with a death wish," Catrina said. Empress spat on the ground. For some strange reason, when Red Diamond glanced back our way, her red vision settled on Empress. Enmity danced in her strange-colored eyes as she raised her hand, and used her fingers to form a mock gun—*Pow! Pow!* I imagined her whispering as she aimed at Empress and acted as if she'd pulled the trigger *two times.* Egypt took a step forward, but Nukkey stepped around me and into her path. Facing her, he gave a seductive smile before extending his hand toward her.

"Peace, Ms. Lady, I'm RNO Nukkey, and I'm asking for a reprieve for my crazed sister." He paused to nod back toward Red Diamond, who'd suddenly lost interest in us and had turned back to the casket. Egypt's orbs were dangerous as she glared down at dude's hands as if it were a vile notion, but Nukkey was a protégé of my king. The bottom row of his teeth glistened with soft pink VVS twos as he began to run his mouth. "Now what type of nigga would I be to let you self-destruct?" His question was odd, and obviously, one that rubbed my sister wrong.

"Self-destruct?" She jabbed a manicured finger toward Red Diamond.

"If you knew better you'd be more cautious with your—"

"Peace, Lady!" Nukkey cut her off, lifting his hands in a calming motion.

"I said *self*-destruct. As in, destroying *your own* vibe all in the name of a mu'fucka that doesn't respect your *peace* because they can't find all the *pieces* to their own puzzle of tranquility. So, you join their vibe and never realize that you're destroying yours until you're so deep in a mess that it's too much to just wipe up with a napkin." He spread his hands apart as if to say, *Feel me?* I could see for the first time in her twenty-seven years of living, Egypt had allowed a man to out-talk her. Though still frowning, her eyes trailed from ole girl and connected with dude's.

"Yea, well, maybe you should be preaching those philosophies to the bitch that has the problem, 'cause we—" She pointed a sassy finger toward the rest of us. "We don't do the petty, Boo Boo."

"Overstood. I'll make sure to have a talk with my sister."

"You never answered my questions," I interrupted their vibe. RNO Nukkey's eyes drifted to me with a raised brow, so I clarified. "I asked you who this lady is?"

"And I was telling you that you should *never* ask a mu'fucka you don't trust, or a person that hasn't done anything to earn your trust, a question that has the power to turn your world upside down." His answer was vague, but even more, it pissed me off.

"Fuck! What is that supposed to mean?"

"Dig, sis, what if I was a nigga that's trying to win and snatch you from ya man? See?" He shrugged. "That would be my way in *even if I lie!* I can say, yea, that's ole girl ya nigga fucking with, and even if you don't wanna believe it, it's human nature to *expect* the negative, and with a real playa, all he needs is a crack to slip through to get at whatever he wants. *Why* open those types of doors when you can just ask the main parties?" His point was punctuated with a dimpled smile.

"What are you saying, like, she can't trust you to tell the truth?" Egypt asked.

"Naw," Nukkey shook his head against the question. "But again, *why* would she trust *any* man's motive outside of *her* man's? "Who are *you* anyway, smooth talker?" I rolled my eyes at Egypt's ass. Here I was, trying to figure out why this red-haired bitch is crying over my dude's casket, and *this* girl wants to flirt. *Eye roll* with a suck of my teeth. *Bitches!*

"I'm RNO Nukkey, and—"

"RNO business!" The monstrous proclamation came was a roar, as a hundred-plus people shouted at the same time! I jumped in surprise as my eyes shot toward the mass of people that had surrounded the casket. Khalief's cry let me know that his mother wasn't the only scary person in the world.

"Here, sis, it's raining, let me take my nephew to the car," Catrina offered after making her way over to me. I smiled before kissing the top of my son's curly hair.

"Thanks, sis, I'll be there in about ten minutes," I said. Catrina was my backbone. We'd grown closer since our mother's death, and she was the only one to know my secrets. I trusted sis and knew she was all I had to place my trust in, *in those times.* I watched her walk away, making baby noises to quieten my baby before my eyes shifted back to the strange scene down by the river.

"Hey, I don't want her to be the one to—" I began, but *too late!* Red Diamond waited for the crowd to give her some space before she reached behind her head and untied the knot of the black bandanna. Pulling it free, she held it by one of its edges before using the butane lighter to begin the end of the ceremony. The flame danced beneath the bandanna for seconds before the material caught fire; the flames casting flickering shadows across her face. Time slowed as she gently tossed the burning material toward the platform and in my eyes, everything happened in slow motion. The bandanna fluttered down on the casket and the flammable liquid I'd had it soaked in was instantaneous. Flames licked over its surface as Red Diamond stepped back, watching with a deep sadness in her gaze. I frowned as something clicked inside me. *She and Ghetto had something going; something deep!* The thought seemed to reach down and grab my heart, and I honestly didn't know if it was jealousy, or the prick of betrayal that created the strange feeling I was feeling, but whichever it was didn't much matter. My trigger finger itched, and I silently prayed that I was just in my emotions. As the flames consumed the casket, and an entourage of men helped push the platform onto the water where it bobbed above the flow of water, fire fought against rain as a dark-skinned brotha; the color of a midnight sky, stepped forward. His attire was all-black designer, from the black BITS hoodie worn with the hood pulled up over his head, down to the Dior fitted jeans, and the matching black Dior kicks. My confusion was evident as RNO Nukkey turned and used his fingers to create the RNO insignia just as the young brother had done earlier. Though the sight appeared juvenile to me, when the large masses of people followed suit, the act was impressive.

"RNO business!" they shouted in unison. The dark-skinned brotha gazed out at the burning casket before he began to speak passionately.

"From ashes we came and to the dust we'll return!" He seemed to be reciting some type of rite. Pausing, dude reached down to the earth and smeared his fingertips in the moist dirt. *"The blessings, Flesh, is that we struggled as one, starved as one, and made it out of the wilderness as one! One life, one love, one death! So, what's real? Real is when a nigga stands on all ten, no matter the odds!"* He shouted as he stood, lifting his face to the heavens and allowing the drizzle to gently splash against his dark face. The wind seemed as if it had ADHD; one moment it would be a strong exhale of breath, and the next it would become a beautiful dancer, twirling around with no direction. *"Real is choosing righteousness over fuck shit, even if the numbers are against you, and it's easier to just go with the majority! Real is only what real can be! Real isn't an opinion, it's a code that can't be changed, moved, or erased! Real is never compromising you for momentary satisfaction!"* Brothaman's eyes cracked open, his face appearing dramatic beneath the gray sky. *"Open your eyes, Flesh, and you'll be able to see life in a dark room. Don't forget you, and you'll never forget me! For you*

are Flesh of my Flesh!" Thunder roared like an angry gorilla pounding its chest, as a spider web of lightning split across the heavens like a pit of fleeing snakes.

"Though you ain't blood of my blood! Through this thing of ours, I've learned that family isn't defined by DNA, it's the love and loyalty that locks us in! Table talk, though we don't discuss table talk amongst civilians! From the flesh, we were accepted and at the table, we passed the cup of our Prosperity. Sip slowly, Flesh, for death isn't the enemy, but the next phase of our journey, where Flesh is traded for soul, and we rejoice in realism. RNO shit!" He shouted at the top of his lungs, and as if to punctuate his point, a tall, muscular brotha with blond-tipped dreadlocks stepped from the crowd clutching a sexy-ass street sweeper. Aiming toward the heavens as if he were about to have a shootout with God himself, a streak of lightning cut across the dark clouds just as he yanked back on the pump. *Boom! Boom! Boom! Boom!* Each shot was offensive to the ears. The rifle was so powerful that the dread head's body jerked with each shot, and in that instant, as if the gunshots had cracked its surface, the sky opened up into an all-out downpour. The large crowd began to disperse, some running, others walking, allowing the rain to hide their tears, but I stood still, watching as the flames lost to the relentlessness of heaven's cascade. I stood there so long that before I knew it, the rain had soaked through my clothes, and the stampede of people had thinned out to just a few stranglers. Then as the sky cried and lightning flashed like a live wire dropped onto a pool of water, I spotted her. Her red hair had fallen about her head and face, and the slanted rain began to pelt us. My feet moved without me realizing it; me and this Red Diamond chick was about to get some straightening!

Renta

Chapter Two

Red Diamond

Deep Conversations

2:30 A.M.

V Live in Dallas was turnt that Friday night. The lights were dim as the LED-effected stage flickered in different colors of reds, a flash of purples, then a quick blink of yellow. The two beauties that worked it were exotic; one Latina, her body shining from the baby oil she applied, and the other was a thick redbone with some kind of tribal tattoos intricately covering only the right side of her body.

Drop, shake your ass then (Shake your ass then) / Drop, with your best friend (Best friend) / Stop, that ain't your cousin, ho / That ain't your brother, ho / Y'all be fuckin', ho—Yo Gotti and DaBaby's *Drop* single had both ladies making their asses clap as they raked it up. The stage was surrounded by D-boys who created a thunderstorm of ones and twenty dollar bills as if making it rain was the exact reason they hustled in the first place. With a seductive smirk on her face, the red bone made her way to one of the poles on the stage and slithered her sexiness up its stiffness.

"Yeah, I'm her friend-friend (I am) / I wanna fuck her again-again / Introduce me as her brother friend—" Thugga was on ten as he rapped along with Gotti's verse. He was beyond tipsy as he clutched a bottle of DOM in one hand and twelve hundred ones in the other. The RNO squad was lit for the night as they celebrated Ghetto's death day. As the red bone turned upside down on the pole, her ass cheeks bare to the crowd, she wrapped one of her long legs around the metal before erotically humping it. The crowd went stupid as she did acrobatic tricks. RNO Nukkey and RNO Klutch sat crouched low in their seats, catching a vibe on their own hype.

As Nukkey observed his surroundings, his studious vision digested it all. He and Thugga weren't from the Dallas / Ft.Worth branch of the family, so they were practically strangers to most of the extended portion of La Familia. Yet, it was overstood that they were two of the originators of the table, so even though the younger wolves were wild, they saluted the OG's. RNO Klutch was the sixth and final *head* of the table whom Ghetto and Nukkey brought in after Kiest's demise, and Tay—the first head of the table— was serving a sixty-one-year bid. These were the 360 degrees of the heads of RNO, and the body loved them all.

"I ain't got no mind! BGM in this bitch! Welcome home to my guy BGM Big Mook!" Fat Dawg shouted from across the room, and Nukkey watched as he slapped his hand against the back of a big muscled up cat that sported all blue. He wore a Sunni beard, and when Klutch's vision trailed towards them, he clenched his teeth so tight his jaws hurt.

"Pussy ass niggas!" he spat before taking his bottle of Rosé to the head.

"Welcome home, Mook!" a chorus of partygoers erupted, followed by applause, whistling, and cheers. Ass and titties stampeded to their section, knowing BGM would change the forecast. Klutch mugged. He had blood in his eyes and smoke on his mind. "Flesh, we should've *been* cooked that nigga Fat Dawg's lunch a week ago!" he spat, reminding Nukkey. Yet, Nukkey's vision settled on a thick, raven-haired diva who sashayed toward Mook. Mook, was enjoying the company of a jazzy little thang with small breasts, and skin so pale she could pass for a vampire. Lady popped her goodies on his rigidness as the jailbird turnt a bottle of Patron up to his lips. Yet, the raven-haired stripper was oblivious to all around her, all but her target! Her chinky eyes drank him as she stopped before him, cocking her right leg out in a sassy pose and allowing him a beautiful view of her stature. Her bronzed skin seemed to glow beneath the lighting of the room; her sex appeal was exotic as she placed her manicured hands on her shapely hips. When Mook pulled the bottle from his lips and his eyes captured the goddess before him, he ran the back of his hand across his lips before pausing the light-skinned chick in her dance for his bands. Her glare was fierce as she allowed the disrespectful chick before her to see what she didn't appreciate, but when Mook placed a stack of bills in her hand and slapped her on the ass, it took a bit of the sting out of being dismissed. As she passed the Hennessy-hued diva, she rolled her eyes before sucking her teeth in her pursuit to find a new sponsor. Mook's eyes were fixated on the five-foot-three Barbie before him and as his orbs digested her, she was reminiscent of a dangerous feline! She made her way over to dude, and leaning forward, she ran the tip of her wet tongue around his earlobe before whispering something in his ear. Mook was *literally* putty in her hands as she massaged his masculinity that stood strong beneath his Champion sweatpants. From across the room, RNO Nukkey smirked as Klutch digested it all. He impulsively gripped himself at the sight of mami's rear view; lady was a masterpiece.

"Damn," he mumbled. Nukkey chuckled.

"Vibe with me, Flesh, let me share a piece of fruit the Blow Ghetto once shared with me," Nukkey offered, slouching back into his seat before patting the short gap between them to indicate that his mans should do the same. RNO Klutch obliged, before taking a gulp from the Rosé bottle. Nukkey watched Mook be led off to the unknown by shorty.

"Yea, that's my nigga, Mook the Spook. Mane, do that, Baby Boy, get that jailhouse up out ya system!" Fat Dawg shouted, lusting on the roundness of the lady's backside as she led his dude off. As they passed, with Mook whispering freak shit in her ear, the goddess smiled seductively and winked at the two RNO affiliates. Klutch spat the liquor out in surprise, causing Nukkey to jump back.

"Damn, Flesh!" Nukkey laughed as his man's eyes shot to him questioningly. He shrugged nonchalantly. "What, you ain't ever seen a bad bitch before?"

***

Ghetto

"Awww man, you're doing it again!" The sound of the child's voice caused my eyes to flutter open. I felt groggy, sluggish from a slumber I couldn't even remember falling into. I blinked rapidly against the brightness of the sun's light, and once my eyes were at peace with it, they drifted to the child that sat beside me; swinging his feet back and forth as if he were antsy and anticipating my awakening.

"Dang, Fool, took you long enough!" the lil' dude exclaimed and to my surprise, I recognized him. It was the same seven-year-old boy that I'd met when I first opened my eyes to realize I'd been whacked. That time seems so long ago, but as I glanced around, I realized that I was back on the same bench, at that same strange bus stop. The strange street was empty and as my vision reclaimed the child, something dawned on me. I hurriedly lifted my hands to my face, no holes! "What the hell!" I mumbled as flashes of my experience with Jesus played upon the big screen of my mind.

"What ya doin?" Lil' dude was curious. Confused, my vision returned to him.

"Am I in?" I paused, shaking my head and unable to complete the question. "I mean, say, lil' man, where are we?" I was flustered and he looked at me as if I were the biggest dummy on this side of the hemisphere.

"We in heaven, crazy, I told you!'" he said with a childish irritation. I chuckled as I glanced down at the white designer attire I wore.

"Oh yea, *Heaven,*" I mocked before climbing to my feet. "Say, lil' dude, you ain't seen that nigga God round here?" I stretched with the question.

"What does nigga mean?" he asked innocently. I glanced down at shorty. He merely looked up at me with curiosity reflecting in his gaze as he swung his feet back and forth. His shoes were untied, and the strings scraped the ground.

"Nigga is like—" I paused to consider my words. "It's a term people use to identify others."

"Why?"

"It's—It's—" I frowned as I realized that even *I* didn't know how a derogatory term had become embraced by me and my culture. Smirking, I knelt and began to tie lil' homies kicks. "It's a bad *habit,* lil' man, that's all."

"So, why do you say it if it's bad?" His curiosity was innocent as he studied me.

"Well—that's what habits are. Whether good or bad, they're things a person has been taught or taught themselves to do. It takes time to break habits, lil' one." Lil dude shrugged indifferently before hurriedly covering his nose and mouth as he sneezed. Climbing back to my full height, I glanced down the long street as if I were expecting someone. "Bless you, lil' one," I whispered.

"My mama said—my mama said, she said that people say *Bless you* because they gonna want you to bless them later down the road!" he exclaimed excitedly. I laughed hard, and the confused expression on lil' daddy's face only fed the much-needed laughter. Reaching down, I rubbed shorty's head. "Tamir, right?" I remembered his name. Shorty wings nodded confirmation. "How'd you get here, Tamir? I mean, how'd you—" My words trailed off. I was still fucked up about my circumstance. At that moment, the sounds of music reached my ears. I frowned before spotting the car, making slow progress toward us.

"*You* brought me here, Ghetto." Tamir's tone was saddened, and a look of confusion surfaced on his face.

"But I don't understand why, Ghetto, what I ever did to you. Did you hate me?" he asked.

"Huh?" was all I could say. My vision shot to him. Lil' dude hopped down off the bench and stood before me. Time seemed to stand still as I gazed down at him. Tears swimming in his innocent eyes, Tamir wanted me to see his pain.

"What—what you mean, lil' one, how *I* bring you?" I began but froze when Tamir reached out and touched my leg. It was as if my insides began to melt as fire swam through my veins, and that's when I fell to my knees, struggling to breathe as I clutched my chest. My eyes were wide in shock. But now face to face with little dude, I could see his tear-streaked face, and the heartbreak playing in his pupils is what snatched me under, below the surface of the waters of my past gangsterisms.

The day was humid, the sun reigning supreme in the heavens as it beamed down on the flow of traffic that sped down interstate 20.

The vision played within an ocean of lucidness as I remember it vividly. "Sit down, Tamir, and buckle your seatbelt before you get me pulled over!" The growled demand belonged to a light-skinned, chubby brotha. Dude was dripping with ice, from the crushed baguette encrusted bezel, the big boy mountain on his pinkie finger, and on up to the ice cubes reflecting in the Cuban around his neck. I stared from the backseat of the burnt orange Escalade truck as my mind connected and brought me back to the day—the time and reason—I'd not only smashed his father but by default, stepped on Tamir as well. I shook my head as my heart leaked; it was a hit. I knew because I remembered the day I'd carried it out.

"Aww, man, dad, I was just looking at your neck-i-lesss," Tamir huffed before falling back from leaning over the console. He pouted, crossing his little arms over his chest. His father glanced over at him, ready to scold him, but the way lil' dude had his bottom lip poked out, and was mugging, brought a chuckle out of him instead. He reached over and rubbed the little man's head.

"My fault, lil' man, but these troopers are just looking for a reason to harass any man with just a hint of color to his skin, you don't want ya pops going to jail do you?" Though the boy was too young to truly grasp the concept of jail, the tone in his father's voice told him that whatever jail was, wasn't good. His eyes grew wide at the question as he vigorously shook his head by way of saying no! His father, a man known to the streets as Pop Cee, chuckled as his eyes continued to deviate between the road and his little reflection. "And it's necklace, not neck-i-lesss."

"No, dad, it's neck-i-lesss! Dad!"

"What did I say, Tamir?"

"But-dadd—"

"But dad nothing, lil' man, you have to speak correctly so people know what you want." Tamir frowned slightly as if considering his old man's advice before glancing at him.

"Dad."

"Yea, Tamir?"

"Are you rich? My mama said—my mama said she gonna take yo butt to court, 'cause you a rich ass and—and don't pay the support for us. She said—she said you a sorry mothafu—"

"Tamir!" Pop Cee demanded, cutting little one off before he could repeat the foulness he'd learned at home. He glared down at the child, who merely glanced back with an innocent look that reminded dude why he didn't fuck with his baby's mother in the first place. I need to take her ass to court for being an unfit parent! He shook his head in disbelief at the thought, if only I wasn't so deep in this street shit! he mentally summarized.

"Watch your mouth, boy, little boys shouldn't talk like that!" he scolded.

"But mama said—"

"I don't give a damn what ya momma said, Tamir, and stop telling on her. That's called snitching, and real men don't rat!" The man's tone had more bite than he'd intended, and it brought tears to his son's orbs. Tamir's little chest began to heave, and his shoulders rose and fell as a storm fell from his wide eyes. Pop Cee exhaled a long breath of warm air. He loved the little world he'd created with his BM, but he hated the fact that he'd created something so precious with someone so worthless! She was a money-hungry, low-down, ratchet "thot" that he'd never intended to create with, but through her, he'd learned that a man has to respect his nut more than the feeling of it, 'cause though splashing inside a woman's ocean may be one of the best euphorias known to man, it's what that splash can create that will have a nigga stuck with bad luck for the next eighteen years. Again, Pop Cee shook his head in frustration. Gots to be mo' careful! he thought. "You know I love you, right?" he proposed, and almost laughed when Tamir shook his head no.

"Well, I do, shawty, and just 'cause I get on ya ass when you're wrong doesn't take away from that. That's what a father does."

"But—But—" Tamir hiccupped. "If you love me, why you don't live with me and my mama? Mama said—"

"Tamir!" Pop Cee cut him off, his eyes reminding him not to repeat what his Queen says to him. The child dropped his head. Unbeknownst to him, his question had cut a slice in his old man's heart,

for it was the exact sentiments he'd had when he was the boy's age, and wondering: "Where the fuck daddy at?" It only made him hate Tamir's mother on a deeper level. "Sometimes, Tamir, a man and woman create beautiful things they have to share even if what they were doing before that beautiful creation existed was never meant to last." He attempted to make sense to the seven-year-old. Pop Cee chuckled bitterly, knowing that trying to explain to a child how a man could become so entrapped within the feeling of some good pussy that he foolishly becomes an erupting volcano within the small island of a bullshit bitch, was truly unexplainable. Patting little man's knee, Pop Cee smiled with pride. "You are that beautiful creation between your mother and me, but me and her worlds were never meant to mix. Me not staying with you has nothing to do with you nor my love for you. You know why?"

"Why, dad?" Tamir asked while wiping his eyes.

"It's because my love for you is bigger than the world, lil' one, so it's with you wherever I'm at!"

"Can we go to McDonalds, dad?" he asked hopefully before running the back of his arm across his runny nose. Pop Cee shook his head in amusement; he didn't fault the kid on the sudden change of subject. Chuckling, he focused on the road. "Yea, lil' man, we can do that."

***

The Present

Twenty Minutes Later

Back at The Club

"What you say your name is again, lil' mama?" Mook slurred before gulping from the bottle of Rosé.

"Boyyy!" Queen pulled the bottle from his hands before tilting it to her lips. After quenching her thirst, she dropped the empty bottle on the floor of the car. "This your third time asking my name! So, since you keep forgetting, why don't you just give me a name *you* like?" She purred before leaning across the console and rubbing the back of her hand down the side of his face. The interior of the mango-colored, S63 Benz was dark, save for the illumination of the moon. Mook and his seductress had escaped the club's madness and found their own vibe within the luxury of the AMG; the music low, Yung Bleu's *Beautiful Lies* feeding their energy as he allowed his eyes to rape the vision of the goddess. Hair pulled to the top of her head; twisted into a tight bun, with two silver chopsticks she'd crossed into it, gave the lady an exotic appeal. Mook's eyes swallowed her, and once they settled on her thick thighs, he involuntarily licked his lips.

"How 'bout—" he paused to run a jeweled hand over the soft flesh of her left thigh. "Juicy? Yea, that fits you, mama. So—" he allowed the words to hang in the air as he appreciated what lust offered. Lady wore next to nothing! The boy shorts cut up into the crevices of her essence, revealing the plumpness of her crotch, and the skin-tight baby tee she wore was so short that it showed a fraction of her chocolate areolaes. *Damn!* he thought. "So you gonna let me sample the—" He was cut off by the Cardi B ringback tone on his phone. Frowning, he contemplated letting it go to VM but knew he'd regret it later. Pulling it from his hip, he answered. "What the bizness, Baby Mama?" He answered, and as he fabricated a tale for his lady, the one beside him rolled her eyes with an amused shake of her head. *Niggas aint shit!* she thought. Mook caught the side-eye looks she gave him and held up a finger to let her know he wouldn't   be   long.

"What!" he spat into the phone. "Yo cousin, who? Ray Ray said that? That boy lying, baby, you know ya people don't wanna see us together. I'm on my way to the house *now*. I ain't left the club with no one." He continued to lie, and from the shadows of the passenger seat, the lady smirked mischievously. "Yea, and you know what else? I got that liquor in my system; I'm on my way to punish that pussy!" he vowed with a crooked smile. Though she couldn't hear the caller's side of the conversation, the diva in the passenger seat could tell they'd been pacififed, and she had to stiffle a giggle at the other woman's stupidity. Mook lied and lied, but the lady beside him was too through, and when her eyes fell on the slight bulge in his pants, it caused her to bite her bottom lip seductively. *Fuck it!* she thought before lifting her knees up onto the soft leather of the seat, and on all fours, she leaned over and began to massage the bulge in his pants. Mook's eyes found her before he placed a finger to his lips, indicating silence. Mischief danced in Queen's eyes as his snake rose beneath the material of his joggers: *Gotcha!* she mentally praised. As if he could read her mind, Mook reclined his seat, and gazing down through the shadows as she slipped her soft hand beneath the waistband of his joggers, he slightly rose as she tugged them, along with his boxers down to the middle of his thigh. His dick was swollen and though it was nowhere near the length of the snake it appeared to be while hidden behind all that material, Queen appreciated its girth and as soon as he plopped back down in his seat, she attacked him! While massaging his nuts, she planted soft kisses around the swollen head of his nature, causing Mook to clench his teeth. "Man, I just tol-told yo asssss—yo cousin is a hater, dude ain't seen me leave with no bitch!" he growled from the pleasure. Yet, when his dick coveted the baptism of the lady's tongue, it became a task to focus on. "Yea—Yea, Tamara, I—I love you, but—" He stammered as his lower self was swallowed whole. He reached down grasping the back of her neck and forcing the queen's head down until her lips kissed his shaved pelvis. He almost lost it when her full lips hugged all he had to offer, before she slowly eased back, leaving a wet trail up his rigidness. She had no respect as she intentionally popped her lips when pulling him free of her wet imprisonment. Mook released her, urgently tapping a finger to his lips, trying to shush her. Red Diamond smiled with a seductive glint in her gaze as she rose from her position and practically had to pry the iPhone from the man's hand. Mook was hesitant, but with his dick throbbing, like most *simple* niggas, he became proof that a woman's touch was one of the most powerful weaknesses known to man. Releasing the phone in defeat as his temptress jacked his muscle with one hand, his eyes drifted shut. Oblivious to her texting with the other, Mook gave into ecstasy as the lady jerked him with rapid urgency. Her strokes were magical as she let the phone fall to the floor. Regaining her position, the lady got straight to her business! Wrapping her lips around the head of his sausage, she *squeezed* the base with gentle pressure while licking, sucking, and kissing his flesh. Mook's head fell back against the headrest as the freak tongue-kissed his love muscle. The low music playing intermingled with the seductive sounds of mouth service.

"Goddamn, bitch!" Mook growled through clenched teeth before placing his hand on the back of her neck. Her head bobbed up and down at a feverish pace as she attempted to suck his soul from his physical. Mook melted in her hands as she punished his dick, his eyes rolling to the back of his head as his toes curled in his retro 9's. The diva smiled inwardly, her blood hot in her veins as she felt the throbbing of Mook's gun as the bullets surged from his nuts, and just when he was about to shoot her in the throat, she released him from her soaked captivity as if his dick wear a convict being released from prison. Her hand took the place of her mouth, jerking him fast but artfully. Glancing up at him through the shadows, she studied him predatorily.

"This is a stick-up, daddy, give me this nut or die!" she demanded before running the tip of her tongue across her top row of teeth.

"Fucccck!" Mook bellowed; milk shooting from his barrel and coating the lady's hand as she milked him.

"*All* of it, nigga, give me all this nut or I'll suck ya *soul* out this fat ass dick!" she spat as if she were robbing him.

***

Ghetto

Click-Clack! The sound of me snapping the see-through mon-key nuts into place was resounding. I admired the double drum cartridge; it made me fall deeper in love with the Kel-Tec PLR 16. As Red Diamond followed the Escalade, I rested the pipe across my lap. The stolen Roush Mustang GT was powerful as it trailed the burnt orange truck that sped ahead of us, and just as I retrieved the ape's mask from beside me, my jack rang.

"Yea?" I answered. "Fuck you mean how he'll know? Tell 'em to just watch the news, nigga! Matter of fact, just tell 'em to have my check ready or he won't have to worry about payin' in cash, he'll fuck around and pay in blood!" I demanded before disconnect-ing.

"What did he say?" Red Diamond's voice was soft. It was her first words to me since we'd had our disagreement. She wasn't feel-ing my jones for Heaven, and though we weren't on no exclusive shit, Red Diamond had always wanted more from me than I was willing to give.

"It's a go, but Flesh checking to make sure the Fetti is right before we flip this boy, just don't lose him," I answered. Lady rolled her eyes at me to let me know our little civil war was still in full effect. Nevertheless, she pressed her foot down on the pedal, caus-ing the engine to growl as the midnight blue GT showed off its stage three, 710 horsepower. She gripped the wheel with both hands as she focused on the truck ahead of us.

"You know what I find crazy, Ghetto?" she asked, as I slipped the ape's mask over my head.

"Why you dry stressin', ma? You already know my heart." I tried but failed. Red laughed bitterly.

"Do I?" Her eyes flickered to me before returning to the target.

"If I have to remind you, then it wasn't much important to you from the genesis, right?" My vision found her from behind the mask.

"Or maybe it's just way too important to me in the Omega of things," she whispered. I shook my head in defeat. No matter how much a nigga learned of the opposite sex, he'll never know her. Yet, I've learned that too much quality time spent between a woman and man is a no-no in terms of friendship! There's no such thing as

we're just friends when a man and woman are sharing portions of themselves that should only be reserved for relations beneath a different title. I chuckled as I studied her.

"I see this dick has you on some other shit, but let me ask you something—" I paused to lift the tool into my clutches. "When we were just thuggin, no sex, or none of the extras, we were good, but now you're all in your feelings 'cause I found my rib, why?" Her hands tightened around the wheel as her eyes began to leak. I hated to see love cry, but how does a man stop love from loving him when he knows that he and love's love would only be destructive?

"Nigga, don't flatter yourself, the dick wasn't all that," she rasped. I tilted my head to the left as I gazed at her, and when her eyes drifted to me, Red laughed despite herself. The orangutan's face had two rosy red spots on its cheeks and with the mock tongue hanging from its mouth, I knew I looked more like curious George than King Kong. Wiping the drizzle from her eyes, she shook her head in disbelief; she'd never been able to stay mad at me for long. "I mean, yea, I know we agreed on the no-strings-attached thing, but damn, Devonte, I'm a woman." I knew shit was real when she'd used my government name. "A woman with feelings," she added.

"Aww, naw, not the big bad Red Diamond, not the redbone with good hair that feels she can have any man she wants." I teased. She smiled.

"Any man but you," she mumbled. "Ghetto, I know I'm out of pocket for stressing you like this, and maybe it's just 'cause my period is here and a bitch just emotional, but I don't care, dammit!" She pouted with a slap to the steering wheel. "You're the first and only man that's ever made love to me! The only nigga that's ever taken his time to really get to know me. You're just different, and I guess I just—" she paused, considering her next words before shrugging indifferently.

"I fell," she whispered.

I focused my vision on the truck ahead of us. Two other vehicles separated us and I knew Pop Cee intended to take the next exit. Massaging the side of the Kel-Tec, I gave Queen a piece of a God's perspective. *"Red, how does a person make love through inter-course?"*

"Excuse me?"

"Excuse me, my ass! You heard what I just said, Ms. Lady." The question was just as simple as it was deep, and I wanted a piece of her truths, so I could exchange them for a piece of raw realism. *"Matter fact. Since you are on the extra, what's good with you and Kitty? Last I checked, y'all were in too deep."* I knew I was being petty, but shid, the pressure was on. When Red cringed, I knew I'd hit a sore spot.

Exhaling, she shrugged. *"Kitty? I mean—"* she thought before speaking. *"She—we cool, and I enjoy her company, but she's not a man, Ghetto."* She downplayed her relations with her gal. I chuckled.

"Now answer my questions, lady." I got back to it. Red Diamond rolled her eyes.

"Look, man, all I'm saying is, you make me feel like—like—"

"A woman?" I helped. Red smacked her lips.

"Yes, Ghetto, like a woman. When you make love to me, you—"

"See, there you go again with the "make love" bidness."

"Will you stop cutting me off!" she snapped as her red glare cut to me in irritation. *"Damn!"* she spat. I chuckled, lifting my hands in surrender. Again, Queen rolled her eyes. *"Devonte, you're just different. Like, you see beyond this bad girl persona and though I try to hide it, you see my heart. The real me! When you touch me—"* she shivered in thought and I wondered if it was merely to punctuate her point or was it merely involuntary; the memory of my touch? *"It's like—like you just need me to cum! It's like—"* she paused once more and exhaled. *"Like love?"* Her vision drifted to me, inquisition doing the cha cha in the gaze. I leaned back in my seat before pulling the mask off; my wild dreadlocks fell about my face like a real rude boy. *"Can't you see, nigga, I'm that bitch for you? Like, damn, Ghetto, any nigga would kill to have a Bonnie like me, but you just sideline a bitch like I'm some—"*

"Cause I'm not just any nigga, Red. See, that's just it, many niggas want Bonnies, never considering that Bonnie's story wouldn't be the same if it weren't for Clyde. That lady only become who she was because she reflected her man. Bonnie was a good girl turnt bad by a bad boy turnt bad by a bad system. Bonnie was only loyal to "her" nigga. She was Clyde's bitch, and her love for him led her to be everything he needed her to be. "His" reflection." I paused to wave a hand toward the truck we were pursuing. *"But in my eyes, Bonnie invested too much into a nigga that was headed nowhere fast."* I shook my head disappointedly. *"Any time the nigga you getting your gangstress on for begins to love the thrill of being an outlaw more than he pursues the goal of protecting the queen on his board, you're queening for the wrong empire. You have a prince rather than a lord! The crazy part about it is, if Clyde would have chosen to be a lawyer, guess what, Nubian?"* I lifted a brow as I smirked. *"Bonnie would've been his assistant! If he wanted to be a doctor, she would've studied to be his RN. She was foolish to follow such a man that couldn't see beyond being an outlaw. I've never wanted Bonnie, Red, I want a bitch that not only wants more for us as a team but more for her as a woman!"* I jeweled with a confirming nod. *"More for me than the slums! Not just a woman that can secure a bag and fuck me, but I'm grown enough to know—naw—"* I shook my head against the choice of words. *"I'm real enough to know that just 'cause you're special to me, just 'cause you're beautiful, and will slide crooked for me, none of that shit means we should travel beyond the point of no return. You're a street bitch, ma, that wifey shit not your vibe. Plus,"* I focused my eyes on Queen, *"I'm no good for you. I'll fuck up your heart on accident."* I kept it a buck, but not even realism is enough when a woman's heart is the gamble. Red Diamond's blood shots bore into me.

"But, little Mrs. Heaven is, huh? Oh, you'll take good care of her heart 'cause—"

"See, Nubian?" I cut her off, pointing a finger at her. *"That's what I'm telling you! You claim to love me, but don't respect my top."* I pointed to my head. *"It's never about the bitch when it comes to a real nigga's decision. I'd never spit on our bond by implying*

that the next female is better than you, but—" I needed Nubian to overstand what most misunderstand. "I'm a grown man, Red, I know what's best for me." Red Diamond sucked her teeth.

"But you can't tell me what's best for "me", Ghetto."

"Maybe not, but "maybe" that's why the other niggas you're given yourself to, depreciated what they should've been appreciating. Maybe it's not the niggas you choosing, but you that needs to realize your worth."

"Nigga, fuck you!" she glared. "Fuck you."

"I can only be a real nigga, Nubian!" I shrugged indifferently. "Now, if you want me to, I can continue jumping up and down in that pussy, give you my dick while giving Heaven my heart, but will you be content with being the side bitch? You see my fucking you as making love, but I don't believe a mu'fucka can "make" love through intercourse. Your pussy should be sacred to you, mama, and when a nigga is fucking you, he's 'pose to make you feel as if it's just as scared to him." I allowed my hand to slip between her legs. "When a woman opens herself to a man, she's at her most vulnerable because there's no deeper form of submission than relinquishing her womb." I nodded toward her pussy. "When a nigga cutting you, if he's doing it right, of course, you're gonna feel some typa way, especially if y'all fucking on the regular."

"So," Red Diamond paused me with a lift of her hand as if she were giving me the sista girl hand, "what you're telling me is, you don't feel the same as I do or what? I'm just another lame bitch? You don't think I'm good enough, Ghetto, huh? You think I'm just another piece of pussy to you?"

"Bitch, don't put words in my mouth!" I demanded, growling in frustration. Red shook her head but kept her jaws on pause nonetheless. It never ceased to amaze me how a certain type of female had to be talked to stupidly to get some understanding.

"I'm saying, if love can be made through sex, what's to say of when I'm no longer fuckin you?" I vibed before my vision fell to the mask in my lap. "People just fall in love while fucking because the feeling feels so good that they became possessive of it! That's not love, that's just possessiveness, Red. How I make you feel is merely

a reflection of what you "should" feel from "any" nigga that "en-joys" fucking you. You're my baby but," my eyes lifted to capture her, "Heaven is where I want to be, and as my ride or die, you should respect that, 'cause I respect you." A long tear ran down my baby girl's face, but should I have lied and spared her tears? Or kept it "G" at the cost of the rain dripping from her eyes? She swiveled just as my jack vibrated. "Yea, yea?" I answered. "2:21, Blow." I ended the call before glancing at love; she felt my eyes on her but kept hers focused on the road ahead. Her knuckles turned red from gripping the wheel so tightly, and as her gaze was being baptized with troubled waters, I could tell she waged war against the impulse to blink.

"It's a go, you a'ight or what, ma?" I needed to know her mind. Red Diamond nodded her confirmation so vigorously that tears snaked down her cheeks.

"Yea, I'm cool." She sniveled before quickly using the back of her hand to wipe away the diamonds. "It's nothing, and—and you're right. Forget I said anything," she offered, but the drizzle falling from the sockets of her vision was my kryptonite. I exhaled a hot breath in exasperation before pulling the mask back over my head.

"I should've never put my dick in you, ma," I whispered. "I wish I hadn't."

"Me too, Ghetto, me too," she whispered before mashing her foot down on the gas. I lifted the stick into my clutches. I could feel its torque. The growl of the engine felt alive beneath me as the lady zig-zagged through traffic to catch our target at the exit onto Cooper.

***

The Present

Moments Later—Back at the Club

"Take-this-puuss-ssssy, nigga!" the diva cried as she bucked on top of him. Reclined with the driver's seat pushed all the way back, Mook's body was rigid in ecstasy. Shirtless and pants at his ankles, the man was lost in the rapture. The liquor submerged his brain, and he'd allowed queen to use her baby tee and thong to tie his hands behind the headrest, and the act of being her slave only added to the pleasure.

"Grrrrrshiiiit!" he growled, dick pulsating as his nut came to life. Queen smirked, feeling his intent, but not ready for him to give in. She lifted off his lap, and using her knees for balance, she hurriedly reached down and squeezed the base of his dick.

"Uh uhhh," she shook her head. "I don't want you to nut yet." Her tone was firm.

"Dammmmmmn, Baby!" Mook cried. Shadows played across his sweating face as he clenched his teeth against the pleasure. The woman gazed down at him from her straddling position as her kitty leaked, and her juicy breasts swung down toward his face. Lady could see the euphoric torture he was within.

"I wanna cum too, daddy, but first—" she purred, releasing his hardened flesh before reaching up to pull the chopsticks from the bun atop her head. Mook studied the gleaming sticks with a look of confusion, and when a warm squirt of semen shot from him and splashed against the lady's inner thigh, she smiled seductively at her captive. Though his loins were thirsty for more of that pussy, Mook's gut spoke to instinct—*Something ain't right!*

"Wha—What's that?" He wanted to know as the woman held up the sticks for him to see. The smile on her pretty face was devilish as the sharp tips twinkled in the moonlight.

"I have to tell you something," she began before positioning him beneath her woman's cave. Shadows played over his face as she fell upon him, impaling herself upon his thickness. "Hhhhaah!" she sucked in a deep breath when he opened her up. Lady began to rock back and forth as suspicion danced within Mook's eyes at the sight of the two chopsticks in her hands. "Damn, Boy, you hav—have a fattt—assss—dickkk!" She moaned, and with a metal rod in each hand, she placed her palm on his chest. Her titties swung tauntingly just above his lips and she imitated a cowgirl. Arching her back, Queen popped her pussy up and down his dick, the sounds of her ass cheeks slapping against his thighs creating a beautiful fuck melody. "Ssss!" she hissed through clenched teeth. Mook's face revealed the war between ecstasy and uncertainty as the call of his dick faced off with common sense, and when Queen noticed the strain he was putting on the bondage she'd applied to his wrist; *the possibility* of him getting loose only served to feed the freak in her. "I-*sssss*–I lied! My-my name isn't Toya," she revealed, and the war began. Her revelation murdered ecstasy, and panic appeared within the eyes of her prey. Mook's inebriation evaporated and his fight for freedom became urgent as he attempted to buck her off his lap.

"Get the fuck off me, bitch, get—off!" he growled, but his bucking only served to drive his love stick deeper; stabbing her in the sweet spot. The woman spread her knees further apart while locking her feet beneath his thighs.

"Yes, *juicy* does fit, but only for this pussy." She giggled before an erotic moan escaped her. "My—My—name is—*ssss*—she sucked air through her teeth—"is Red Diamond, and I'm here-herrre on RBO business. Sure you heard of us, hmm? *Real bitches only* type shit." Mook fought his damndest to knock her off her horse; unconsciously fucking her.

"Yasss—yas—dad-dy!" she cried as her rose gold capped, ruby-stuffed canines gleamed in the twilight. "We warned you niggas," she reminded him. "*Two weeks!*" she said, and that's when the sounds of the binds tearing brought a sinister smile to her lips. The evil in her eyes caught Mook's panic, and he yanked against the binds with all he had.

"Grrarh!" he growled and with the speed of a serpent, Red Diamond lifted and swung the first rod down, "Arruh!" Mook cried when the metal pierced his jaw and blood squirted. The sight of the liquid to Red Diamond was like an open vein to a vampire, and she ravished within the act of the bloodletting. Over and over she pummeled his face with stabs; blood squirting onto her stomach, breasts, and neck. Mook cried out in agony until one of the sharp picks punctured his throat, putting a hole in his larynx. A wet-wheezing noise emitted from the small hole just as his left wrist broke free, and in the man's desperation, he swung a hammer-like fist into the she devil's face. The blow rocked her back into the steering wheel, causing it to honk.

"Ahhh!" she growled, but blood lust was too powerful to overcome. She fought back with a feral passion, driving the picks down into the man's flesh in a windmill motion, and in the lust of death, she and Mook swung simultaneously. His blow dazed her, but her wild swing of the metal was her savior. *Phish!* A squishing sound could be heard as the rod came free of her hand.

"Rrrugh!" Mook cried like a wounded animal, both hands flying to his left eye where the rod had jammed. Blood poured, instantly slicking his hands and face as Red Diamond fought through the dizziness, and when she set eyes on the grotesque sight, something evil spoke to the spirit: *"Finish him!"* it demanded, and she obeyed. With everything she had, she plunged the remaining rod into the soft flesh between Mook's neck and shoulder. Warm blood shot forth in a dark splash as his lungs began to fill. He fought the good fight, but his body was quickly weakening as if his soul was pouring from the many holes she'd punched in his body. Spent, and on the threshold of the reaper's playground, the man fell back into the seat; choking on his own blood. His breathing was wet-ragged as his killer's chest rose and fell as she attempted to catch her breath. Red Diamond's eyes fell to her blood-splotched chest, gazing curiously as the crimson liquid dripped down her breasts like warm water from the shower. The sight stirred something crazy within her, but it was the rigidness between her legs that caught her by surprise. Reaching down between her thighs, she found Mook's dick standing tall. With a mischievous smirk, her vision lifted to her prey. "Don't move, okay?" She held up a finger. Mook could only gurgle on his blood as the woman reached down and retrieved his phone. She held it up so he could see before tapping it to bring the screen to life. The screen opened to the messaging app, and though where his spirit was headed, it wouldn't matter; Red Diamond smiled.

__: *Girl, this nigga is a deadbeat!*
Baby moms: Excuse me?
__: *"Listen bitch, I'm 'bout to fuck this nigga to death! Forget him and find you a real nigga!*
Baby Moms: WTH? SMH! Mook, Y u playing?
__: *K! since you don't understand, just listen!*
Baby Moms:??? I'm lost! Who is this? Ok, Mook, I'll play your game.

Red Diamond showed how devious she could be. "I texted ya bitch when I took your phone so she wouldn't waste too much time crying over your bum ass." She smirked before putting the phone to her ear. "Um, baby mama?" she sang, and the soft crying on the other end made her roll her eyes.

"Mook, I can't believe you," the lady sniveled. "You're a hoe ass nigga. I held you down for four fucking years while you were in jail and *this* how you do me? *Us?* Our son?" she cried. Red Diamond gagged in disgust, but when it dawned on her that the heartbroken lady had mistaken the tussle for rough sex, she laughed.

"Umm, I don't mean to interrupt, but he's not worth your tears, Boo Boo. Go find you one of them big dick square niggas, 'cause niggas in the streets are expiring faster than milk left out too long." She giggled as she began to grind against Mook's five-inch, chubby dick. The woman on the other side of the phone lost it!

"Bitch, I'm gonna toast yo ass when I catch you! I'm gonna beat yo ass!" she screamed into the receiver. Her words were so slurred that they came out in a meshed jumble. Red Diamond pulled the phone away and stared at it with a stank face. *Fuck!* she wondered before putting the phone back to her ear.

"See?" she spat with a roll of her eyes before reaching down and positioning the dying man's masculinity at the wound where God split her at. "*That's* why I don't fuck with too many bitches as it is. *I* put you on game and you wildin on *me?* Bitch, *I'm* not the one that cheated on you, but—" she paused as her vision fell to Mook. He began to convulse as she massaged his dick.

"Right now I'm 'bout to fuck ya nigga."

"Put Mook on the phone, please," the girl sniveled.

"Oh, now you have some manners? Ugh! Look, chick, this nigga has expired, don't wait up." Red Diamond disconnected the call before easing down onto the hardened flesh beneath her, her eyes drifting shut in bliss, and she gave into a wicked ecstasy.

"You really do have some good dick-goood-di-dick." She purred, her pace quickening.

"Do—do me a favor, daddy, tell Ghetto—" she momentarily lost thought, speech, and control while bouncing harder. Red felt Mook's muscles losing rigidness from blood loss, but she was determined to get that orgasm. The car bounced slightly as the hurricane stirred within her ocean, and winding on that dick, queen's nether region became a rain storm as her eyes rolled. "Huhhhh!" she moaned erotically as her fuck face became an ugly prettiness. "Ouuu-ou!" pleasure surged, heaven cracked, and rain was the forecast as her orgasm reached its highest elevation. Red Diamond's body trembled atop him just as Mook took his last breath. She came hard as a thick trail of blood eased from the corner of his mouth. Shortly after, her eyes cracked open and a devilish smile crested her lips. "Tell Ghetto a real bitch sent you."

Bam! Bam! The sound of someone slapping the trunk of the car made her jump in surprise. "I see you, boy! Welcome home nigga, BGM shit!" someone saluted.

"Bruh, let fam get that off, quit cock blocking!" another spoke as a group of BGM's finest left the club. Red Diamond's heartbeat galloped as she thanked God for the five percent tint.

Chapter Three

Tamir's Forgiveness

Ghetto's Reflections

Just when Pop Cee signaled for his exit, Red Diamond cut him off; the Mustang zooming in front of his SUV at breakneck speed and almost causing the man to crash into the rail of the exit ramp. Pop Cee was furious! Smashing his palm against the horn while tapping the brake to keep from rear-ending us, brotha man spat curses. As Red Diamond expertly switched gears, downshifting as she navigated down the ramp, I shook my head in dismay when the burnt orange truck sped up in his pursuit. Anger is a fool's emotion, leading mu'fuckas to make irrational decisions and as Red Diamond's vision lifted to the rearview mirror, the smirk on her pretty face was evidence that she agreed with that philosophy. "He's gonna pull up beside me on some ra-ra shit," she predicted.

"You sure?" the physical me questioned, and Nubian sucked her teeth.

"Naw, Ghetto, he's so mad he's about to just ram his pretty little truck into us for cutting him off!" she retorted sarcastically before rolling her eyes. "Yes, daddy, I'm sure. He can't be that mad," Lady assured, though I knew road rage has driven people to do worse. My spirit self took it all in, watching the other me chuckle before cracking the passenger's door, and even now, as a spirit, I can recall what took place.

"Good, then maybe you can use those tears to do us some good. How 'bout you conjure up a few real quick, I'm sure this sucka will fall for it."

The physical me added his own form of sarcasm. Red Diamond cut her red vision to me and I could tell I'd cut her, but she hid it well as she clicked on the hazard lights. She'd eased the whip to the shoulder of the road and just as Pop Cee's truck approached, I crouched low and slipped out of the car; on the lurk. Just as Diamond predicted, the man swerved around our car and brought the truck to a screeching halt at an angle that blocked any attempts of escape.

In the backseat of that car, I shook my head at what I knew would transpire; the devil would dance, and for some strange reason, I craved to be near Tamir. I wanted to see what I'd missed that day, and as my eyes drifted shut, the cliche of being careful what you wish for became the devil's laughter!

***

When my spirit materialized in the passenger seat of the Escalade, my eyes popped open in a desperate search for Tamir. The boy was in the back seat and so engrossed in the screen of his tablet, he was oblivious to the madness going on at the other side of that truck. "Tamir," I began, just as Pop Cee jumped out and upped his burner. "Get down, lil' daddy, shit bout to get stupid," I warned, though I knew the child couldn't hear me. He merely laughed giddily at whatever he was watching on Tik Tok, and that allowed me to look out at the scene playing outside the truck. Clutching the black and gray .40, Pop Cee rushed over to the driver's side of the Mustang. Wasting no time taking aim at the tinted window; from his body language, I could tell that if Red Diamond wouldn't have eased the glass down to enchant homie with her beauty, he'd have given it to her. All lead—no words! Yet, beauty is the very "weapon" Cleopatra used to manipulate Caesar into helping her outsmart her brother for the throne of Egypt. It's the same shit that allowed the beauty to tame the beast. As a matter of fact, beauty is the exact key that Red Diamond used to unlock the door to Pop Cee's defenses and allow the reaper in!

"Bitch, are you crazy!" he raged but once he beheld the feline before him, he retucked his pistol. Red Diamond's face was wet with tears as she gazed up at him with pleading eyes, and I chuckled bitterly when she began to put on an Oscar-winning performance. "He—he doesn't want me anymore and I-I'm—" Her words died as pain gave birth to a storm. She rested her head against the steering wheel as if Pop Cee wasn't worthy of witnessing her pain, but as if

he wanted to prove otherwise, he reached in, placed a finger under her chin, and lifted her head. The moment became surreal, taking on a slow-motion effect as Red Diamond's head lifted to reveal a wicked smile that was Siamese twins: Bitterness conjoined with deviousness. Pop Cee's smile was instant but waned when he spotted conspiracy dancing within her irises. A suspicious frown contorted his face just as I popped up like the jack-in-a-box.

"Shit!" he spat before backpedaling while going for his pistol. Bittah! The first volley of .223 shells cut through his chest so viciously that the impact knocked him back four feet. Blood splashed from his chest as he slammed against the side of his truck, staring horrified as I swept the stick in a half arch. Btttah! The sound of the windows shattering intermingled with the rapid mantra of bullets penetrating metal as they punched through the truck. Pop Cee tried to scream, but I was relentless with that cutter. Bittah! It sang, spinning the man and spraying his internals onto the pretty paint of his Escalade. The man fought to stay on his feet, but it wasn't to be! As if his legs had deserted him, Pop Cee fell to his knees, face trapped within a grimace of agony. I don't know if it was pure adrenaline or pure will, but he stumbled back to his feet, blood pouring from his wounds copiously. I watched homie stumble forward. "Tamirrrrr!" he cried in a wheeze. I frowned in confusion, dread surging through my being at the thought of what I already knew I'd find, and when my spirit self glanced in the backseat, my heart turned upside down. Tamir's eyes were wide, but his soul had aborted his body. The boy was slumped to the side, his noodles spilling out his head where the .223's had scalped him. And when a thump at the back window drew my attention, I found the child's father staring in horror at the carnage. He placed both hands on the only intact piece of glass and a lone tear spilled from his right eye before blood slipped from between his lips.

"Quit playing, Ghetto, and finish him before we wind up in a jail cell!" Red Diamond's irritated voice drifted to me. There was a brief silence before—Btttttah! The volley of bullets rocked Pop Cee to sleep, and as he fell awkwardly, a thought was born within the

alleyways of my mind: "Maybe the world was better off without nig-gas like me?"

***

Ghetto

"I'm not mad at you, Ghetto, God said—God said that *every-one* makes mistakes!" The sound of Tamir's young voice caused me to crack my eyes open. I was back in heaven and back on my knees staring into the eyes of the boy whose life I'd stolen before it could even get started. My eyes were so wet with my diamonds that my vision was blurry, and when little dude reached up and wrapped his small arms around my neck in a tight hug, the dam cracked, my diamonds dripped, and for the first time in my days of thuggin, I wanted someone to see my pain.

"I'm sorry, Tamir, fam—I fucked up, lil' man," I apologized, though I knew that an apology could never be sufficient enough to compensate for what I'd robbed him of.

"It's okay, Ghetto, but—" Little dude accepted while pulling away from me. I ran my sleeved arm across my eyes to clear the salt water before giving Tamir a sad smirk

"But?" I was curious.

"But, you owe me a new tablet, fool!" Little dude's demand caused me to frown but when it dawned on me he was speaking of the one I'd cost him during my moment of wigging out, I burst into laughter! I nodded my agreement to little dude just as a car horn sounded and drew our attention toward the street. My jaw fell at the sight of the metallic-colored Maybach S650. Though the wheels were factory, the beauty of the foreign had the power to cause any true playa to fantasize about slipping through the city in that mu'fucka, with something fly, jazzy, and cool sitting pretty beside him.

"They waiting on you, man," Tamir drew my attention, my eyes settling on him.

"Who are they?" I asked before my eyes drifted back to the Benz.

"Grown-ups!" Little dude slapped a palm to his forehead as if to say: *Duhh, stupid!*

"I'll see you later, man, and don't forget my tablet." Tamir pointed a finger into his palm to punctuate his point. "You promised!" he reminded before suddenly turning and sprinting off. I frowned slightly as I watched him pause midway down the long street, and to my amazement, a familiar, burnt orange Escalade materialized beside him. Tamir turned to wave one last time before hopping in. The truck swung around the Maybach and came to a halt! My mind was on go as I reached for the tool on my waist, only to find that I was caught down bad without it. I stood with a goofy ass expression as the window eased down, and Pop Cee glared back at me from the driver's seat. When his scowl turned to an understanding smirk and he nodded *What's up*, I became lost in the sauce. *Huh!* I thought.

"Peace, black man, peace," Dude chuckled. But I stood speechless. Again, homie nodded some type of understanding. "The price of the streets, my man, seldom comes cheaper than a life, and sometimes it takes that moment when it's too late for a man to realize that he should've never waited until it was so late to make big boy decisions." Pop Cee shrugged sadly at the words. "Karma doesn't play favorites, fam, and most times while we're running wild, we don't give a damn bout Karma, so—" He paused before waving a hand from himself to me. "So, she doesn't give a fuck 'bout us when she comes to collect. Stay up, playboy." These were the man's last words before easing the truck away from the curb and slipping off into the distance. I watched the truck until the driver of the Maybach lay on the horn impatiently, snatching my attention. I studied the car until it dawned on me—*shid, I'm already dead, what I got to lose.* That was the thought that propelled my feet to move, and when I made it close enough, the rear door opened by itself.

Lord, they really think they fooling you by coming to church on Sunday/Praying and laying hands on folks, stomping and jumping around fakin' the holy ghost /but it's a thin line, between walkin it, and talkin it / living it and giving it or just pretending it's alright /and did they really think they can pull the wool over your eyes lord/Did they really think that by fakin they were saved, that they would get the same reward— Lyfe Jennings' soulful melody spilled from inside the machine, and stooping low to see who was beckoning my company; there God sat, posing like a gentleman, with a glass tumbler poised halfway to his lips. "You gonna get in or continue to let my air out?" He wanted to know. I slid in before securing the door and when the whip pulled away from the curb, my older reflection, the man that called himself God, took a sip of the amber liquid in his glass. Savoring the taste, his eyes drifted closed for a brief moment before opening again. "Help yourself," he offered with a nod toward a small stock of drinks. My eyes shot to him before I chose the bottle of 1942 and got straight to the business. Damn a glass, I had no manners as I took the bottle to the head. God chuckled as I pulled it away and tapped my chest a few times with my fist. "Careful, youngsta, that's that grown man right there," he chuckled. I still wasn't feeling how dude allowed Stick Talk to take my piece off the board, so I wasn't on no friendly shit. Resting my head against the soft seat, I rested my eyes.

"So, this is what all the hype is about, huh?" I chuckled as the deity's orbs drifted to me.

"Excuse me?"

"Heaven, this shit," I waved a dismissive hand around the car before jabbing a finger toward the curtained window. "Just a rewind of niggas' mistakes?" My eyes cracked open with the question. God smirked.

"Who said this was *Heaven?*

"You did."

"Did I now, and when would *I* have said such a thing?" He asked as he sipped.

"I believe that was *Tamir's* claim and when you couldn't understand his pronunciation, I corrected you.

"Look, my dude, fuck is wrong with you, huh? What's your aim, mane! We in heaven or we ain't. You're playing games and I ain't feeling this shit!" I wanted to punch him in his face but knew

I had no win. He sipped. I seethed. He glanced. I glared "I ain't Jesus, bruh, I'm not a pawn in your game of chess you're playing with my life, and I'll fuck around and snap, fam, that's why I'm begging you to let's get it over with." I was absolute and for some strange reason, dude almost choked on his drink. I frowned as he composed himself and glanced at me with soft eyes.

"My son Jesus made his own decisions, but let me ask you something." He paused to down the rest of his drink. "Have you ever noticed that *every* religion has a man that they praise, follow, and claim that *I* sent to give the message?"

"Fuck that has to do with what I just—"

"You can't tell me *how* I can answer your questions, sun, and just to keep it a buck with you, you *can't* keep trying to handle me either. I'm a sensitive God, Ghetto, so let's be gentlemen." He cut me off, his eyes telling me that even God demanded respect. I chuckled with a shrug.

'Yea, I noticed it, bruh, but again, what does that have to do with *me?*"

"Everything!" He said, and as I tilted the bottle to my head, he continued. "Christianity, Islam, Catholicism, Jewish humanism, and even Rastafarianism, and Satanism. Jesus, Mohammed, Satan, the Virgin Mary, the Torah, Bible, or Quran—the only beef between these groups of people are *the men and books* they believe. Yet—" He paused to rest his glass down. "All books, men, or women that lead *to me* are the truth! *Everyone* is a pawn in one way or another, Ghetto, 'cause just as a pawn is meant for a purpose, so are people, and no, sun, this isn't Heaven, but it's close." He chuckled.

"So, where the hell are we, mane, what's all this extra bidness you got me on?" I lifted my hands as if to say: *What the fuck!*

"This, Ghetto, is the middle passage, the space between Heaven and earth, above hell, but a bit of all. *Your* decisions lead you here, sun, where your fate is being determined."

"Like in a court of law, huh?" I chuckled bitterly as the liquor coursed through my veins like a warm balm to my frustrations.

God shrugged before nodding —"Well, yes, like a court of law."

"So," I tilted the bottle toward him, "you must be the judge, huh, Gangsta?" The liquor was in full effect by then.

"*Your* decisions, sun, see, right now, you'll give it all for my forgiveness and for me to give you the things you desire the most, but—"

"I ain't asked you for shit, but let's get it over with. Forgiveness?" I spat the word as if it were a sour taste on my tongue. "Nigga, *you* the one that needs forgiveness! *You're* the one who created fuck niggas! It was *you* who made disloyal bitches, fam." I'd counted off and held up two fingers before swigging from the bottle. "Poverty made the ghetto crooked, it turnt my people's culture dark, and when them crackas brought the dope in, that shit created a monster!" I spat before running the back of my hand across my mouth. "That shit made fiends and convicts out my people while you sat high above all the bloodshed and serpentine shit it created, watching us rot down there! Nigga, all the mothers, and grandmothers that's praying to you, the streets, real men that needed you in the clutch, you ain't said shit!"

I studied homie, wondering how he could find fault with *anybody* when his sins were greater than all 'cause he's the creator. Taking a sip from his glass, he had the form of a poised, old-school playa with white dreadlocks pulled back into a neat braid. The cognac-colored slacks he wore were cut perfectly and rested impeccably atop the same colored gators on his feet. I respected his drip as my vision took in the ice-white turtle neck beneath the brandy-hued leather vest. The man was clap doctor clean and I nodded my appreciation. God tilted his glass toward me, and with a chuckle, he spoke.

"I've always found it funny how people betray me for the flesh. For the love of money, and even because their hustles are poor; so their pockets are on flat, and then they pray to me and think there should be no penance. Forgiveness, Ghetto, is nothing more than *understanding* that people make mistakes and giving a damn about them in spite of. Yet," he wet his tongue with his drink, "we all, *myself*, you, and the rest will have to answer for *who we are* versus who we were. Most people pray and still live crooked. You say I ignore the plight of the ghetto, sun?" He laughed bitterly. "Well, news flash, brothaman, there are third-world countries *where starvation is common* and people are oppressed by their own government! I'm *one* God, Ghetto, and the sad truth is, I can make the *entire* world rich *today*, and by tomorrow, someone will be murdered for being rich. I can make everyone happy *today* and by tomorrow, someone will *find* a reason to be angry. There's no cure for human nature, sun, for much is given, much is taken away." Dude paused to look at the Rolex on his wrist. "Well, I hate to cut this short, 'cause I do enjoy choppin game with you, but I have a chess game to finish. Where would you like me to drop you off?" The question fucked me up. Yet, I answered him from my soul!

"Home, God, I just wanna go home." God smiled with a nod.

"Yes, Ghetto, home is where the heart is, so let's get you home, sun."

Renta

Chapter Four

The Animal in Me

Ghetto

The Maybach picked up too *much speed*, and it felt as if we were on a ride at Six Flags! I glanced at Lord, but he seemed unfazed as he savored his drink. "Say, mane, tell your people to slow this bitch down before we wreck—" I shouted, eyes wide as they bounced from him to the front seat. The driver was no doubt a woman, but all I could see was her profile, and even from that angle, and with her hair pressed and framing around her face, I could see that she was gorgeous.

"Aaliyah, beautiful?" God called.

"Yes, Lord?" Her voice was soft like velvet and one I'd been in love with since I was a little dude lusting after her in the movie *Romeo Must Die!*"

"How much longer until we arrive, sweety? I really do need to get back to that game of chess." God's response really ran me hot, but before I could check his ancient ass, the woman turned to give me a sexy smile. I never had the time to appreciate it because her foot slammed down onto the brakes, causing the car to spin out of control before coming to a smooth stop. My eyes snapped to my reflection; *God*, before drifting back to the beautiful woman, and she winked before glancing at yours almighty.

"We're here"

"Say, Aaliyah, look, ma," I began but just like the hater he was, dude cock-blocked.

"We're here, Ghetto," God cut me off and I glared at him.

"And where is *here*, OG?" I probed.

"Here, as in *wherever* here is, you gotta get ya slick ass up out this car." He chuckled before nodding toward the window. My gaze became suspicious, but I turned to pull the curtain back nonetheless, and Aaliyah and God became afterthoughts when I set eyes on my crib. It was late, moments before dawn and the gray brick ranch house looked almost ominous; shadowed by shades of night and morning. A flock of dark birds flew overhead. Without further ado, I reached for the door handle, but when God touched a hand to my arm, I paused and glanced at him irritably.

"What's up?"

"There are conditions."

I lifted a brow. "Conditions? What you talking 'bout, bruh, ain't no—" God snapped his fingers and I felt my spirit crack into a million pieces. I felt like a shattered stone before I crumbled to pieces.

"Say, fool, what kinda games—" I began until I blinked, and found myself standing in the familiar room I shared with my earth. The room was dark, save for the light of morning that spilled in through the open window. Everything was just as I'd left it; all my things were still in their place, and that's when my eyes fell upon the sensual curve of my baby's body beneath the black fur blanket. The moonlight barely kissed her beautiful face and as I studied her, I wondered if she knew that she'd gotten away with a gangsta. I loved lady without flaw, and my heart cracked at the thought of not being able to show that business.

"Love is a funny thing, Ghetto, it's a gift that a lot of times, comes at an unexpected time. It's just like Cinderella at 11:59pm." God spoke from behind me. I never took my eyes off my rib.

"Eleven fifty-nine p.m.? Cinderella?"

"Yes, at twelve the fairy godmother told her she'd change back into her natural self. Love—when not loved properly—will change as well."

"You said there were conditions?" I wasn't trying to get into all the parable-type shit.

"There are."

"Conditions *for what*, my dude?" I asked and as if she could hear us, a slight frown eased onto Heaven's face. Her eyes cracked open for a brief moment before drifting shut again.

"Never," the word was barely audible as she turned to her other side. I smiled. Queen was talking in her sleep. "Fantasy," she mumbled before rolling onto her back.

"I wonder what she's dreaming 'bout," I spoke more to myself than him, but God chuckled.

"Had a feeling you'd say that, so—" He clapped his hands before rubbing them together anxiously. "Conditions!" he smiled. My eyes drifted to him curiously. "No matter what y'all do, *you can't* reveal who stole your life. No matter what! Not even a hint! If you do, you lose her *forever*." His bargain was strange.

'Man, what the hell you talking about?" I was confused. God nodded to her.

"Step in."

"Huh?"

"You said you want to know what she's dreaming about, right?" His question caused my heart to pound as I nodded my confirmation. He nodded back before glancing down at his watch. "Well, Sun, I have a game of chess to finish. I'll catch you in traffic." He chuckled at his own attempt at being hip, before turning on the heels of his gators and making his way to the door.

"Say, God—" I paused him. "How—I mean, what am I 'pose to do?" I didn't understand how she'd hear or see me. God smirked.

"Ghetto, you stay on the woman's mind, so—" He shrugged. "Just step into it"

"Her mind?"

"Well-yea, sun."

"How?" My eyes drifted to the woman I'd gamble it all for.

"You remember the story of Sleeping Beauty?" God finally got a laugh out of me.

"Say, you're a mu'fucka. Why are you always playing games, bruh?"

Silence! I glanced back to find the dude had vanished.

Step into her mind? I wondered. *Sleeping Beauty?* "Man, this dude—" I began but paused when I remembered how Sleeping Beauty had been awakened. Still skeptical, I made my way over to my Nubian and studied her natural beauty, and I realized at that moment that whether it worked or not, I'd been yearning to kiss her since I'd left her that night. So, that's what I did. I leaned down, the moon playing over our faces, and placed my lips against hers, and the strangest shit happened.

***

Ghetto

The dawn of morning had arrived, casting the heavens into shallow and dark grays, a hint of soft pinks, intermingled with a slash of baby blue. Below its majesty, the wilderness was wild, untamed, beautiful! Massive, ancient trees rose high into the sky, some three hundred feet high, and the thick, tropical vegetation surrounding them gave the jungle-like land the perfect kiss of danger trapped within a gorgeous imperfection. There were hundreds of different species of wild plants; some hot pink, some greenish-orange, and others with the appearance of ordinary ivy vines, but all had poisonous attributes. Heaven couldn't seem to understand how she'd gotten there, but even more, as her vision fell to her naked flesh, she wondered why she stood in her birthday suit; body shining with a slight sheen of perspiration. A loud cry from above drew her pretty eyes up toward the canopy of trees, where she found a large flock of colorful parrots; some watching her curiously, and others paying her no mind. Their sing-song bird calls merged into a tropical symphony that brought life to the morning, and as Heaven's vision fell to take in her surroundings, she found the source of humidity.

About ten feet to her right; lay a steaming hot spring that sat directly below a cascading waterfall. Her lips parted as she began to take timid steps toward it, eyes digesting the aquamarine-hued water. Reaching its edge, she cautiously dipped a pedicured foot into its bowels, moaning in appreciation as her eyes drifted shut. Yet, as she appreciated, unbeknownst to her, she was being appreciated.

The jungle was alive with predators lurking within its shadows. A massive, yellow and white python slithered through the thick plants, its forked tongue flickering and tasting the air as it crawled in an unearthly motion toward the warm water. Not far away, moving on his feet and knuckles, a huge gorilla with menacing eyes

120

hurled through the hanging vines and thick brush; huffing and grunting as it moved. Suddenly, he paused, dark eyes searching as he sniffed the air. The ape caught the alien whiff of a woman in the air and the strange fragrance brought a deeper scowl to his angry face. The beast huffed hot air before moving forward, excited by curiosity, but there was another predator that had beat him to the feast. A seven hundred-pound, black panther crouched low, its emerald green eyes studying the woman as she slipped into the warm water. His acute hearing caught the 'hsss' that escaped through her gritted teeth, and the panther growled deep in its belly before running its tongue over its sharp teeth. His dark fur was a strange contrast amidst the multicolored plants and flowers, but it somehow helped him blend in with nature. As he stalked from the tall grass; watching his prey disappear beneath the surface of the water, it was then that he chose to hunt. Gliding from his place of hiding; with blinding speed, his powerful muscles moved beneath his fur in beautiful dangerousness. And just as Heaven re-emerged, the feline skidded to an abrupt stop at the stone and grass edge of the spring. Dust rose from the earth as his prey screamed in surprise; eyes open wide in fearful shock. The panther roared with a flash of razor-sharp teeth before feasting his beautiful eyes upon her, and within his gaze, Heaven shuddered at the hunger thriving there. Her hands clapped over her mouth in an attempt of imprisoning the scream crawling its way up her throat. "Oh my God!" she murmured from behind cupped hands before taking fearful steps backwards. The panther growled as killer instinct whispered to its nature; goading him to dip his massive paw into the steamy water. Heaven dove beneath the warm surface, and the beast let out a monstrous roar, revealing its razor-sharp teeth before pursuing his food. Heaven felt the water shift as the predator hunted and her heart sank. On impulse, she swam as hard as she could toward the waterfall, hoping to find deliverance from the animal's intentions. When her fingers touched a rock, she shot up, breaking the surface in a splash before swallowing a deep gulp of air to soothe her burning lungs. The overhang of the waterfall shadowed her, and the water pouring down before her revealed she'd swam behind the cascading water. Her eyes desperately searched for a way out, but the rocky cove held her captive and made her easy prey for the determined animal. Her eyes grew wide when she spotted the surge cutting beneath the water and heading straight for her. Heart pounding against her chest, Heaven cursed herself for the rash decision of swimming into her own defeat. With nothing else left, and trapped within a moment of despair, something wild and vicious eased into her spirit. She was a mother that would not desert her already fatherless son! She was a spoken-for woman who knew that for her to give up would mean giving up on her future with Ghetto. "I won't," she whispered as she braced herself. The turbulence in the water was upon her, and just when the predator burst up from the waters, Heaven swung with all she had. She cried out when the painter's hand caught her wrists in an iron grip, and as she swung with her free hand, it dawned on her in the heat of battle that something was unnatural. She cried out in shock when the beast roared, but it wasn't the fear that rendered her speechless! It was the vision of the man-"me"-standing nude before her. Heaven gasped in shock as my wet dreadlocks swung wildly about my head, dripping warm water. Smirking down at her, "peace, Earth, I've missed you."

***

Heaven

As the water fell from above our heads the sun chose that moment to rise above the world. Ghetto gently released my wrists before pulling me to him- "I swear, I've missed ya pretty ass with my soul, lady."

His words knocked at the door of my heart but I was afraid to answer. Speechless! That's the only word that could describe me at the moment and when I didn't return his hug, Ghetto slowly pulled away with a perplexed expression on his handsome face. "Sup, ma, you didn't miss me?" He sounded wounded. Yet, I merely studied him, willing him not to disappear on me, and only when I felt confident he wouldn't, did I lift a hand to caress his jaw. With eyes forming their own baptism, I etched every detail of his chocolate-hued face into my memory. Pushing away a stray dread, I couldn't take my eyes away from the only man that had ever been able to crack through the stone I'd built around my heart; he was beautiful to me.

"Ghetto?" His name slipped from my lips upon a breath I wished I could suck back in so I could savor it for all time. He nodded his acknowledgment as a slow smile broke out across his face.

My left eye released a slow leak as I smiled up at him and without warning—Pow! I'd slapped fire from him. I was out of control as I cried and swung wild and cried my little heart out. "I-I hate you! Why you-you left us! I tollld-yoou-no-not-to-to leave, Ghetto, I-I told youuu!" I cried. Again he wrapped me up within his embrace, fighting to keep my arms at my side.

"Chill, peace, Heaven, I know, baby, I know," he whispered as I surrendered to his touch. He held me to his chest, allowing my tears to drip down his pecks.

"I-I hate you sooo much," I whined like a big baby. Ghetto released me before holding me by the arms.

"Naww, you don't, Heaven, don't say that shit, baby," he begged.

"I hate you! I hate this feeling you've created inside me for you! I hate you! I hate that you left me and yours alone in this cold world! I ha-hate you! I hate you! I hate you!"

"Stop, Heaven! Just-stop, bae!" he demanded, his eyes filling with an agony that was too wide for Christopher Columbus to lie and claim to have discovered geography so vast. I paused, staring at him from eyes leaking my own pain. The waterfall fell just behind him, framing my warrior within its wilderness. "What, you think I wanted this shit, Heaven, huh?" He roared like the king of his jungle, but I was drowning in our love.

"I hate your ass, Ghetto, I-I wish we never met! Wish I never let you fuck me."

"No!" he growled, shaking his head in denial, refusing my fire.

"Yes!" I nodded; battling against his head shake of "no". My fire fought his ice, both elements powerful upon our battlefield.

"Don't say that, baby, I'm in love with you, Heaven!"

"Fuck love!" I roared like a lioness and Ghetto's hand lifted like he wanted to choke me. I glared, daring him. "The streets ain't got no love-no heart, so I ripped mine out so I won't have one either!" I swore and this time his hands did wrap around my neck. But just when he applied a bit of pressure, Ghetto did what only Ghetto does. His hand slipped behind my neck before he pulled me to him. My hands went to his chest to push him away, but his ice melted into water that extinguished my fire, and before I knew it, his slippery tongue was sensually wrestling mine into an erotic submission. "Umm ummmmm!" I refused his dominance, but my man knew the path to my submissiveness.

"Uhhm!" He nodded yes before backing me up until my back was against the cool rock of the waterfall. Upon releasing my tongue, he sucked my bottom lip before stepping away from me, "Turn around," he demanded. Eyes still wet, I shook my head no before becoming verbal.

"No!" I refused, yet, Ghetto is a warrior of the hood niggas tribe and they believed in their women being submissive. That's law!

"Turn-yo-ass around!" he growled before his hand became a blur and found a fistful of my hair, and the pain of his pull caused me to obey.

"Ahhh'I cried, but my body craved. Ghetto wrapped more of my wet hair around his fist for a better grip before using his knee to force my legs apart, and once my ass was tooted back, he pushed the palm of his other hand down into the small of my lower back.

"Baaaaby!" I moaned when he opened me up. His strokes became deep and crooked as he gave me too much at once. I cried, moaned, purred, praised Ghetto, and took that dick like a big girl. "I've missed you so-sooo-oo much!" I cried in painful pleasure. It was something about cumming that had the power to make a girl forsake her grudge, anger, and thoughts altogether.

"Nawww!" Ghetto growled before—smack! He slapped my ass with a force so strong my mouth fell open in a silent "O", but the way he worked that dick kidnapped my ability to talk. Pulling out to

the tip of his arrow, my Cupid drove in powerfully with a quick suc-cession of stabs before pulling out and slowly driving back into me until my lower lips kissed his nuts.

"Uhhh! Uh! Uh! Ohh-oo!" I cried in painful ecstasy and that's when his strokes became so beautiful that they became poetry in motion.

"Give—me—thisss—cum!" Ghetto demanded and with each inward stroke, poetry played within my mind. Almost as if he were whispering it in my ear.

***

"I know one day I'll be the kind of man you need...I just hope I wake up in time to become that man before you decide to leave.

The mere thought makes it hard to breathe. So, I inhale our memories and hold onto the daydreams of what I dream us to be.

A revolutionary black love drifting upon the waves of a vast sea! I'm trapped within a fantasy, a picture splashed upon an un-tainted canvas...A painting depicting me stranded...on a deserted island where I've been banished. I won't lie, without you, life just doesn't feel the same, but somehow I've managed...Just me, day-dreaming on my deserted island, where a wounded animal can cry in peace without his pride being damaged. The animal inside of me."

***

Ghetto

I'd carried baby onto a smooth rock that was positioned just beneath the waterfall, she watched me curiously as I laid on my back and beckoned her to climb aboard. Fear, intertwined with cu-riosity, danced within her gaze. But she obeyed nonetheless. At-tempting to place her knees on either side of me, I paused her. "Naw, Queen, just squat over me. Put your feet right here," I in-structed. "Put your hands on my chest." I guided her until she was in a frog-hopping position with hands planted on my chest. Reaching between us, I positioned myself. "Now rise and allow me into your world, love," I requested in a gruff tone. Heaven seemed unsure and her facial betrayed her.

"I'm-I don't know how to—"

"Shiiish," I shushed her. "Never fear what you should be trusting. Where I shall lead, just follow me. You don't trust me or what?" Heaven nodded before rising to the tip of my south pole and slowly sliding down, allowing me to explore her battlefield.

"Hhuuu," she sucked in a deep breath, her eyes half-mast as she surrendered her vulnerability to a real nigga. When her essence had digested me down to the hilt, Heaven sat there, her pussy molding around me like a sculptor's clay. Her eyes told me she wanted me to lead, so I became baby's navigator as warm water fell upon us from above.

"Now bounce for me" I instructed. Her bounce was slow and sensual in the beginning, but as pleasure clashed with pain, love's pace quickened. Balancing on her tiptoes, Heaven dug her nails into the flesh of my chest while she nibbled the corner of her bottom lip. That shit turned me on. My eyes fell to her nipples; they were the size of Hershey's kisses and when my eyes reconnected with her, she knew I craved to suffocate them with my lips.

"Uhh-uhhh!" she moaned as she bounced a dance, and before I knew it, Heaven had begun to twerk on my nature. "Ghet-too I nee-need you, baby. Nee-need you sooo-oo-much!" she revealed through gritted teeth as I reached down and wrapped my fingers around her ankles. I held on tight as our eyes wrestled.

"Can you see? Can you read my mind, Heaven?" I growled and baby merely nodded her head as she lifted and fell upon me like a giant wave of the ocean. Her waters oozed down my inches, bathing my nuts and made me sticky.

"Yo-Yes, I-I'm coming!" she cried and her eyes danced with mine as I mentally willed her to understand what I felt for her.

***

"I want you to trust me, baby, but please don't trust me, baby, I'm irresponsible when it comes to love...

I've traveled the world and broken a million hearts, it took me meeting you to learn what I really was.

I don't want you to trust me, baby, but please trust me, baby, let's erase and replace what I said above.....

A contradiction trapped within my confliction, like finding pain lounging within the waters of love.

You just wanna be loved.

I'm just scared of love.... We're facing off on a battlefield, tug of war for something fragile and precious...

A prayer within the church of intimacies imperfections, the whole while, cupping our hands, anticipating catching intimacies blessings.

We've created an earth with no wind, but consumed with a whole lot of fire. Ms. Right gives chance to Mr. Wrong, dancing within the flames of carnal desire. Fucking you is like listening to the devil cry...Making love to you is like hearing God laugh...

Making you happy is like reaching up and grabbing the sun, and with the other hand grasping the stem of a rose, then pulling with all my might and making the earth and the sky crash.

I'm speaking to you from the animal inside me."

***

Heaven

"Is this a dream, Ghetto?" I asked a rhetorical question. Bodies glistening with sweat after I'd pulled his spirit up into my Heaven, I sat wrapped within Ghetto's arms. Back to his chest as he rested against the warm rock, I felt him shrug.

"I don't know." For some reason, his answer turnt my skies gray. Gazing out at the strange spring, I traced my fingers over the arm he held around my waist.

"Can I ask you a question and you keep it real with me?"

"Real is all I know, Heaven, and you should know that. What it do?"

"Who's Red Diamond?" The question got a flinch out of him, but I merely smiled sadly.

"She's a woman I have history with."

"Have you ever fucked her?" Even before the words slipped from his lips, I had my answer. Men's body language often speaks their truths before their lips do, but in Ghetto's case, it was his silence.

"Yea, we've fornicated."

"Fucked," I corrected, not letting him soften the blow.

"Fucking is when sex becomes animalistic." He was adamant.

"Oh," I spat with a roll of my eyes. "So, now you're defending the bitch?"

His chuckle was deep and it pissed me off. I attempted to pull his arm from around me, but Ghetto held fast.

"Sit yo ass down, woman."

"Let me go, Ghetto"

"Don't be like a simple bitch, Heaven." His words caused me to stare at him from the side eye, and though he took in my offended expression, Ghetto was a God that reigned over his earth versus his earth reigning over his Godism. "A simple bitch would think I was defending what needs no defense. A simple bitch feels with her heart instead of her mind." He tapped a finger to his temple. "Most of all, a simple bitch wants the truth, but loses the ability to "think" after they receive it. Like—" He paused to kiss the back of my neck. "Like you just asked me if I've ever fucked this woman, and the truth didn't cause you to think of if I'm worthy enough to keep moving forward with but instead caused you to find another misunderstanding to stack on top of the one we're already having. You're so fucked up bout me piping this lady, that you don't even consider that I had a life 'before' you." His realisms were absolute, but hell, I'm all woman!

"Do you love her?" I needed to know. Ghetto considered the question and that alone ran me tea kettle hot! "Oh, so, you have to think about it?"

"What type of bitch wants a man that doesn't think? Yes, I'm considering 'how' I answer you, 'cause you showing me that you're not gonna 'think' in your reaction to something that hurts you."

"Answer my question, Ghetto?" I wasn't trying to hear it.

"Yes, I love her."

"Wha—"

"I have history with Red, Heaven, she's my family, and before that she was—"

"Your bitch, the bitch who loved you unconditionally and—"

"There's no such thing as unconditional love, ma." Ghetto released me and I stood up before facing him. I could tell he recognized he'd cracked my heart, I didn't care; before me or after me, no woman wants to know that the man she loves was, or is capable of loving the next bitch. It's the same with a man, no matter what, he'll always wish he was the first and last nigga to fuck the gal he loves. I'm a woman that loves unconditionally, and not only was the man I love telling me he loved another bitch; he was now telling me my love is a lie. Wrong answer! I was saying when Ghetto climbed to his feet, the waterfall behind him sent sprays of water against his skin.

"What, Heaven? You fucked up I'm keeping it "G" with you? Red Diamond is a bitch that has killed with and over me, so yea, I love her as the type of bitch she is. Yet, I'm "in" love with you, and the word 'in' is what changes the entire concept of love. It means I'm actually in the love I have for you, my nigga, it means I choose you over it all! When you're "in" something, it sits surrounding you; it's your world to fix and tend to, and manifest "within". Shid, I love my dogs, my clothes, my money, but all that shit has its limits." He stepped closer to me, masculinity swinging between his legs and causing the nature between mine to moisten in spite of myself.

"Ghetto, that's cool, but you can't tell me how "I" should feel. Truth or not, that shit still bothers me. Now, I'm far from naive and I understand your vibe, but I'm selfish with you. This bitch told me how her love for you is unconditional and how you—"

"There's no such thing as unconditional love, ma, even God has conditions. If you piss him off and don't follow his plan, he sends

129

you to hell." He gave me a new perspective. "If a nigga ain't loving you how you feel he should be, you'll either fuck over him or leave him. If you're not following the rules of mama's house, she puts you out." He chuckled.

Conditions. He made his point. I smacked my lips before switching lanes.

"Ghetto, if this is a dream, at least tell me who killed you or—" I corrected myself. "Or who 'tried' to? Let me show you that all love isn't conditional."

Ghetto frowned before a smile eased onto his face, a sad one. "Bae, the word "condition" has a definition of working something into shape or influence. So, if love is an action word, it has to be formed into a working condition...As for who killed me?" he asked with a thoughtful expression. "It was—"

"RRRRAAROAR!" A vicious growl shook the ground, cutting him off. I spun around just in time to see a monstrous ape explode from the tropical forest, and that gorilla was humongous! It slammed its knuckles against the ground challengingly as my jaw dropped in awe. It then stood upright, almost seven feet tall before the beast began to pound its massive fist against its chest. "RRRRROAR!" Its roar was demanding as it fell back to its knuckles and flashed its sharp teeth. Then "GRRROAR!" Another roar shook the earth, but one more feline, and coming from behind me. I spun to see if Ghetto was safe, only to find him gone and that giant black panther baring its razor-sharp canines. Its emerald eyes took me in from behind a menacing frown of its beautiful face. The muscles moved beneath its sleek fur as its eyes shot to the gorilla, and my heart pounded against my chest in terror.

"Ghetto?" I murmured, and as if my voice was the war cry, both animals charged. At first, I thought I was the feast, but to my surprise, I was merely the meal they would battle for.

"RRROAR!" The gorilla roared as it leapt into the air, its massive fists held high above its head as if it would clobber the panther to death.

"GRRRROR!" The panther growled as it flew into the air, one massive claw reared back as if it would shred the beast. The cat's

teeth were on full display as the two beasts crashed like the big bang theory!

"Ahhhhh! Arrrhhh!" I screamed as I exploded up from my bed. "Heaven?" A familiar voice cut through my hysteria and my eyes flew open. My body was saturated with sweat as my heart pounded against my rib cage.

"Take a deep breath, sis, you were having a bad dream," Catrina, my sister, calmed me as she bounced my son against her shoulder. I took those deep breaths, calming the gallop of my heart as I registered the morning sun pouring in through my open window. The cool breeze that flowed through it caused the drapes to flutter, and the smell of the Brazos River was a welcomed company.

"You okay?" Catrina wanted to know, and when our eyes connected, I could see the concern on her pretty face. Nodding, I used my hands to wipe sweat from my brow.

"Yea, I—it—it was just sooo real!" I frowned. *That dream was tooooo real!*

"You sure?" she studied me quizzically. ever since the strange episode at the hospital, she'd been worried about me.

"Yes, Catrina, I'm good, sis," I confirmed, and Khalief stirred at the sound of my voice. He'd throw a fit in a moment, and I needed to clean up a little before doing mama's duties. "Let me take a quick shower and I'll take him," I told sis, and she nodded, giving me one last gaze before turning to make her exit. "Catrina?" I called to her just before she did. She glanced back at me. My baby sister had grown her hair, and it was framing her head in soft, curly tendrils. *Beautiful!* "Thank you, baby girl, for being my rock. I really appreciate it, sis."

"Heaven, you're my sister, there's *nothing* I won't do for you. You and this little pest are all I have left." she kissed the top of my son's head.

"Get yourself tougher, girl, I've cooked breakfast." She smiled before retreating. I fell back onto the mattress. I could hardly believe it when I turned onto my side and placed my hands between my legs. The crotch of my boy short was soaking wet; that dream was so real!

Renta

"Wake up, Ghetto, I need the animal in you."

Chapter Five

Cock Fight

Heaven

After we'd showered and eaten breakfast, I got me and Khalief ready to go sit with Ghetto. "Well, we're off, Catrina, call me if you need me." I told my sister as I put Khalief in his car seat. She stood in the doorway with a smile on her face.

"Girl, you're acting as if you're going across the world, you're only—" Her voice trailed off as her eyes lifted beyond me. Though the sun had risen high above the earth, when I followed her stare, a chill ran down my spine at the sight of the black SUV making its way up the drive. It was followed by a multitude of other cars, and all of them had red and blue lights flashing from either the front or the top of their shining roofs. My mouth fell open, and as if he could feel the wrongness of the approaching motorcade, Khalief began to ball his little eyes out. The SUV was the first to screech to a stop, and two men in pants and windbreakers jumped out.

"Ms. Domingo," the man from the passenger side acknowledged. I frowned when he held up an official piece of paper, but even before he spoke his next words, the three letters on his jacket were self-sufficient: *FBI.* "Mam, I'm Agent Crosby and this here is my partner Joseph. This here is a search warrant for this house, the deed is in the name of a Genevieve Bousard, but we can't seem to find her." He gave me a questioning brow.

"Can I see that?" I extended my hand for the paper, but even before it was in my hand, the search was on. What seemed to be a million officers descended upon the house, drug dogs, and strange objects in tow. As I read the warrant, my reason for attending the university kicked in; criminal justice required me to learn the law!

"You know the fourth amendment, right? *Protection from unreasonable search and seizure? That one.*" I showed him I wasn't just some lame bitch. Agent Crosby smiled as he accepted his little warrant back.

"Of course, but I'm sure you're familiar with the term *probable cause* and *Rule 41* of the federal rules of criminal procedure?" He smirked before nodding toward the house. "Not only do we have reason to believe that Devonte Bousard purchased this property with illegal gains, but we also have reason to believe that within his criminal activities, Genevieve Bousard and Heaven Domingo—" Again, he paused to smirk, nodding at me. "That's you—are accomplices." His *assumptions* set fire inside me, but not as much as his next words. "Devonte Bousard is wanted for question in a string of murders and heists throughout the states of Atlanta, Mississippi, Louisiana, and Texas. We've tracked him here." The prick seemed to be enjoying his job. When officers began walking out the house with boxes of things, I lost it!

"Uh uh! Why the fuck are y'all taking our shit! Ghet—I mean, Devonte isn't here and our things have nothing to—"

"Everything to do with this case. *Seizures of items in plain view* doctrine, Ms. Domingo, was first used in the *Coolidge vs. New Hampshire* case as well as Texas vs Brown." He was well-versed in his duties and when his partner stepped around him and made his way over, I knew things were about to get worse.

"Ms. Domingo, I'm Agent Joseph of the Federal Bureau of Investigations, and we need you to come with us." He said this before gently taking me by the arm.

"Wha—What!" I stuttered. I struggled against his attempt to *cuff me*!

"What the hell y'all doing? I'm gonna sue you mu'fuckas! Hey, let my sister go!" Catrina stormed out of the house just as I was about to bop the agent in the mouth. "What the hell's going on, Heaven?" I could see the uncertainty radiating from her gaze as she wondered if this fiasco had anything to do with any of our past crooked dealings. I gave her a quick nod against the idea, and it was only when I registered the cries of me and Ghetto's creation that I relaxed and allowed my abductor to cuff me.

"Watch Khalief for me and I'll be back as soon as I'm free."

"Yea, that may be a very long time, Ms. Domingo," Agent Crosby said.

"Oh my God! I thought. I was, for the first time ever, escorted to the back of a police car. *May be a very long time, Ms. Domingo!* His words played in my mind as my son's cries faded when I was secured in that back seat. I gazed out at Catrina holding him, no doubt attempting to convince him and herself that everything would be alright.

***

Empress

Yes, the day I helped Heaven and Catrina fight those girls back when we were in high school, *I was just a boy.* But as soon as I became old enough to do it, I began my transformation, and now I'm *all woman.* I can give two fucks about the opinion of the next bitch or nigga. I'm a bad bitch and if a hoe disagrees, I'll fuck her nigga to prove it. Period! Me and Stick Talk had become an item, and just like any other nigga, after a bitch put these fluffy lips and this *new* cootie cat on him, the man forgot our little dilemma. That's how we found ourselves somewhere in the country at that old man Clifton's illegal spot. Stick Talk is a street nigga through and through, so romance wasn't his forte. Yet, I enjoyed what my baby enjoyed. The room was smoky and loud as bets were made and tobacco and ganja were smoked. The fighting pit had just been raked to cover up the blood of the animals that had just fought to the death. *Weird*! I thought, as two Mexicans entered the pit from opposite sides. Each man held a large bird in his hand; those big ass roosters were beautiful, and as soon as they were released, all hell broke loose. The first one to be let free had feathers that were a mixture of blackish blue that faded into a strange plumage of white on his fluffy tail, and the other cock was a rust hue with a plumage of red feathers. Both birds spread their large wings and screeched threateningly before taking flight, sharp talons aimed at each other. The crowd was drunk with excitement and as my eyes swept across, I spotted the old man Clifton chomping down on a cigar as he nursed a short glass of cognac. *Shreeek!* The war cry of the pugnacious *combative* birds drew my attention back to the ring, and that's when I noticed the razor-sharp knives attached to their feet. The blackish cock seemed more aggressive, but the brown one was well-trained. Knives sliced through the air as both male chickens screeched and flapped their large wings. A blade cut through the plumage of the blackish bird, and blood squirted free, but as if he wouldn't be satisfied until he got his lick back, that beautiful cock clawed and fought until the razor attached to its feet sliced through the flesh of his opponent. The blades cut and shot blood everywhere as the two cocks fought to the death! Amid the action, I glanced over to see how old man Clifton was faring, and what I saw froze my blood. The seat next to the old man which was empty just a moment ago was now occupied. It wouldn't have bothered me if the man who'd just taken his seat hadn't been none other than the cat I'd come to know as RNO Thugga. *Now, why would an RNO nigga that's from an entirely different state come all the way out to the country to have a sit-down with the last man that saw Ghetto alive, outside of me and Stick?* I wondered as the two men leaned close and began to have what appeared to be an important conversation. I got Stick Talk's attention and nodded in their direction, and his jaw dropped at the sight of his brother in arms. Then the surprise wore off and that killer shit eased into his gaze, and when the two men rose and disappeared through the crowd, Stick Talk leaned and whispered: "Thugga's whip is the burnt orange Benz with the swangas on it. Do your work." He sealed the mission with a kiss to the cheek before going on the hunt. I smirked just as the rust brown cock's blade cut through the neck of his *op*, and thinking of Stick Talk's Gangsta ass, my hormones kicked in! *Damn, I'm beginning to love this boy!*

***

Heaven

"Don't fucking lie to me!" Agent Crosby shouted before slapping the table. They'd kept me in the cold investigation room for an hour before they'd begun their routine, but I'd watched too many episodes of *Law and Order* and too many movies not to know the tactic! Ghetto had once told me it's called the tactic of anxiety, where they keep a suspect waiting for long periods to allow fear to reach its zenith before they entered the room on their good cop, bad cop routine. Hence; what I was going through now. Joseph was playing the role of the good cop whereas Crosby played the bad one routine. *Blam!* Crosby slapped the table once again. "You think we're stupid, Ms. Domingo, we're the fucking FBI, for Christ's sake!" he spat, a light sheen of perspiration covering his face from the effort he put forth.

"Crosby-Crosby, come on now, that's no way to speak to a lady, partner, let me handle this while you cool off, go have a coffee or something." Agent Joseph portrayed the calm of the storm. Making his way over to the table, he placed a file on it before opening it. "I know you're thirsty, Ms. Domingo, would you like a coffee? A coke perhaps?" he offered.

"Mother of Mary, Joseph, the lady, and her friggin boy toy are modern-day Bonnie and Clyde on steroids, man, and you want to offer her—"

"Chill, man, I'm a pretty good judge of character and I don't think Ms. Domingo will be a problem, especially after she sees the *evidence* we have on her," Crosby pump faked. I sat back in my seat, arms crossed over my chest and legs crossed as I bounced my foot. I rolled my eyes at the two lames. The entire hour and thirty minutes they'd been trying to *break me,* I hadn't said one word! I knew that anything I said would be and could be used against me in a court of law. Staring daggers at the man, I *appeared* as solid as stone but internally I was so lost! Just when you thought you knew a person, life threw you a curve ball and as soon as you caught it, you realize you truly didn't know a thing! The things they accused Ghetto of were wicked! Yes, I saw the killer in him. A lioness can *always* recognize the king of the jungle, but damn! They were making my man out to be a *serial killer!* The good thing about it is they couldn't have known that he was laid up comatose in the hospital.

"See, Ms. Domingo, we here in the Bureau have a ninety-five percent conviction rate, so, that's saying—" He paused to pull something out of the folder, and that's when my world was turned upside down. "When we got ya, we got ya!" He chuckled. "Save yourself, Ms. Domingo, you're young and too pretty to go down for that scumbag," he offered, and my heart fell because the pictures I was staring at had *nothing* to do with Ghetto, but everything to do with *me and my girls!*

***

Grrrroof! The massive pit bull barked viciously. The blue pit's muscles were prominent beneath his sleek fur as it reared back as if it were preparing to attack, sharp teeth bared as it growled menacingly. Eight other of its species followed suit. Many of the dogs were of the bully breed, and others of the razor bloodline but all were vicious and all were posed to attack. Many barked, others growled while showing an impressive display of vampire-like teeth, and as the two men strolled through their habitat, they were ready to protect it. *Snap!* The jaws of a dog almost the size of a hyena snapped shut as it lunged at Thugga. He jumped back in surprise at the sudden attack but when the massive animal slammed against the wall of its cage, the man breathed a sigh of relief. Thugga's eyes took in the dog kennel in its entirety, amazed at the number of barking pit bulls. To his left stood an all-white beauty that appeared to be on steroids! As it bared its sharp teeth, long drips of saliva dripped from its jaws as it growled. Clifton chuckled as he pulled the wet cigar from between his teeth. "So, it's true?" he asked, cringing at the mere thought of it. "He's dead? They killed my boy?" the man asked, not wanting to believe a man as sharp as Ghetto could allow suckas to get the drop on him. Thugga nodded, *feeling* the love for his brethren radiating from the man. *This old head couldn't*

138

have had a hand in bro's demise! his heart summarized. Though they were strangers, the vibe revealed.

"Yea, OG, that's why I'm here. Me and my people got the taste of blood on our tongues and we're turning over the earth to find out what happened." He revealed his reasons for being there.

"And the old soil lead you here?" old man Clifton asked, before facing off with his visitor. "To my place of business?"

Thugga studied the man, both having the eyes of a predator. *His first lie!* Thugga's gut screamed. His mind briefly reminded him of the metal tucked on his waist, and he was prepared to down the old man right there if he had *any* doubt that he had Ghetto's blood upon his hands.

"Ole man, Clifton," he began before strangling all pretenses and upping the M&P Shield .45. The older man's eyes fell to the metal in the stranger's grip before recapturing the young wolf's cold gaze.

"I know you don't know me, OG, but please believe me when I tell you, I was bred by a savage tribe that taught us how to scalp a nigga. Listen, let's try this." He clicked the safety off. "We know Ghetto was flatlined here but for some strange reason his body was found miles away!" Thugga shook his head, fire swimming through his veins as he thought of his brother's body being dumped like trash as he died like an animal in the cold streets. Old man Clifton exhaled a long breath, gritting his teeth to calm the hurt in his heart.

"I loved that boy like a son, ya hear me? I'd warned him time and time again about the company he keeps. He just didn't listen."

"Fuck that gotta do with my Flesh's body being—"

"Let me finish goddammit!" The old man's demand left no room for debate. Though Thugga had the ups on him, it was the pools in the old man's eyes that made him respect the old head's mind. "That night, I'd got word that someone got shot, and my only thought was to get them far from here. I run a respectable place; feel me, young blood?" He waited for Thugga to nod before continuing. "I didn't find out until much later that it was my boy, and Lord is my witness, as soon as I'd reviewed the footage and seen what transpired, I went *myself* to the place my boys dumped the body and took him to the hospital!" The man raised his right hand as if to make a pledge. "I swear on my mammy's grave," he vowed but Thugga's ears had become deaf to everything after the word *footage*.

"*Footage?*" he asked before tucking the tool back on his waist. Clifton nodded, a sad smile curving his lips.

"Have you ever heard the story of Shaka Zula, Thugga?" Clifton asked before his eyes trailed to the white pit bull. The dog eyed him, calming at the sight of his owner. Thugga shook his head in confusion.

"Naw, OG, but what does that have to do with this footage? If you got—" he began, but Clifton lifting his hand gave him pause.

"See, Youngin, Ole Zulu was a bad mu'fucka! Back in the 1800s the man was a savage that created more savages, but it wasn't the African king's viciousness that allowed him to rise to power within the ranks of the men in the bush, it was *his mind!*" he schooled before unlocking the cage that kept them safe from the massive dog. *Grrrr!* The beast growled and Thugga took a step back before resting his hand on the burna.

"Say, Og!" he cautioned as the man opened the cage. In a blur, the white beast rushed out, skidding as it slid in its haste, and just as it went to make dinner of Thugga, Clifton snatched the beast by its spiked collar. *Snap!* Its teeth clamped shut only inches from the man's chest. The beast had lifted onto its hind legs, poised in a lunging motion as the old man restrained it.

"At ease, Zulu, sit, boy!" The demand was met with obedience. The dog barked before licking its chops and plopping down onto its hind legs in a sitting position. Thugga's eyes were wild, but he didn't miss the gleam of the nickel-plated .357 the old man Clifton had strategically slipped from the small of his back. "The mind was Zulu's key to success," Clifton smirked at how he'd just hoodwinked the young fella, and the shock written across Thugga's face only made him chuckle. *I've been duped!* it read. Clifton had used the dog as his strategy to get to his weapon. Thugga smirked, having to respect the raw game.

"I ain't make it this long in a treacherous game not having a few tricks up my old sleeves," Clifton laughed and to Thugga's amazement, the man rested the tool on the ground.

"Shaka Zulu began with a small little tribe, but his mind and ambition were beautiful! The warrior began laying the law down on all the other smaller chiefdoms, forcing them to either get down or lay down, same shit Russia is trying with Ukraine! Zulu whacked every one of those smaller tribes that bucked his system! The one that was with the new regime, he trained with his own men, teaching them the art of strategy. The man went as far as to learn the game from the white boys from England, that equipped him with guns to aid him in conquering his enemies. You wanna know the downfall of Shaka's reign?" He asked, and Thugga nodded, certain that the man was leading him somewhere. Clifton chuckled as he scratched the massive dog under its chin. "A man should have *a limit* to everything he does. Even the sky and oceans have limits to how deep a mu'fuicka can travel before shit gets funky, but just as it is with anyone who doesn't cap off their ambition, Shaka Zulu created *too much fear*. And fear turns respect into desperation, and desperation will cause your closest allies to become your closest enemies!" The OG nodded when the dog barked. "Shaka Zulu killed his brother to take over the Zulu tribe. He killed those who opposed him, and you know why Ghetto should've followed Shaka Zulu's example and killed the boy he once loved?" The old man's tone was as cold as stone as his vision lifted to Thugga.

"Why's that, old head?" Thugga was all ears. Clifton smiled bitterly, and it made the other man's skin crawl. Even the dog, tongue hanging from its mouth, turned its blue eyes upon its owner, and a chill ran down Thugga's spine. He knew the next words from the man would flip his universe.

"Cause just like ole Shaka Zulu was assassinated in September 1828 by his own brothers," the OG's eyes fell to his gun, "Ghetto was whacked by his brother over jealousy."

***

Heaven

I tried all I could to keep a straight face. The picture was taken from a strange angle, but even at night, the clarity of it was unblemished! It had been taken the night me and my girls had robbed Ghetto and Stick Talk. There were other pictures of us leaving our home, but the one that caused me to sweat was the one of me, Catrina, and Empress standing outside of Ghetto's spot, masked up while clutching heat as that snake— Hurk—rang the bell.

"That's-th-that's not me!" I stuttered and my voice sounded strained even to my own ears. "I want to talk to my lawyer," I demanded, though I didn't even have a lawyer.

"For fucking Christ's sake, lady!" Joseph declared while staring at me in disbelief.

"Here are the pictures of you and the other women *without* the masks before leaving home." He jabbed a finger down at a photo. "And this one is you and your little gang in the act of premeditated murder!" he spat before leaning toward me until our faces were mere inches apart. "Where'd you hide him, huh? We're gonna find his body and when we do—"

"What will you do then, Agent, huh? Are you threatening and badgering my client?" the door flew open and a tropical storm blew into the room. The handsome brother wore a navy blue, pinstripe suit as he strolled in, carrying a titanium briefcase. "My client has nothing more to say," he demanded, eyes fierce as he and Crosby eye-wrestled. Agent Joseph wiped sweat from his brow before fixing him with a distrustful stare.

"And who the hell are you!" he demanded as Bryant, a middle-aged Hispanic man, and director of the Bureau followed the man into the room.

"He's Brandon Tyler, an obnoxious son of a bitch from Ft. Worth, and he's her lawyer."

Bryant introduced. Agent Joseph glared.

"Well, this woman is a suspect in the murder of—"

"But is she under arrest? Being under arrest and being a suspect are two different realities, especially in the court of law." Brandon challenged.

"Yes! No—I—" Joseph stuttered as his eyes shot to his superior. Bryant shrugged with a strange smirk on his face.

"Let her go!" he demanded causing Joseph and Crosby's jaws to drop in shock.

"But-sh—she—" Crosby tried.

"Let it go, Crosby!" his boss demanded with a sharp glare as Brandon helped me out of my seat. His cologne wasn't too heavy, but it made him smell mouth-watering! As I was leaving, me and Crosby's eyes met and the smirk on his face held a secret that if I would've known then, rather than months later, *I would've taken my chances with twenty-four white jurors and two racist judges.*

"See you around, Ms. Domingo," he chuckled.

"Don't hold ya breath!" I spat as my knight in shining armor and strapped with a law degree, whisked me out of there.

***

Clifton Short was deep in thought as he fed his pups; he loved those dogs. He'd just given Thugga a copy of the footage capturing the night Ghetto got stepped on, and it took some of the weight off his back.

"Young niggas got the game fucked up nowadays," he spat and the massive brindle-colored pit bull he was feeding barked in response. "You feel me, huh, gal?" The old man chuckled but frowned when the dog's body language became aggressive. "What's wrong, girl?" he asked before reaching up to pet the animal he'd raised, but the dog's teeth bared and before ole Clifton could stop her, the beast shot passed him. "Bitch!" he cursed in confusion, but when he turned around, he was just in time to see the dog leap into the air, mouth wide, set for a vicious bite as it lunged for a man who'd appeared unannounced. *Boom!* The gunshot blew the side of the airborne dog's face off, but its momentum kept it in flight until it crashed into the fence. When Clifton recognized the murderer, he went for his pistol and it cost him. *Boom! Boom!*

Two shots hit him and he fell to his knees. Stick Talk was all business when he stepped into the cage, and over to his victim. Clifton clutched his stomach as his other hand rested inches from his gun, but common sense warned him not to move. On his knees, the old man coughed up a spill of blood "You-you rot-rotten, punk!" he sputtered with blood on his lips. Stick Talk kicked him in the face so hard, his head snapped back and sent a splatter of blood into the air. The man fell to the side, but wanting to look into his eyes, Stick Talk used his foot to maneuver him onto his back. The old head fought to breathe as his eyes glazed, and he wondered how he'd let a fuck boy get the ups on him.

"You should've minded your business, old man, now look at ya," Stick Talk teased, knowing Clifton was the last link that could tie him to Ghetto's slaying. He glanced down at his kicks and wanted to smoke dude for that alone. "Bitch ass nigga got blood all over my retros!" he spat.

"They gon-gonna kill you suc-ka!" the wounded man fought to speak, and smiled a bloodied smile before spitting a spray of bloody saliva toward Stick Talk. He was ready to die. Stick Talk respected his gangsta and nodded his acknowledgement before shrugging.

"*Maybe* but *you* won't be here to celebrate with them," he chuckled before stepping on the man's stomach and ending all chit chat. *Boom! Boom! Boom! Boom!* All face shots.

***

Empress

Thugga slid behind the wheel of his whip before tossing a manila envelope onto the passenger's seat. He slapped the steering wheel aggressively.

"Bitch ass nigga!" he spat with a disbelieving shake of his head.

"Red Diamond was right!" he growled before hitting the push start on the Benz. The sexy bitch came to life in a slow purr as Thugga pulled out his phone.

After his fingers danced across the screen, he placed the device to his ear and waited for an answer. Seconds passed before— "Look, Nubian, mask the apes up, I know who killed Ghetto. The nigga—" he was saying when I slithered up from behind his seat and placed the barrel to the back of his dome. Thugga froze, our eyes clashed in the rearview mirror, and to his credit, dude tried it. "What the—" *Boca!*

His memory bank splashed against the windshield when I gave him the coup de grace. The man's body fell forward, his face slamming into the steering wheel before I reached over and took the envelope off the passenger seat. Hurriedly, I pushed the door open; it was time to dip.

"Give my love to Ghetto," I whispered before slipping from the foreign.

"Hello? Thugga! Hell naw! Not my nigga!" Whoever the bitch was on the phone screamed. I giggled before pulling open the driver's door. Thugga was slumped over the steering wheel, facing me. I shook my head at the blank stare of his dead eyes as I reached down and intertwined a white gold necklace between his fingers. The deed was done and I quickly fled the murder scene. The pink bandanna covering the bottom half of my face concealed the smile I gave as I thought of the *BMG* chain and medallion I'd just left in the man's hand. It was *a token of their love!*

Renta

Chapter Six

Esquire

Heaven

It was late in the afternoon when the platinum-colored, Corvette Z06 3LZ pulled up to the house me, and Ghetto shared in the country. Under ordinary circumstances, I would've never shown another man where me and my king rested our heads, but this wasn't an ordinary circumstance, and this man had just rescued me.

"Nice crib," He acknowledged when pulling to a stop in the circular drive. I nodded, eyes taking in the beauty of the gray brick ranch house. It was beautiful and held so many good memories.

"What happens now? I mean—" I shrugged. "I know this isn't over, but what do they have on me? My girls?" I asked softly, eyes never leaving the landscape of the house I planned to raise my son in. I could feel the man's eyes on me, appraising me.

"A little, but not enough. Besides—" He sat back in his seat, tracing his perfectly trimmed goatee. His pause drew my attention and again I was struck by how handsome that black man was. He was a chocolate-hued version of Michael B. Jordan, but with hair like Ginuwine's was back in his heyday. *You're out of pocket, bitch!* I chastised myself for lusting. Spreading my hands in question, I lifted a brow to let him know I was waiting. "It's not you or your girls they want. It's this Devonte, *Ghetto* Bousard they're after." He shrugged indifferently.

"What they have on you and your girls is circumstantial, and with no weapon, no body, the case is pretty much open and shut for any decent lawyer," he clarified. I frowned.

"Body? Weapon?" I inquired and received an expression with question marks dancing around it. "What?" I was confused, but not for long.

"Their star informant, Mr. Drew *Hurk* Jones, came up missing. They suspect that the guy went rogue and double-crossed them while triple-crossing his friends in the process. Furthermore, they believe that before the man could disappear into the sun, he was murdered for his half of whatever was taken, but—" Again, he shrugged. "There's no evidence, they can't even be sure the man *didn't* make away with his bounty. There's no body!" he confirmed, not knowing he'd just eased my anxiety.

I exhaled a long whoosh of air before falling back into my seat and allowing my eyes to drift shut. Silence was bliss but short-lived, "Who hired you, Mr. Tyler?"

"You're a unique woman, Ms. Domingo." He chuckled, "but the one that hired me wants to stay anonymous."

"*Mrs.,*" I said just to reveal the line in the sand. Just as much as I'd admired him, I'm a *full-grown* woman, and a woman within the first ten minutes of reading a man knows if he wants to fuck her, if he's merely attracted, or if he's merely being cordial. In Mr. Tyler's case, he wouldn't mind entertaining all three or just the first two. Eyes cracking open and trailing to him, I could see he recognized the line I'd drawn; *Real bitch here!* "How so?" I asked. He chuckled, lifting his hands up in surrender.

"Hey, I'm the good guy!" he proclaimed with an innocent smile. "I'm just saying though, you're a gorgeous sista; I mean—" He frowned, searching for the words sufficient.

"You're supposed to be on the cover of someone's magazine or in a video or *something!* But, here you are, being questioned by the FBI for heinous crimes." He studied me, perplexed. I smiled sadly, he didn't have a clue. "You're a paradox, lady, and your man—*husband,*" he corrected himself, "is a lucky *brotha* to have you." The way he said the word *brotha* was more of a question. I smirked at his *cute* way of being nosey before I pushed open the passenger's side door.

A girl has to know when to place space between her and the opposite sex if she planned on remaining solid to whomever she'd entrusted her heart to, and Ghetto need not worry 'cause he's the only man I rotated around. Yet, I spoke my mind.

"Well, Mr. Tyler, I thank you for your help. I don't know who sent you, but I'm grateful." I extended my hand to him and he took it, but after the shake, Mr. Smooth went to kiss the back of it. I politely slipped it away. Pushing the door closed, I waved but the man let the window down; *Ugh, persistent much!* I thought with a soft roll of my eyes.

"Mrs. Domingo," he called.

"Yes, Mr. Tyler?" I asked, and to my surprise, he extended a business card to me. *Brandon Tyler, Esq. Attorney at Criminal Law* it read. My vision lifted to him and he gave an innocent smile.

"Just in case you're ever in need of a lawyer," he seemed to think for a moment, "or a job—"

"A job?" I asked with a raised brow.

"Yea, uhh, my assistant is becoming a partner in another firm so—" He shrugged as if it was nothing. "The pay is good," he offered hopefully. I laughed softly. The man was cute.

"Thank you, Mr. Tyler, I'll keep your card." I acknowledged before smiling and heading for my front door, but pausing suddenly, and glancing back at him. The man hadn't moved a bit and seeing me stop, he watched me expectantly. I shook my head with a smile on my face.

"For *lawyer* purposes," I clarified before waving and creating that space. The whole while I walked up the drive to the front door, I felt the man's eyes on the jiggle of my ass in the sweatpants I wore. *I hadn't worn any panties!*

***

Ghetto

The night was coal-black, and the sky was starless as the moon sat up in her throne in all her majesty. For as far as the eyes could see, the earth was white with snow as fluffy snowflakes continued to fall from Heaven's floors. The land was blanketed with frozen precipitation, and the dark trees that had lost their leaves gave the white landscape a wicked appeal with their weathered and twisted branches. A baby doe had no shelter from the cold, and as it stopped in its trot across the vast land; thirsty from her long journey, she dropped her head and began to lick at the whiteness on the ground. The snow melted upon her warm tongue and it felt good to the baby deer, but suddenly her head shot up in alarm; eyes wide while listening for the slightest sound. Silence! Cocking its head slightly to the side and listening to the earth, the animal was alert. Yet, no longer sensing danger, the beautiful Bambi dropped her head once more. Nature has a law.

"You eat what you kill!" And if the doe would've been more acute in observation, she would've known that a predator lurked. If she would've listened to instinct, she would've seen the menacing glare of jade-colored eyes studying her. About ten yards away, camouflaged by snowflakes falling softly upon its fluffy white fur, one couldn't differentiate the ground from the wolf. Save for the glowing, pale green eyes that feasted upon its prey. The predator growled deep in its belly, its mouth watering as it inched closer to dinner. As if the beautiful doe could sense the hunger of the beast, it paused, head shooting up in alertness. Snowflakes drifted down slowly as the moon cast an eerie glow upon the scene. A light mist formed just above the snow-capped ground, and as the fog swirled around the baby deer, instinct reared its pretty head. Without warning, the doe fled, with the speed of a bullet, but not even the speed of a bullet could outrun hunger's speed. The wolf sprang from its crouch; teeth on display as it gave chase. The doe was graceful in its flee; at times, seeming to glide through the air as self-preservation motivated her dash, but a famished wolf was a hunter; a hunter that knew if he didn't kill, he wouldn't eat. He cut through the snow, ears flattened against its head, and in a mad leap-slightly twisting in the air with his jaws wide for a massive bite, the animal crashed into the deer. Both animals fell into a tumbling roll through the snow but the doe wasn't as experienced or agile as its predator. The wolf slid across the snow and with a quick snap of its sharp teeth, it was able to clamp down on the hind leg of its prey. The doe cried a wounded cry even as it yanked its leg free. It fell, but rose instantly and attempted to find safety. Yet, nature favors the beast, for in that moment, the wounded animal stumbled in its flee and that's all the carnivorous wolf needed to pounce? It descended upon the *wounded animal with vicious teeth cutting into its deep neckline like hot razors through margarine. Blood squirted across the white snow as the animal kicked; fighting for the right to live, but the wolf's hunger was blinded to sympathy. Blood staining its white coat, the beast ate the life from the weakling, and by the time he'd begun to eat through the stomach of his meal, he'd already digested the spirit from it. "Rrruuurr!" A long howl emitted from somewhere in the distance and with suspicion dancing within its eyes, the wolf lifted its head, blood dripping from its jowls as it growled low. All predators sense others of its kind, and lone wolves sensed them even more because they "chose" to roam alone throughout a wilderness that cautioned against it. The wolf's jade gaze lifted to a full moon, and he howled mightily at its beauty. It was then that his roar was met by a multitude of threatening howls before the distance twinkled to life with glowing, amber eyes. The white wolf growled, flashing its teeth as it took a territorial step forward, just as a pack of gray wolves emerged from the fog. The leader of the pack shot forward, kicking up spurts of snow as he was lured forward by the aroma of blood, and just feet away from the white wolf, it skidded to a sideways stop. Snow shot up and speckled the white wolf's muzzle and he ran a warm tongue over it as he growled. The leader of the pack's fur was as black as the night, but its eyes glowed golden as it sized up the other animal, and in seconds the rest of the pack had surrounded the white wolf. I stood watching it all from the sideline, and as I blinked in surprise at suddenly appearing in the middle of nowhere, I understood there was to be challenge; a fight to the death.*

"What's blessings Flesh, what're the fruits?" the familiar sound of his voice registered before the smell of the pineapple express kush he was smoking invaded my nostrils. I jumped in surprise as Kiest, my nigga that had been snatched from my world by lethal injection, appeared beside me. My mouth fell open as I took him in. We were dressed identically in all-black designer, but my blow's drip was a bit nastier with the diamond-encrusted RNO Cuban frozen around his neck. "Damn, Flesh, you gonna just stand there on groupie mode or hit the gas?" He laughed before extending the blunt wrap filled with exotic. I chuckled after the shock wore off and I accepted

the dope. Sucking life from it, I filled my lungs until they rebelled against the potency. Exhaling, I gave it up.

"The table is sour, but the fruits are always ripe, Blow," I said sadly. For a moment, we allowed silence to thicken as the white and black wolves began to circle each other, but Kiest nodded.

"Yea, I've heard how you allowed the serpent to sit at the table." He shook his head in disappointment.

"Nigga, I can't help that, that pussy boy Stick Talk was a jealous sucka, Flesh, no one sees the snake in the ones they love until love is gone and the snake reveals the enmity between them." I hit the blunt as my Blow nodded, his eyes digesting the wolves. They clashed in midair, teeth snapping at each other's throats as snowflakes swirled around the war.

"He whacked you 'cause his love for his bitch was deeper than the brotherhood. That boy saw how you was eating and all it took was the whisper from soft lips for him to surrender to what's always been hidden in his heart." Kiest chuckled as he accepted the blunt back. "Ever since the serpent got into Eve's head and lead her to cross God, the roles have been reversed, and now the eves are getting in the serpent's heads and leading them to cross all they believe in." He nodded just as the white wolf bit down into the furred neck of its challenger. The black wolf howled in agony and in an act of loyalty, one of its minions dashed in and nipped at the hind legs of the white wolf. The beast growled furiously before releasing his captive and spinning to face off with the new threat. The new threat was a gray and white-furred beast that flashed his teeth, and the cocaine white wolf returned the challenge with its own flash of razors. Blood stained its white muzzle as his Jade eyes glowed beneath the moon. Snowflakes drifted from the dark sky as the challenge was accepted.

"Ghetto," Kiest captured my attention, though my vision was fixated on the battle.

"Digest these fruits of a real niggas labors, Flesh," he offered before sucking the spirit from the blunt, and passing it back to me. "One of the cruelest things God has ever done is give sight to a

*starving man so he may see the prosperity of the next mu'fucka."
He spoke over a lungful of kush smoke.*

I frowned. "Why you say that, Blow?"

*"Think 'bout it, bro, even the mafia ate itself alive for this exact
reason! Every cat that obtained the title, boss of all bosses, got
whacked because either their capos or the op was either envious or
felt they were better suited for the title, and guess what happened to
the next one who wore the crown?"*

*I shrugged, the question was rhetorical. "They got knocked off
by the next one up who had the ambition and nuts to buck the system."*

*"And the cycle repeats itself! The Cartel, Bloods, and Crips,
Folks, Latin Kings, all that shit that began with success as the motive," Kiest added with a chuckle. "What you think the first nigga
that ever robbed someone was thinking? Why'd he do it?"*

*"Shid," I laughed. "I bet their stomach was touching their
back! They was thinking, I gotta eat, or this nigga ain't built for the
throne!" I chuckled. Kiest didn't.*

*"Naw, lil' bruh, see you got my vibe all wrong." He finally got
me to look his way. He smiled softly. "Starvation isn't only food! It
can also be for love, lust, power, money, and immortality! Nigga,
hunger breeds ambition, but starvation breeds greed! Genghis
Khan was a starving ruler that starved for dominance."*

*"No matter how many empires he conquered, he was never sa-
tiated. He had his eyes set on taking over the world, just as Adolf
Hitler attempted to do, and that was their biggest mistake! Why?"
he asked me as our eyes fell upon the warring wolves. I hit the blunt
two times before twisting bruh's brain.*

*"Cause the world is too massive for one man to hold in his
hands." We chuckled.*

*Kiest nodded his agreement—"Yea, and the same starvation
got Julius Caesar, Napoleon Bonaparte, El Chappo, and Great
Britain taken down!" he added before pointing to the wolves. The
white and black ones were locked into a fierce battle, teeth slicing
into fur, and vicious snarling as they fought to the death! All the
while, the five gray wolves feasted upon the slain doe, yanking flesh*

free as why watched their leader attempt to prove worthy of leading them. The black wolf lifted onto its hind legs and with a menacing snarl, swiped a clawed paw for the killing blow. Kiest tapped my chest with the back of his hand, "when God gave vision to the starving man, he created an evil that will feed betrayal for eternity!" He concluded just as the two wolves fell into a tumble and ended with the white wolf on top of the black. He'd planted his massive paw into the chest of the beast, the snow fell softly as that albino animal glared down in victory. Bloodied saliva dripped from its lower jowl and fear was born in the eyes of the black animal as defeat smiled. The pack of gray wolves encircled the two alpha males, their eyes aglow and their teeth bared as they growled threateningly. The white-furred warrior wasn't to be deterred, and with a savageness only born to natural killers, he lowered his head and sank his teeth into the fur of the fallen leader's neck before savagely tearing out his throat! Blood splashed against the white blanket of snow as he ate greedily, and only after he'd swallowed his snack did he lift his jade-colored orbs to the rest of the pack. Blood wet his muzzle as he lifted his head to the heavens and howled at the full moon, and when his eyes fell to the remaining animals, he stared challenging before nudging the dead wolf with his nose. Taking a few steps back, he growled. The pack returned his menace with guttural growls of their own and the flashing of sharp teeth. And with an untamed hunger, they attacked. Me and Kiest watched in awe as the pack fell upon the slain form of the same black leader they would've killed for only moments ago. The white wolf reared its head back, his ears flattened against it as he howled his call of dominance at the moon. He was the new alpha of the pack. I smirked before my vision drifted to Kiest who was just turning to leave, but paused to speak from over his shoulder.

"And mind, stomach, and dick are his weak links, they're the portions of a man that if controlled by another, can turn him into a puppet."

"What about a man's heart, Blow?" I wanted to know, though my eyes didn't abandon the savagery before me.

"A man's stomach is powerful enough to make him take down God himself if he could." My flesh nodded as if talking more to himself. "A nigga that can't control his dick is a women's gift, and a dude that can't control his mind is a hurricane that will destroy everyone that loves and follows him." He nodded to the pack of wolves who were tearing their former partner apart. I chuckled as my vision drifted to him. "What 'bout his heart?" I repeated. Kiest glanced at me from over his shoulder. "Niggas like us don't have no use for no shit like that, you'll climb higher if you learn to ignore it."

***

Heaven

10 A.M.—Next Morning

The sun had risen and its glow promised a beautiful day, but still in my sleeping clothes and still having my hair wrapped in a black scarf, I knew that the sun would be ignoring my side of the world. I watched from the passenger's seat of my Aston as the FEDS walked in and out of my and Ghetto's home, carrying away our possessions like worker ants. It was a moment of deja vu that took me back to the night all those years ago when these same *crooks* with badges, appeared under the blanket of night and turnt me and my family's lives upside down. Now, here they were again-tilting my world until the ceiling became the floor and the floor became the ceiling. "This can't be real, just—can't—be," I whispered while gripping the steering wheel so tightly that my knuckles turned red. "Ghettooo" I cried like a little girl before I rested my head against the wood grain of the wheel, and allowed my mind to replay the events of that fateful morning. *I'd fallen asleep on the couch after Brandon had dropped me off and I'd fed my son. The events of the day had drained me and though Catrina and Egypt had cleaned up most of the mess the feds had made in their treasure hunt for "evidence" for Ghetto's crimes, there was still much to do. Yet, it would have to wait; sleep beckoned me, and the last thing I remembered was Catrina waking me to tell me she was taking Khalief home with her so I could get some peace. Then? Slumber! Until around eight fifteen A.M. when the sound of someone pounding on the door snatched me from a deep sleep. I jerked awake with a start, eyes wild as I tried to recall the events of the day before, but the pounding was persistent. I made my way to the door and peeping through the peephole, I rolled my eyes at the two agents. I finger-combed my hair before unlocking the door, and that's when the "unwelcomed" stepped past the welcome home mat. Agents poured into my home with no regard.*

"We're giving you twenty minutes to get dressed and vacate this property. This house and everything you can't show proof of purchase by legal means now belong to the Federal Bureau of Investigations" Crosby spat happily before holding up an official document that had the words, *"Search and Seize"* stamped boldly across the paper. *My heart fell as I read the fine print of the IRS and Federal Government.* Crosby chuckled. *"This is only the beginning, Ms. Domingo, we're going to turn you and your murdering boyfriend's lives upside down!"* That was two hours ago, and now, as I sit behind the tint in my car with hot tears cascading down my face, I was forced to take a quick look at my life. *Girrl, get it together, you've been through worse!* I mentally encouraged myself, but I was a twenty-three-year-old mother. With no job experience, and a man in a coma. "Lord, fix it," I whispered and I don't know if it was the thoughts of going back to my old ways or mere desperation, but when I took my phone from the passenger's seat, I was on autopilot when I highlighted his number in the device's address book. *Why'd I saved his number?* I don't know, but when he answered, I broke down.

"Hello?" he answered.

"I-Bran-I—" I tried but it seemed as if the weight of the past few months had finally broken my back. Ghetto...The mess with the house…Trying to be a good mother….Everything! It was just too much pressure.

"Heaven? Is this you?" Brandon Tyler was unsure. It took a moment, but I got it together enough to reveal my reasons for calling. Hugging myself as I watched those people violate me and my family's home, my tears dropped silently. *The cons of loving a street nigga!*

"Yes, it-it's me. Ummm" I spoke softly before sniveling.

"Are you ok?" His question seemed to only make my reality worse. So-I answered him with every ounce of honesty I had within my being.

"No!" I cried, vision blurred by the Niagara Falls that poured from my eyes. "No, I'm not okay-Nothing-*nothing* is ok, Brandon." I shook my head as if he could see me. "Nothing!" I cried, and for a moment we just allowed our breathing and my cries to marinate.

Then. "Brandon?"

"Yes, Heaven?"

"Is that job offer still good?"

"Yea-yeah! Yes, when can you start?"

Renta

Chapter Seven

Fried Chicken

Six Months Later

The sun hadn't yet risen above the horizon, but from the large, curtainless window in the bedroom, one could see how its slow rise had turned the purple sky a beautiful reddish gold, and in moments, would reign supreme. It takes 499 seconds for light from the sun to touch the earth, and by that time, Kitty would have sucked the waters down from Red Diamonds paradise. Kitty, Red Diamond's girlfriend, was a five-foot-six masterpiece! Chocolate skin was as smooth as silk, and the lady was slim thick with an ass that could balance a glass. Though she rocked an Amber Rose hairstyle with intricate designs cut into it, her most striking feature was her chinky hazel eyes, and at that moment, they were feasting upon the delicacy she feasted upon. The sleigh bed with the sheer, dripping drapes suspended from above it sat high above the floor, and with her head down, and ass up, it was easy for Kitty's pretty feet to dangle over the edge as she sucked a sleeping Red Diamonds clarity. "MMMMAA" Red Diamond moaned in her sleep, her pretty face contorting into a mask of ecstasy. This only fed Kitty's hunger and her tongue flickered faster-wet-as she bathed her lovers pearl. "Ouuu" Diamond moaned, unconsciously spreading her legs further apart. "Da-Damn, Ghetto, baby" she mumbled, and though the mention of another's name usually killed the vibe, it only fed Kitty's determination as she licked and sucked-kissed and gingerly touched, until Red Diamonds skies parted and the great flood broke free. "HUAAAUUUU!" she cried, eyes shooting open in shock as her back arched off the bed from the power of her release. Kitty lapped it up, catching her juices on her tongue while watching Red Diamonds eyes fall to her. "Baabyyy!" The woman cried, toes curled as the tremors subsided. Kitty swayed her ass from side to side before smiling, her woman's nectar sticky around her full lips.

"Good morning, baby" she purred before crawling up Diamonds body; pausing to suckled her left nipple before releasing it with a pop. Once they were face to face, Red Diamond pulled her down and slid her tongue in her mouth

"Mmm," she moaned at the taste of her own juices. "Good Morning," she acknowledged once the tongue wrestle was over.

"What's on the agenda for the day?" Kitty smiled down at her. Months had passed since the war between RNO and BGM had begun, and though the RNO faction was up a few, BGM had proved to be a formidable foe. Blood called from the streets of Dallas/Ft. Worth, and no one was safe.

"We can go blow a bag at the Gucci outlet, they have these cute little boots"—she began, but the phone vibrating on the nightstand gave her pause. Glancing over at it, Kitty gently kissed her neck.

"Just us today, baby, let's" *muah-* "Just"-*Lick-*"do"-*muah*-us. She punctuated each word with a promising kiss. Red Diamond smirked seductively before pushing Kitty onto her back before rolling on top of her. Their lips locked while Diamond's hand trailed down south until it found planet *pussy*, and using her fingers, she explored. Kitty grinded her mound as Red Diamond finger fucked her. Their moans intertwined as their tongues sensually danced, and Red Diamond's fire was ignited! Fingers sticky, she lifted them to Kitty's mouth and together they licked Kitty's juices away. "Put that sweet pussy back in my mouth," Kitty demanded and Red Diamonds was happy to oblige. Lady stood straight up in the bed and placed her feet on both sides of her lover's head. Kitty glanced up at raw femininity, licking her lips as her lady squatted down on her face. Red Diamond's lower lips kissed the woman's lips and Kitty tongue kissed them with fervor. The wet sucking sounds created erotica as in the frog position, Red Diamond's vision fell to watch the vulgar tongue kiss. She reached up and squeezed her left nipple to add a taste of pain to the serving of pleasure.

"You-ou ouuu"- she cried as Kitty's lips pulled on her clit. "Youuuuu-know-how-to eat-eat-eattt this pus-syyy, girl!" Red Diamond's facial contorted into an ugly beautifulness, but when Kitty's finger slid into her ass, the beautifulness departed and left only the ugly. "Bi-t-ch!" she cried as her fuck face told the tale. Knees apart, she leaned forward and gripped the head board before beginning a slow gyration on Kitty's face- "you want this-thissscum-, hu-huh? You want it?" she'd abandoned her manners as she began to ride the woman's face with a feverish pace. She could feel liquid passion converging in her clouds as a thunderstorm formed, and in the midst, the ringing of her i-Phone became trapped within the moment. She knew the call could be what she'd been anticipating, yet she was trapped within the thralls of sensation that threatened to release her precipitation. "Kiy-tyyy!" she purred before hurriedly snatching the phone up. *Flesh* flashed across the screen.

"Blowww" she whined, hand trembling as her body betrayed her.

"Fuck? What you got goin on Nubian?" Nukkey asked in confusion.

"Call me backkk, nigga, I'm get-getting some head!" she fought her concentration. Nukkey chuckled.

"Nasty ass, look,I'm textin you that info, it's on you."

"KKKKK" she moaned before killing the call and tossing the phone. Red Diamond began to rock her hips so powerfully that her wet pussy lips began to slide back and forth over Kitty's chin to forehead.

"Baby!" she cried, riding her face so fast that the headboard slapped against the wall. "I'm-bout-to-bust on your face!" she cried as the storm fell from her heaven and almost drowned Kitty. Red Diamond's body tensed, teeth clenched, and her ass cheeks vibrated with her release. Kitty took it like a big girl, tongue gliding from clit to ass hole. When Red Diamond slid away and fell beside her, Kitty's face was coated with stickiness.

"Damn, Bitch, you tried to *baptize* me!" She laughed; out of breath. Red Diamond smiled, strands of her hair sticking to her sweaty face.

"Come here" she demanded before pulling her lover down and began licking the stickiness from her face. "Since we can't catch up to Fat Boy" she spoke between licks. "Nukkey texting me his mom's addy" *Lick!* We'll pay

Lick! Her tongue bathed Kitty's face. "Her a visit." she giggled sinisterly before purging the remaining cum from Kitty's flesh.

***

Heaven

Brandon locked the door to his office before making his way down the highly polished hallway; his day had been good to him and winning one of his most prestigious cases was cause to celebrate. So, when he rounded the corner and came into view of my desk, our eyes met and he smiled. "Hey there hard worker, fancy meeting you here?" He flirted. I laughed as he made his way over and leaned against my desk.

"Yeah, whatever, dude, but here's your messages, and the file on the Smith's case you asked for." I handed him a file and a slip of paper. He scanned them before reclaiming me with his gaze. Ever since that horrible morning six months before; when the FEDS had stormed my home, Brandon had been a blessing in disguise. He'd helped me get a new apartment, furnish it, and the job. And though the pay wasn't what I was used to, I was determined to never go back to sticking niggas for their cheese. I still stripped as a side hustle, but at an entirely different club.

"So," he began, his smile contagious, "We're now official.

My eyes grew large in surprise. "They made you a partner of the firm!" I shouted excitedly and had to control my tone. Brandon Tyler smiled proudly, he'd worked hard for that firm and it was his dream to become a partner. Nodding, he made an attempt at modesty.

"It's nothing, Heaven, but yes, it's now, Perry, Kyle, *Tyler,* and associates." His eyes misted at the accomplishment, and before I knew it, I'd risen from my seat and made my way around the large receptionist desk.

"That's what's up, boy, I'm happy for you!" I congratulated him before hugging him. His arms found their way around my waist and Lord knows how much I needed that hug.

"Thanks," he whispered, and to my surprise, when we disentangled, Brandon kissed my forehead. "This is cause for celebration" He announced before I could react. Stepping back, I didn't know how to react. As innocent as it was, I knew Brandon had feelings for me, and he had no problem showing it. Me and the man had grown close over the past few weeks, and though almost a year had passed since Ghetto had been hospitalized, my love and respect for him still ran too deep for me to allow the man standing before me to surpass the notion of friendship. Yet *that kiss! His lips were sooo soft!* I glanced at the ground to hide what he may have witnessed in my gaze. "There's an act tonight at one of my favorite spots, come chill with me, Heaven, you say your husband is deployed somewhere in the army, right?" He tried it, and though I hated to lie to him, the truth would only feed his ambitions in pursuing something that could never be his. *Me!* Lifting my eyes to find him smiling at me innocently, I nodded the lie, "yes, but that doesn't mean that it's ok for us to"—

"Aw come on, Heaven, it's not like we're going on a date or anything." He paused, lifting a brow as his lips curved into a sexy smirk, "Unless, you want it to be?" He paused when I burst into laughter. The boy never stopped.

"You're too much." I laughed.

"For real though, beautiful, I don't mean any harm, and I promise to be on my best behavior." He vowed as I gave him a skeptical look. Brandon raised his fingers to his heart, "Scout's honor."

"You're not a scout, Brandon Tyler."

"No, but I'm a man with honor." The man smiled and maybe it was that smile that made me nod my acceptance of his invitation.

"Just to celebrate your success, no date." I cleared the air but didn't know if it was more to convince him or myself.

"Yes!" he exclaimed like a big kid. I laughed. *I won't cross you, Ghetto, it's not a date, baby.*

***

Two Hours Later

163

"Yes, may I help you?" The woman that answered the door was a beautiful, middle-aged queen with smooth skin and a hint of gray streaking through her long hair. Her eyes were soft but studious as she studied the beautiful woman standing on her porch. Red Diamond smiled.

"We're so sorry to bother you, mam, but we're students at Texas Wesleyan University and we're selling these delicious cookies to raise money for a project a group of us has to do. The money will go towards helping single mothers get school supplies for their children." She revealed before holding up a box of cookies. The older woman's eyes took in her and Kitty's big smiles and couldn't resist.

"Well, chile, I like the cause, but I'm allergic to chocolate." She nodded to the box of peppermint chocolate chip cookies. Red Diamond's eyes shot to Kitty- *I told you, bitch, sugar cookies are neutral!* She thought with a roll of her eyes.

"But—" The woman's tone drew both girls' attention. Smiling, she held up a finger. "My son loves peppermint chocolate, I'll get a box for him."

"Girrrrl, is that fried chicken I smell!" Kitty playfully rubbed her stomach. The older woman laughed, enjoying the vibe of the younger girls.

"Baby yes! I can burn! Are you hungry?" Her hospitality would be her undoing. Kitty giggled.

"Are we! We haven't eaten all day, and it's almost three in the afternoon!" she exclaimed.

"Y'all come on in, I made enough to feed a houseful even though I live alone, and I bet you girls will love my recipe!" the woman of the house offered before stepping to the side. Kitty's vision found Red Diamonds before she stuck her tongue out at her playfully. *Yea, bitch, like I said, peppermint chocolate chip!* she thought, all the while thankful Red Diamond hadn't pulled the baby nine out the cookie box and shot the woman in the face.

***

The black SUV was as silent as a graveyard, save for the barely audible clicking of slugs being stuffed into clips. Fat Dawg sat in the passenger seat, taking a *Backwoods* blunt to the face as he stalked the ragged house.

"What's the plan, Fat Dawg, we steppin' on *everything* or just goin' for that hoe ass nigga RNO Klutch?" Choppa, one of the BGM affiliates spoke from the back seat. Fat Dawg exhaled a cloud of Hydro smoke before tuning into the question. "Blood, we dogs, we eat *everything* on the menu!" he spat. Four deep in the Ford Expedition, all heads nodded in agreement. Each clutching pipes with either drums or banana clips sitting on their bellies, the shooters were war ready. They'd been lurking a few houses down from a known RNO spot for half an hour and though his shootas were anxious to get active, Fat Dawg knew miscalculated moves could lead to a nigga taking an eternal snooze.

"Them boys will come out and when—" he was saying when his jack vibrated. Pulling it out, he frowned when his mother's FB showed she was calling via video chat. He wanted to ignore it, but something in his gut compelled him to answer "Y'all niggas be quiet," he told his goons. "Sup ma, I'm busy right now, let me—"

"Heyyy, Fat Boy, this not mother dearest, but don't you worry, she's here, just kinda tied up right now." Red Diamond smiled sinisterly. Fat Dawg sat up straighter in his seat, the blunt falling form between his lips at the sight of his adversary's face versus his T-Jones. He clumsily scrambled to reclaim it before it burnt through his clothes.

"Fuck!" he cried when he refocused on the screen. "Bitch, you bet not"—

"Un ahh, temper temper!" Red Diamond wagged a mocking finger before diverting the camera to show him his mother was tied up; *literally!*

Her eyes were wide in fear as she attempted to scream from behind the panties stuffed in her mouth. Diamond shrugged sheepishly. "She wouldn't shut the fuck up, so—" she giggled—"we had to be creative!" she revealed before the phone lowered and she lifted her skirt to flash him her waxed oasis, "No panties, daddy." She giggled as tears baptized Fat Dawg's vision when it dawned on him that her panties were in his mother's mouth. The phone shook in his hands.

"Fuck-you-at-my mama's house for, bitch!" He spat. His goons' eyes were glued to the screen as they leaned to catch a view. They all knew Red Diamond was a she-devil, and her motive was always murder.

"Now that's a stupid question, Fat Boy," she giggled. "Me and my girl was just in the neighborhood and decided to stop by, just so happened, mama dearest was cooking dinner." she smiled; resembling a black version of Harley Quin. "Boy, you know her recipe for fried chicken is to die for!" she said before lifting a fried drumstick and biting into it. After having her fill, she tossed the food before glancing down at the bound woman. "I know you're hungry, so—" her eyes drifted back to Fat Dawg. "Y'all been fucking the city up, and you knooooow how I feel 'bout a nigga touching one of mine." she laughed at the tear that dripped from the fat man's eyes. Shaking her head while pointing an admonishing finger at the screen, "Y'all already know how RNO coming, and y'all still wanna play with the demons? Cool! "Kitty?" she called.

"Yes, Baby?" Kitty's purr was seductive.

"Bring mama dearest some chicken, she's hungry."

The request was met with the camera switching views, and capturing Kitty walking towards them, carefully! With oven mitts on her hands, she tried to hold the handle of the skillet steady. Hot grease popped as the chicken continued to cook, and once she was standing over the older woman, she paused, holding the frying skillet away from her body to keep from being burned. The older woman's eyes were bloodshot as water leaked from them, and Red Diamond focused the screen so her son could see her sufferance.

"For the flesh of my flesh, the blood of their enemies will turn the city red in vengeance, Fat Dawg-BGM"—Red Diamond's tone had taken on a devilish edge. "For your sins, I hear-by sentence the mother of my enemy to death by torture!" She shouted at the top of her lungs and Kitty tilted the skillet. Fat Dawg and his team watched it happen in slow motion as the scalding cooking grease spilled on top of his mother's graying hair.

"Mmhhhhh!" Her agony emitted from behind her gag. Smoke rose from her head as patches of hair and scalp melted away.

The lady went into instant shock as the hot liquid ran down her pretty face, peeling skin away as it flowed.

"BITCHI'MGONNAKILLYOURWHOLEBLOODLINE-YOU-SICK-B-IT-CH!" Fat Dawg cried; his words coming out in a jumble as he rocked so hard in his seat that the SUV bobbed on its springs. Kitty laughed as two pieces of chicken, a breast and a thigh fell into the woman's convulsing lap. The shock had morphed into a full-blown heart attack, and in the aftermath, the older woman resembled a pinker version of Fire Marshall Bill. The skin of her face had completely melted away, and outside of a lone patch of gray hair, her bloodied head was raw and inhumanly pink. Red Diamond laughed hysterically "Fried chicken anybody?"

Renta

Chapter Eight

Twice As Funny

Heaven

10 p.m.

The room shook with applause as the comedian finished his act and departed the stage. The night was festive, and the energy was positive as the hundred or so attendees enjoyed themselves. The *Twice As Funny* comedy lounge in Killeen Texas was packed and vibrant with good cheer. Brandon had shown up to get me, debonair in designer; a black pair of Burberry slacks, complete with a gray wool Burberry turtleneck and gray loafers. The fit was causal but still GQ, so I killed it in a charcoal gray catsuit with tears at the knees and a pair of peep-toe Fendi boots. The rose gold tinted designer frames covering my eyelashes were their own statement, and after he'd wined and dined me, Brandon had shown me the front row seats at the lounge.

"Aiigght-aiiight now, I see you good people enjoying the show!" the host shouted from the stage and was matched with a louder round of applause. I smiled, and though I was enjoying myself, the mood was overshadowed by the remembrance of the comedy event Ghetto took me to in Louisiana. The thought only made me miss my baby more, and though it hadn't been a day that passed I hadn't gone to sit with him in that hospital, my heart needed him to wake up and remind me of so much.

"You enjoying yourself, beautiful?" Brandon leaned to whisper in my ear, and the feel of his breath against my flesh seemed almost sinful. I nodded with a smile, though my heart was crying.

"Well," the host recaptured our attention, "as they say, we've saved the best for last! We have a real special guest here at the lounge tonight and he's come all the way from Brookhaven Georgia to show his talents. So, you mu'fuckas, give it up for my boy— *White Boy Corn Bread!*" He introduced and the crowd went wild.

Even I burst into laughter when the white man appeared on stage, clad in a Stetson cowboy hat, a pearl button, button-up, a pair of cut-off jeans, and a pair of snake-skinned cowboy boots. Smiling big, the man nodded at the warm reception.

"Thank you—thank you." He waved. "Mannn, I just came home from a fifteen-year bid, and—" Before he could finish, the room exploded with cheers and choruses of *welcome homes.* The man loved it!

"Yea, man, I was caught with an ounce of dope; me and my girl were riding in her car, just enjoying freedom, man, 'cause let me tell ya, there's nothing more beautiful than freedom!"

The crowd cheered.

"Amen!"

"Trying to tell ya, my man!"

"Tell the truth!" People shouted. Corn Bread laughed.

"Yea, I see a lot of you motherfuckers are just coming home from a bid too!" The joke was well taken. "Man, so, me and my girl are riding around getting high, and out of nowhere man, a fucking cop pulls us over. We're white folk, ya know, so we weren't too worried when we were asked could the car be searched. But, then they found the dope!" He paused with a wide stare. "Y'all know what, I'm a motherfuckin man, so I claimed my shit! I think any dude that allows his woman to take a fall for him is a goddamn coward! A real man takes his licks!" he shouted passionately, and the crowd's applause was powerful in agreement.

"Tell it like it is, Corn Bread! Tell-it-like-it isss!" a woman encouraged me.

Corn Bread saluted her as he paced the stage with a sad expression on his face. "Prison is filled with beautiful women who takes the rap for no good fucking men! So, recently when me and my girl were riding around, just enjoying freedom, getting high and shit, the police pulled us over again, and again asked us to search the car. Mann, I'm sweating bullets 'cause I have an eight-ball of dope under the seat with a pistol. FUCK!" Corn Bread shouted with a shake of his head. "The fucking dogs found it and when the officers asked us whose it was, hey"— He paused to give a sad shake of the head as his eyes fell to the stage. "I'm a fucking man!" he declared as his eyes shot to the crowd and his chest swelled with pride. "So when my girl's eyes found mine, I was already lifting my hand to claim my shit, but then, the officer said— *this will get ya thirty years!*" The comedian's eyes bulged as his chest deflated. *"Thirty years!"* He screeched. "That's when I gave another sad shake of the head y'all, *no wonder so many beautiful women are locked up behind no hood men!"* he declared to the roar of the crowd. The man chuckled — "I told my girl—*Baby, I told you not to bring this shit!"* White Boy Corn Bread had touched our funny bone. Then, pointing to his left, he said— "Officer, the car's in *her* name, and I told the silly bitch to go to rehab, now look!" He exclaimed, and I was hunched over in laughter. "What?" Corn Bread lifted his hands, "I still put a few bucks on her commissary!" He swore, and I had tears in my eyes as he began to pace the stage, chuckling. "Say, man, I'm tellin' y'all, prison fucks folks up! Man, in prison we wear shower shoes cause we shower in *community* showers, and you can't imagine the things people do in those things! Wait"— Corn Bread held up a hand. *Don't* imagine what people do in those things!" he cautioned. And we laughed. "So, after wearing these shower shoes for so long, it becomes habitual! So, upon my first night as a free man, my *new* girl"— the crowd laughed at the hint. "She wanted to be all romantic and shit, so she decided to take a shower with me. Y'all know, the steamed filled the bathroom and things were perfect until this nasty bitch slips into the shower with me. Y'all know the first place my eyes went, right? He paused as his eyes shot to his cowboy boots. We laughed when he nodded as if the answer was obvious. "Yeaaah, her feet!" He exclaimed before a stank expression eased on his face. "Bitch, where's ya shower shoes?" White Boy Corn Bread demanded his imaginary lady. "I'm tellin' y'all, me and the bitch didn't last another day! I was too busy tryna figure out *why* this nasty bitch was so comfortable *not* wearing shower shoes, whereas, she was trying to figure out *why* I was so hell-bent on wearing em!" It was the serious look on his face that had us doubled over in laughter. The man chuckled with a shake of his head— "I'm tellin y'all, man, prison fucks us up! I'm *still* shocked by my first experience of food shopping after those fifteen years!" Corn Bread chuckled, with a bitter look on his face. "That shit fucked me up, folks, I was the only motherfucker in Wal-Mart with a *commissary bag*! I bought all the wolf brand chili, squeee cheese, Ramen noodles, and corn chips I could buy! Shid, ain't no tellin when there's gonna be a lockdown!" He laughed while acting like he was filling up a bag. "No peanut butter and jelly for me!" The comedian laughed at his own joke. "I'm tellin' y'all, prison fucks you up! And I knew I was institutionalized when the only way my ole Johnson could rise for my ole lady, was if she dressed up like a C. O, and act like if it were count time!" The man was goofy as he mimicked getting caught masturbating on an officer." He chuckled before removing the hat from his head and holding it to his chest as if he were swearing. "I'm tellin' y'all, folks, prison fucks you up!" He swore. "Man, they truly have some strange, kinky shit out here. Shit that wasn't even thought of before I went in, so when me and my ole lady stopped by a sex shop to pick up some lube, I was cool with it. Ya know? Bitch may want it in her ass or somethin'"— he shrugged with a chuckle. "So, we're in the car, headed home, and the freak bitch wants to do her thing! She shows me the lube and it's called"—He raised his *left* hand with his hat pressed to his chest, *"Glow in the Dark, Bacon flavored Lubrication!"* The look on his face tickled me. "I swear, man! So, the whore lubes me up while I'm driving, and had my cock looking like a lifesaver on Star Wars! We're already as high as a satellite next to Mars! So everything is crazy looking! Hell, after she lubed me, I was more fascinated with my glowing Johnson than the bitch was!" He had the crowd as he *smashed* the hat back onto his head. "Man, this cum guzzler began sucking my dick, slurping on it like it was the next best thing to a lollipop, before stopping and saying; *it really does taste like bacon!"* Corn Bread gave us a big-eyed stare. "Bacon? Hell, I swung the car over to the shoulder of the road and told the whore to take off her shirt! Squeezing a little of the lube onto her nipples, I began licking it off, and before I knew it, the whore's *entire* chest was soaking in spit and half the damn bottle was gone"— White Boy

Corn Bread nodded his head vigorously. "It really did taste like bacon!" he shouted. I was too through. Corn Bread laughed— "The shit was so good, I damn near bit the whores nipple off!" He ran a hand over his mouth as if wiping away crumbs. He raised a hand in caution—"Do not"— he warned, "I repeat, *do not* try bacon flavored *anything*! The shit will turn you into a cannibal!" The man began to gnaw on his own arm with a growl.

***

Opelousas Louisiana

The morning was cool and the scent of nature was potent as it wafted off the still waters of the swamp. The sun hadn't yet risen and the drab sky cast dark shadows as a slow breeze carried the chill of November across the lowlands of the Pelican State. The cool air made for a welcomed relief from the sweltering heat that had plagued the south for the past year, and at that time of the morning, only God could foretell what the day would bring. Yet—at that moment, a black spotted dog trotted from the woods surrounding the putrid waters, and with its tongue lolling from its mouth, he carelessly made his way to the edge of where the moist ground gave way to the cool H2O. Pausing, the animal sniffed at the water before dipping its tongue into it. It was cold below the surface, and though the darkness of the plains surrounding the swamp made it eerie in the twilight, the dog drank his fill. Around him, jagged pieces of broken trees sprouted out into the distance, surrounded by dark and vibrant patches of algae floating on top of the saturation. The dog lapped earnestly but paused when a rough log floated a few yards from him. Tongue slowly retracting, he glanced up curiously, eyeing the harmless piece of wood while sniffing the air. Barking, the animal reared back onto its hunches as if preparing to pounce, but baring its sharp teeth, it merely growled menacingly. Yet, seeing that the harmless piece of wood was incapable of danger, the dog relaxed its posture, and with its head cocked to the left, it studied curiously. With timid steps, he eased back to the water's edge and returned to its drink. A soft wind swirled from the East as the sun finally peeked over the horizon, and it was then that the log reptilian eyes cracked open. The dog's senses came to life as it captured the slits for eyes of the beast, and it attempted to flee—to no avail. The alligator exploded from the water with a powerful grace—its jaws wide and it was as silent as an assassin as its razor-sharp teeth snapped down into the neck of the animal. The sound of the dog's neck snapping was profound, and before dragging him into the murky water, the reptile shook it savagely while dragging it into its habitat. The beast spun the dog beneath the dark waters for good measure, turning the cool liquid blood red. About twenty yards away from the act of nature, Genevieve's home leaned slightly from the weight of age, and up its rickley steps, and through the scarred wood door sat a woman with aged, yellow skin. Her hair was as white as a cloud and her green eyes held secrets that ran too deep for one to uncover. Erzulie Bousard, Genevieve's eldest and only sibling, sat rocking in her late sister's favorite rocking chair, humming an old folk hymn. *Erzulie* had gotten her name from her grandmother who was a practitioner of Voodoo. She'd christened her grandchild the name after one of the leading guardians of the Voodoo Queen, Marei Laveau of New Orleans. The guardian, Erzulie Freda Da homey is present in New Orleans voodoo as well as Haitian Vodou and is held in high regard by the Dahomey people of West Africa. It's said that she cried tears of the world because people simply don't do right, and since Genevieve's sister used to cry at the sight of any slight, she'd been named after her. "I told jah, Gen, de boy was trouble, Jea," she whispered as her snake-colored eyes trailed to the large glass encasement that held about a hundred and fifty hand-sized, slave dolls. Their grandmother had collected them throughout her 104 years of living and passed them down once she'd passed on. When Erzulie found her sister dead in the rocking chair, she immediately knew the cause. She'd warned her baby sister about making deals with the dead that she couldn't be sure to make good on, but Genevieve had a dark side that snaked through her veins and wouldn't listen. So, after burying her, Erzulie moved back into that decaying home of their childhood. At that moment, the dolls stared back at her, some smiling, and others frowning, but all were lifelike replicas of the black slaves of old. Again, Erzulie began to hum, but this tune belonged to the song; *Mistress of Erzulie* by the Canadian singer, Alannah Myles. The song spoke of a New Orleans encounter with voodoo, and as Erzulie hummed and rocked, rocked and hummed, she mentally called upon the loa *spirit of* Erzulie Freda Dahomey to show herself. She did so because the spirit bones had revealed to her that Heaven would fall from the skies and appear in the form of a woman. Erzulie smirked wickedly as she eyed the strange dolls, and the woman could've sworn that one of the nappy-headed, dark-skinned slave men winked at her.

***

12 a.m.

Heaven

We'd left the lounge and I'd allowed that man to talk me into going to a club! Outside of the strip club, I haven't been to a club in so long, but it felt good to just be free for once!

"So, did you enjoy yourself tonight?" Brandon shouted over the music. We sat at a table just off the dance floor and as couples danced to a song I didn't know, I sipped from my third drink of *Pink Panties*. Dancing in my seat, I smiled at him before nodding.

"Yes, you're not too bad, especially for a newly appointed partner of a prestigious law firm." I winked at him. He chuckled as his eyes took a slow journey over the satin material of the catsuit I wore. I knew my nipples were imprinting the fabric and when my eyes found him—*yep!* He was sightseeing. When he noticed my gaze, Brandon jumped in surprise, a guilty expression forming on his face, and I decided to toy with him. "You like what you see?" I asked, and Brandon licked those LL Cool J lips of his before smiling.

175

"You're the most exotic work of art I've ever set eyes upon. You like to dance?" He asked, noticing me doing so in my seat. I gave him a seductive look.

"Maybe," I fed his fire, and as soon as I took another sip from my glass, the DJ played an old Wale song that I loved! *Is it bad that I've never made love, no I never did it/but I sure know how to fuck/I'll be a baaaad girl"*— I smiled with mischief playing in my eyes. Giving Brandon a suggestive look, I sang along "I'll prove it to you, I can't promise that, I'll be good to you. 'Cause I've had some issues, I won't commit" I slipped from my seat and headed for the dance floor, but paused to give him a seductive smile before- "Think you can hang?" I asked over my shoulder.

***

Ghetto

Fuck! Was the only thing playing within my mental as I watched Heaven and that fuck boy flirt. *"This bitch betraying me, fam, while I'm down bad!"* I spat, heart crooked in my chest as I watched them step on the dance floor. They began grinding against one another and the cold part bout it is the goofy ass nigga she was defiling our union with was as stiff as an ironing board! At that moment I realized that loyalty was a dying thing, and as the thought manifested, God appeared beside me.

"You've been out of pocket for going on a year, Ghetto, she's waited, prayed, and still waits for you. What do you expect from her?" He questioned. I frowned.

"Loyalty or commitment? They're two different things, ya know." He was pissing me off and when I glared, he chuckled with a shrug. *"See, men have weaknesses within their pride, so they feel if their woman"* He paused to nod at Heaven and her new boy toy, *"Does the simplest things with another, its defilement. Yet, for him to do the same thing with another woman, it's harmless. Double standards rob most men of truth because you're programmed. So I*

must ask, sun, is it your gal you don't trust or the man's potential?"
He lifted a brow.

"Nigga, another man's potential can never give me insecurity!
It's just some things, spoken for women, shouldn't do! Certain doors
shouldn't be opened because no matter her 'intent,' temptation is
an animal that becomes untamed when opportunity and secrets
meet."

"Yet, you didn't deny not trusting her."

"Cause me trusting her or not won't domesticate her pussy."

"Yet, if she's gonna betray you, Ghetto, it's gonna happen re-
gardless. But a man who finds a good woman finds a good thing.
You have that in Heaven. Though she's living at the moment, love
conquers all!"

I spat on the floor "Bullshit! That's a lie."

"Why do you say that?" God asked with an amused expression.

"Cause the same love a mu'fucka had for you that helped y'all
weather the storm, the same love that made someone special to you,
is the exact love that's conquered by lust, a moment in time, or weak-
ness." God nodded his agreement before pointing at Heaven.

***

Brandon was a great dancer, but a bit stiff. He didn't know I
was a dancer, so when I spun around and put this ass against his
nature, making it clap, the man's eyes grew as large as an owl's. His
dick swelled instantly and though we were having fun, I eased away,
placing a foot between us. It was one thing to tease, but another to
touch; I was woman enough to know my limits and I belonged to a
man that deserves fidelity, so I respected that limit. Brandon was
turnt on; standing on the precipice of lust and I knew that lust was
a contagious thing when a man and woman were having fun. So-
when he pressed himself against me, I turnt to face him, letting my
eyes tell him what my body couldn't; *Real Bitch here!*

***

177

"*Ghetto, love isn't strong enough to stop anyone from cheating, but a woman or man's morals are. Sun, every man should know the type of woman he has, and in knowing her, you'll never have to question her. If she's solid, you know she'll be your reflection no matter the temptation, and if she's hoeish, is even more reason not to question her cause nine times out of ten, you knew she was hoeish before you gal'd her. So, why question what you should already know?*"

God's truths were official but still didn't curb my—I won't say jealousies, but—my, foul mood. Heaven was out of line-period! I was hot when they grabbed their things to leave.

"*Let me ask you something, Ghetto.*" God paused to watch them leave. "*Do you love her?*"

"*Mannn, that ain't got nothin' to—*"

"*Do you?*" He was adamant. My eyes drifted to him before following Heaven.

"*Yea*"

"*So, does your love want her to suffer for the rest of her life just cause you're a piece off the board or is your love real enough to let her be happy no matter what her happiness may be?*"

I thought about it, knowing it was a catch-22. No matter how I answered, it would boil down to me having to accept Heaven without a Ghetto.

"*God, my nigga*" I turnt to him, but shook my head when I noticed God was gone.

Chapter Nine

Mr. Burglar

The morning was born with a warmth that seemed bipolar. One moment the kiss of the breeze was a warm caress over her soft skin, and the next massage of its breath would carry a slight chill. The sun was high and as Red Diamond sat on the bench beside the pond behind the house on Ghetto's property, she watched two black ducks fight over the bread she'd tossed into the water. It had been six months since the FEDS seized and violated Ghetto's house and as soon as it was placed back on the market, the RNO family dropped a bag on it. No one lived there, but Red Diamond had always loved the peace that surrounded that pond, and as she sat there watching those birds, she wondered about her life. Even so, she gazed out at the pond; everyone knew how much Ghetto loved the water, and after his physical had burnt to ashes, the ashes had been used to consecrate that small body of water. There was nothing to keep her company but a bottle of liquor and the plastic cup she drank from.

"Cheers, baby, to us" —she toasted before sipping from the cup. Slipping from the bench, she closed the short distance to the edge of the pond and tilted the cup. "And to me joining you soon, Flesh. When I told you I loved you, I really meant that shit. Heaven or hell, freedom or the cell, daddy, I'll follow you." She whispered as the liquor splashed into the murky water. Her eyes were wet as memories of Ghetto invaded her mind. "Can I tell you a secret, Ghetto, you promise to keep it?" She smiled bitterly, heart hoping Ghetto was listening. Reclaiming her seat, she said: "I'm scared to die, Papi." She laughed to herself.

"Like, baby, what if when we die, our soul dies too? Why can't out of all things doctors have discovered within the body, why can't they find the soul?" A tear fell from her right eye as she refilled the cup and drank her fill. She was turnt! "Baby, what if when we die, it's really over? No heaven? No hell? No reincarnation? Just"—she paused to gaze out at the ducks who drank from the water they floated upon. "What if it's just rot?" she scrunched her nose at the thought.

"I'm too pretty for all that, that ain't no way for a real bitch to be. Ghetto, what if there really is a heaven, and it's just a bunch of old people, and mu'fuckas smiling just 'cause they made it?" Red Diamond smacked her full lips and when a gust of wind blew, she never saw Ghetto materialize beside her on the bench. His vision swallowed her. The black Dolce leggings hugged her thighs like the hug of a grandmother, and the white and black, fashionably over-sized Dolce shirt was perfect with the white and black Dolce slippers that gave a playa's view of her pedicured toes. His eyes digested the intricate, three thick braids her red hair had been twisted into. *Keyshia Ka'oir! He* thought of Gucci Mane's wife. That's who Red put him in the mind of. *Beautiful! Loyal! Intelligent!*

"Baby what if there's no loving you in Heaven? No fucking? No partying or shopping sprees? Mann, that ain't no place I want to be! And hell? Who wants to burn! Ugh! I'm too pretty to be crispy." she joked, but even with a smile, her eyes leaked. "It's hard to have faith, Pa, cause God 'pose to be a real nigga, right?" she laughed bitterly.

"Blind faith is what the Caucasians gave to the slaves to keep them workin, ma, and I think Heaven is more in the mind than it is in the sky. I think Heaven is the mind and hell is a person's conditions." Ghetto vibed and his mouth fell open when she answered.

"But why, Ghetto?" The question made him jump in surprise.

"You can hear me? Red, I—"

"Why you let them spank you like that? Who killed you, baby!" Her next words castrated his hopes of finally being heard. A crestfallen expression replaced the hopeful one and the Gangsta exhaled a breath of frustration before running a hand down his face.

"I'm beginning to believe that God is one of the realist niggas I've ever met," he admitted more to himself than anything. *"See, Red, when a nigga living within evil, he's not really living at all. You ask why I let them Spank me? Who did it?"* Ghetto shook his head bitterly as he gazed out at the pond. *"Every nigga in the streets has a shorter life expectancy than most, cause our lives become a*

gamble. And the only mu'fucakas I've seen with the power to control the roll of the dice is God, the devil, Las Vegas, and a nigga that plays with crooks. Boss niggas get whacked by lesser men, the lesser men take their throne of the streets, but gets his crown snatched cause it shouldn't have been on his head in the first place." He chuckled at the irony before pointing at her. *The streets have many objectives, but most of its creatures get expired before they can collect their severance pay because the only "real" objective of the streets is killed by the game of life. When a person lives evil, they're not really living at all, cause "evil" is "live" spelt backwards! I should've taken the letter "e" out of the word; live, and added an "ing" to change the course of my life. You can't spell—"living"— backwards and get evil, ma, there's rules to this shit."* he chuckled. Red Diamond had been silent as she got twisted off the Cîroc, but after finishing the contents of her cup, she slid from her seat. Retrieving the bottle, she stepped to the edge of the pond and while Ghetto watched; she poured the rest of the liquor into the water.

"For you, my nigga, I love you deeply and won't rest until I shed the blood of every man, woman, and child I know were your enemies." She smirked. "And after that, I'll offer you my greatest sacrifice; so we can ride on their bitch ass together! RBO shit!"

***

Heaven

"Wha-t-" I spat in shock, not understanding. Not wanting to understand. My mouth fell open as I studied Doctor Thorton as if he had two heads. Suddenly, the teddy bear and dozen black roses felt so heavy in my hands. We stood outside Ghetto's hospital room as he gave me the most devastating news I'd heard since the night I'd been told Ghetto had been murdered. The doctor gave me a sympathetic look, and it pissed me off.

"I'm sorry, Ms. Domingo, but this is not my decision, the hospital has rules and the patient hasn't shown any change. We're currently understaffed and overcrowded due to Covid and"—

"So, you're telling me that my husband can't be here?" I scoffed.

"Wha-no!" he seemed taken aback. "I'm saying, for medical reasons, we will have to send him to a medical facility that's more equipped in dealing with coma patients or"—he paused, no doubt remembering the time he suggested pulling the plug. I let my eyes warn him of repeating the foolishness.

"So, where would this new facility be and the costs? I asked and the man used so much medical jargon that he lost me, but it was when he suggested sending my man away to a hospital in Baltimore, that made me end the conversation. "NO!" I silenced him with a hand. "Give me a week and I'll either find somewhere closer, or rob a bank so I'll have enough money to equip my apartment with what he needs to breath." I swore and in the midst of him trying to explain himself, I turnt and entered Ghetto's room-leaving the blabbering physician to wonder if I was serious or not. I was— *about both scenarios!*

***

Empress

It was a slow day at Stilettos Strip Club, but I was still able to make a few dollars. Since the pill lick we'd pulled on Ghetto and Stick Talk, I honestly didn't need to strip anymore, but a bitch was about her coins. So, I danced at any club that would have me. That night I was making it clap for a young hustla, when the strange feeling of being watched took over me. Okay—some would think since I'm a dancer, being watched wasn't anything to set off alarms but besides making niggas pay to see my new body, I also stuck niggas for their chips. So, bitch, I know the difference between being admired, versus being studied! *Rolling my eyes!*

So, I used my current trick—yes, Boo Boo, I said trick! Cause any nigga that would risk his freedom for his cho chos only to come make it rain to see or get some ass is a certified trick! *Anywho*-I used the man as my prop as I allowed my eyes to search. Turning so he'd get a faceful of all this ass, I put my hands on my knees and put on a show. I was in my best thot ish, all the while, as dude slipped dollar bills in my G-String, I let my eyes travel. *Bingo!* I thought when I spotted him. He sat in a back corner, nursing a shot of something clear, and when our eyes connected, the man lifted his glass in a toast. I smirked seductively, RNO Nukkey was a sexy-mothafucka! I'd suck the skin off his dick, and though we'd never been introduced, I knew my five foot ten, high yella statue was enough to make any nigga commit treason. I ran my tongue over my full lips as we studied each other, but when I felt a finger glide over my asshole, I had to disconnect our eye fuck to check lil' daddy I was dancing for. Spinning to face him, I gave him the stack face—"Umm, nigga, yo' bank roll ain't big enough to be feeling up a bitch like me; my hair alone costs a check!" I rolled my eyes before flipping a hand through the Peruvian bundles I had recently added to my allure. Playboy held up a D-boy knot before squeezing his crotch with his hand.

"I fuck up a check on shoes, lil baby, I got enough bread to turn ya life into a dream come true." He capped. *Niggas!* I thought with a roll of my eyes before leaning down so that my lips were inches from his ear. Allowing my tongue to glide over his lobe, I used my hand to massage his saluting dingaling.

"Baby, to fuck me, you'll need more than dream money, you'll need safari…Odyssey type currency. Holla at me when you get *that* type of check."

I purred before leaving him staring at my swaying ass cheeks with my name *Empress* tattooed in bold letters across both light skinned, five ass shots a piece butt cheeks. I giggled wondering if he knew the title. *A woman ruler of an empire.* It matters not, cause I wonder more if the nigga I was strutting towards would believe me when I told him who killed Ghetto. *Giggling!*

***

Heaven

183

The midday Sunshine pouring in through the cracked hospital curtains was a contradiction to the feel of the room. With the curtains only opened a fraction, the light only shined in a certain spot, but never reaching Ghetto's bed. I stood at his side, amazed at how feeble my warrior looked. He'd lost at least fifty pounds and though his long dreads had grown so long they almost spilt off the edge of the bed, my man wasn't Sampson, the Israelite warrior whose strength was his hair. It crushed me to see my baby so weak, and as I lay the white teddy bear beside him and replaced the dying flowers beside his bed with the black roses, I wondered if he'd ever wake up. I kneeled beside his bed before taking his hand in mine. "Papi, wake up." I paused as my eyes watered. My mind become a tormented sky with clouds of thoughts rolling into its space. Have you ever wanted to blow your own breath in the lungs of someone you love with all of you? They say I was allowing him to suffer, but I say I'm merely letting him live. "Right baby?" I whispered. "You want to live, you're gonna wake up for me? For our son? Right, pa?" A slow trail of water cut a trail down my left cheek until slipping over my lips.

"I love you, Ghetto, and the unique thing about love is it's a reflection of God. It has no season or expiration date. When it's real; it's a long-distance marathon runner; it doesn't stop or tap out when things get ugly." I whispered. My tears were salty against my lips, and as I climbed to my feet, leaning over him to study every inch of his face…My soft rainstorm drizzled upon him. A tear here, and another there-before long, it was hard to distinguish who the tears belonged to as they fell from my eyes but ran down his chocolate face. Sniveling, I smiled down at him. "Adele has a new song out called, *Easy On Me*. It's beautiful, pa, and that's exactly what I need you to do, take it easy on me. Love is new to me, Ghetto, and ever since you came into my world, you've been a storm within my heart that purges so much of my distrust that I'm as open as a wild meadow. Yet, now you have me regretting trusting where trust can fall." I whined. Ghetto had been frozen in time for a year and it was killing me! My body—I wish he'd never fucked me! Never slid his key into the lock of my feminisms and liberated the monster of desire. I wished he'd never climbed into my mind and made himself at home there, 'cause when a woman loves a man completely and selflessly, she becomes truly selfless! So *less* of *self*, that his power, love, and perspectives fill her up so fully that she reflects him because she becomes seventy percent him, and only thirty percent self. "I wrote you a poem," I told him, talking to him as if he could hear me. Smiling softly, I leaned down until my lips brushed against his ear: "I call it, *Mr. Burglar.*"

***

Empress

Ride on it, don't get tired on it/You're a dancer/Ride on it, don't get tired on it/Ooh he handsome/ Slide on take your time on it/ You a freak too— Erica Banks rapped as I stood before RNO Nukkey. Though his vision was on my face, I knew he'd already witnessed the bulge of my hips, the way my new titties sat up like ripe coconuts, and the cute cute new split of where the doctor split me at. Yes—I'm all women now boo boo. *What!*

"Can I earn some of that money, daddy?" I purred, *intentionally* standing bow-legged. The man was bossed up in Dolce and Gabbana *everything* and his drip would've left a puddle on the floor if it were possible. The RNO Cuban link gave an edgy appeal to the VVS-flooded AP on his wrist.

"I'm good on the dancin' shit, but I'll fuck off a comma or two to dialogue with you for a second." He resisted all of this ass.

What? The nigga had some type of pink stones on the bottom row of his teeth and the shit was so sexy that I wanted to run my tongue over them.

"Okayyy," I laughed before taking a seat beside him and crossing my legs. "You're RNO Nukkey, right? Stick Talk's friend?" I smiled at the quick cut of his eyes before I mentioned Stick Talk.

"Yea, in the flesh, but I'm still wrestling with the second question."

"Huh?" This confused me.

"Stick Talk," he clarified before downing the contents of his glass. Cringing at the kick of whatever he was drinking; he flagged the bottle girl down for another shot. "I'm not too sure Flesh is friend or foe."

"Why not just cop a bottle?" I allowed my vision to take on a journey. My eyes drifted from the water around his neck, and fell towards his dick, before recapturing his. "You look like you can buy the club." I licked my lips and gave him the, *you can get it* eyes.

"I can, but I'm a smart man that's even smarter with where I invest my cake." He vibed before doing the sexiest shit a man can do to a bitch like me. He pulled a dagwood of money out of a backpack I hadn't noticed until then. Slapping it on the table, I couldn't see beyond the first big face, but I was sure every other bill was identical.

Benji, Baby! Lifting a brow, I studied the pretty boy. *This nigga wants whatever he's looking for–Bad!* I thought.

"Okayyyy"— I shrugged; my vision capturing the man I'd just danced for as he approached the bar. RNO Nukkey called to me and as soon as our eyes met, he tried it.

"Who killed Ghetto?" Brothaman wasted no time, and I reared back in surprise. I knew niggas like him could read a bitch like an interesting story, so I diverted my gaze, feigning interest with dude who'd reached the bar and was catching a vibe with the bartender.

"Huh? I mean" I sputtered before reigning in my composure. "What type of question is that, how the hell would *I* know!" I got an attitude, but Nukkey wasn't fazed.

"Cause you were there! Just as you were at that cock fight a week ago when Thugga and ole man Clifton were flipped. Don't you find it strange that whenever the reaper arrives, you're always within his company? We know Thugga was rocked by a BGM nigga 'cause he was able to tell us from his grave, but Ghetto?" He paused to study me.

"How? I mean"— I stared at him confused. "How y'all know BGM did Thugga? Stick Talk ain't said shit!" I said, and the man studied me as if he could see through to my rotten ass soul. He smirked.

"A chain, he snatched one of their necklaces, but it seems like you're avoiding my questions." He wasn't to be deterred, but the arrival of his drink bought me some time. The man tossed the drink back as I crossed my arms over my breast and bounced my leg in thought. I'd heard the RNO family had been dropping bread for info and spinning on everything breathing behind their man. They were out for blood, there was an all-out war between them, BGM, and a few other cliques around the metro, and I knew before long, me and Stick Talk would get swallowed within its deadly storm. Yet, that's when it hit me! *Fuck this bitch! She ain't feeling me anyway, and may never love me the way I do her. Fuck it, if I can't have her*—I rationalized my treachery, and when my eyes trailed to Nukkey, I smirked. His ass was lit! I giggled as he shook his head against the power of whatever he'd just drank, and I figured an inebriated man had the best mind for a bitch like me to play devil's advocate!

"Look, dude, I don't know you like that, and I shouldn't be telling you this, but"— I paused to glance around suspiciously before reclaiming him with my gaze. "I really need this money, and Ghetto was my boy." I shook my head. "He didn't deserve what they did to him." I had a crest-fallen expression on my face as I lowered my head. When I lifted my gaze to him, I noticed his eyes had a glossy glaze to them; that liquor was on his ass!

"Who are they?" he asked, and at that moment, the lights in the club began to flicker as Molly; a cutie with a booty took the stage. The sound of sirens erupted as red and blue lights flickered to the beat of Cardi B's *Wild Side!*

"Heaven"—poison slipped from my lips. "Heaven was fucking one of them BGM niggas and he fell in love with the pussy." My tone was bitter, but I didn't anticipate what happened next. RNO Nukkey slipped a black FN from his waist, Startled, I jumped. "Nigga?"

"Bitch!" he cut me off, and stumbling to his feet, he swayed drunkenly while waving the gun as if he were trying to get a bead on a target.

"Fuck you give me!" He growled as he tried to shake off the effects of the liquor, and after a closer look; I realized something was off —*the drink!* I concluded just when the devil smiled.

"BGM nigga!" someone shouted, and I looked up just in time to see the dude that had tried to put his finger in my butt lifting his gun.

Boom! Boom! He squeezed off. *Boc!* Nukkey fired, and I was the monkey in the middle.

***

Heaven

"When I met you, I was still a child and didn't get the chance to feel the world around me, but the day your fingertips wrapped around my heart, I felt magic surround me, and swirl within my anatomy.

Your masculinity is divinity; a typhoon that threatens to drown me...Within troubled waters, so warm, sensual, tranquil, and dangerous! You entered my soul sista spirit, and I still can't figure out how you found the key to my locks....

You're a burglar that entered my soul without my consent, and now I can't get you out! Like you wandered into the maze of my heart, taking a leisurely stroll as if you're in no rush to make it out.

Now I can't get you out..the house of my mind! Soul brotha with so much potential; trapped within a world where the black power fist has lost its powers...

Yet, when my earth orbits your sun, we create the stars and I can do this for hours...And hours...And hours upon hours!

Yet, you're a burglar, so please, Mr. Burglar, don't run away with my heart," I whispered before kissing Ghetto's ear. *"Cause when it comes to love, a woman can envision until she's lifted into another dimension...Held within suspension, while standing on her tippy toes on the precipice of suspicion.*

Sipping the cup of the future until she's fallin...falling....falling deeper...and deeper into love's craters— a collision of the cosmos, where Cupid's arrow strikes the heart and pussy and dick creates the illusion of forever within naivety. And to wake up?"

My tears blinded me as I poured out my heart, and running the back of my hand down the side of his face, I prayed he could hear me. *"Would be suicide; a sickness with no remedy. All because I believed I could be the Coretta to your King. A woman to help you dream. So, please, Mr. Burglar, you can have all my money...The car...Even my pussy, but please don't run away with my heart.*

You've held it hostage for so long that it doesn't want to leave...A sickness I believe, that's spread to my spirit.

So, now that you say I'm free; I'm free? No. NO! Hands covering my ears 'cause no! I don't wanna hear it! I told you not to make love to me! I begged you not to push me until I fell in love with your power! Yet, your love "forced" me to relinquish my love to you, and now you wanna abandon me on the yellow brick road, where Dorothy can't find her way home, cause the Wizard is a liar!

And—and love is the cousin of desire, and—and there's no courage for the lion...

No brain for the scarecrow, but the tin man is "I" who placed my heart within the hands of a black man's fire!

But please, black man, take my most expensive heels. My sight...You can even have my dreams of forever, but please Mr. Burglar, don't run away with my heart. Please wake up, Ghetto."

Renta

Chapter Ten

Didn't Make the Cut

God and the Devil

"Checkmate, Fool! Ahhaa! I beat yo ass, boiii!" Satan declared in a classic flavor flav voice. God stared in horror at the chess board; he'd made one mistake and the devil had trapped his king with his rook and queen. The devil jabbed a finger against the table triumphantly. "Nigga, you can't fuck wit' me, but I'll chop game with you later, lil' daddy, right now I got shit to do!" he proclaimed before turning to leave.

"Satan," God paused him.

The devil glanced at him from over his shoulder before nodding. "What's up?

"Don't harm Ghetto, or corrupt him, dude's a real one," He said, and the devil turned to face the deity that was omnifarious, omnipotent, and omniscient all in one.

"Dig this, pimp, you lost fair and square, daddy, Ghetto ain't your concern any longer!" he spat.

"Don't make it my concern either," God challenged. The devil chuckled before turning and disappearing.

"Yea, whatever, mu'fucka!" His voice carried on the air. God fell back in his seat, fried out at himself for slipping and letting the evil being defeat him. His eyes fell on the queen's piece the devil used to mate him with and as the wisp of Ghetto's soul formed inside the crystal belly, God studied the scene it became. "Damn!" he whispered.

***

Ghetto

191

After Red Diamond had left, I'd sat at that pond, lost in thought for hours. Yet, somehow, I'd fallen asleep, and when my eyes reopened, I frowned, I found myself in another place entirely. It took me a moment to register that I was sitting on a familiar bench. Glancing around, it dawned on me that it was the exact bench I'd found myself on after Stick Talk had shot me. I blinked in confusion, but as soon as I was sure it was that same bus stop, I shot to my feet and began to foot it! I walked and walked down that long road with no idea where I was headed!

"Fuck sitting round this bitch waiting on God to show me another mistake!" I was gonna find his ass and we were gonna get some straightening! So, I walked and walked along that strange street until stumbling upon a street sign that read, "Heaven's gates- just up ahead." I frowned but kept pushing until I found the end of a long line of people that was backed up for about a few miles. The last person in the line was a beautiful snow bunny that could've gotten some action without asking! Even with all the paid-for backsides of this generation, this lady was exclusive material! She glanced at me from over her shoulder, and once she beheld my playarisms, lady bit down on her bottom lip with seductive mischief in her eyes.

"What's all this? What's this about, love?" I inquired, my vision taking a mission up and down her anatomy.

"Umm," she giggled. "It's ass—" she paused as her eyes bulged in alarm. Her hand flew to her mouth and I frowned. Guess it wasn't proper to curse there. "Oops," she smiled. "I mean, it's butt, all-natural, and what do you want it to be about?"

"Naw, lil' one, I meant—" I paused to wave at the long line. "This line, what is that?"

"Oh!" she blushed, her cheeks turning beet red. "Forgive me, I thought—"

"You cool, Ms. Lady"—I cut her off as my eyes fell to all that cushion she was pushing. You have every right to "know" what you have and yes, that's truly a nice ass." We shared a laugh. I didn't give a damn 'bout the sacredness of where we stood. Lady's vision

swept down the line with irritation in her features; apparently, the line was moving too slow for her taste.

She rolled her eyes, "this is the line of judgment where they decide if you'll be accepted into the golden gates or be sent to the lake of fire." Her tone was apprehensive. I chuckled before thanking her and heading to the front of the line. People cursed and glared, but I didn't give a damn, I'm a boss! I've never waited in a line at the club, at school, or anywhere else, so I wasn't 'bout to wait in one to await the next mofo to determine my fate!

***

Heaven

My name is Professor D.L. Ridge, and I'm a very courageous teacher of sociology at the University of North Texas in Denton. Now—" the five-foot-eleven, tall, dark, and handsome man paused to glance around the large lecture hall. "I don't like white people." This statement created a stir in the room and my mouth fell open in shock. The man held up a hand to calm the room, "I don't like brown-skinned people, and even more, I'm not too smitten with black people!" These last two revelations somehow erased the tension. I'm assuming, people are okay with not being liked as long as they're not the only ones being despised. A trickle of laughter drifted around the room as he continued. "What I'm saying is, I don't see color and I believe that the stigmatization of any racial class isn't only ignorant, but also evil! As one can see—" He paused to point to his skin. "I'm as black as night." He smiled and stole laughter from the students by stating the obvious. "It's February the third, which makes this officially Black History Month! So"—he paused to point out to us. "I'm here for the white people mainly. I'm told that Professor Smith has a very bright class and within this curriculum of history, he's been very fair in his teaching of the races?" His statement was more of a question, and I coughed in derision. *More like altered the teaching of it,* I thought.

"You," Professor D.L. Ridge singled out a Caucasian girl with a pair of dorky glasses pulled down low on the bridge of her nose.

"What's the difference between a nigger and a negro?" The man's question was so unusual that even I felt uncomfortable. The girl sputtered as she stared in horror at the midnight black professor.

"I-umm—"

"There's no need to be shy or uncomfortable. We're here to teach and learn from each other."

The girl shrugged. "I-I don't know," she admitted, eyes wide in fear. The professor smiled.

"For one not to know isn't a sin."

"Google says a nigger is a disparaging term for a black person, and a negro is a black person or a member of the Negroid race. I'll also mention that negro—no—negroid is no longer in use," a white guy further up the rows of seats answered for her while holding up his phone so we could see. The professor nodded thoughtfully.

"Yes, but does Google tell us that the belief of most anthropologists is that whenever a black person; no matter if he's Cuban, Senegalese, Moroccan, or American, accomplishes anything *worthy of notice*, they're no longer considered Negros? What Google doesn't say is a negro is considered a person of the dark complexion of race, who hasn't accomplished anything." The professor chuckled before turning on the smart board. "That means that the only evidence separating the terminologies of nigger and negro is found within the Afro peoples' contentment of the word," he said while pointing to the depiction of an ape on the smart screen. Then, the man asked a question I'd always wondered.

"Who can tell me why most racists call blacks *monkeys*?"

"Uhh, because they evolved from apes?" someone answered, and though there were a few snickers, the professor nodded. I rolled my eyes at the ignorant, pock-marked face, white dude who'd just stated it.

"Asshole!" someone verbalized my sentiments exactly, but the professor held up a calming hand.

"Who said that?" he asked, and though the cock sucker didn't stand on his words, there was a sista beside him that pointed him out.

"He did!" she tattled. More laughter erupted when the dude sunk low in his seat.

"Smart man." The professor's compliment was another jaw dropper that caused even the cowering dude to stare with his mouth agape.

"Yet," Professor D.L. Ridge added. "How can the black man be a monkey without the white man being one too? The basis of black men evolving from apes is a study based on a failing medical scholar of the year 1831. Charles Darwin sailed to the islands of Galapagos, and after landing on San Cristobal, he noticed a strange thing about the animals there. It's said that not only were the animals different from those of the mainland, but animals of the same species behave differently due to the difference in environments." He turned to the class. "Evolution was Darwin's thesis on the birth of humanity, and in 1974, a nearly whole skeleton was found by Donald Johanson *in Ethiopia*. They had apelike features, were taller, and had larger brains than the Australopithecus afarensis. Simple, stone tools were found along with their remains; hence the name *Homo Habilis—Handyman,* when translated from Latin. They are said to have begun the stone age." The professor clapped enthusiastically with a broad smile— "so, bravo, son, you're absolutely correct!" He congratulated. "Homo Habilis had feet and hand bones that were human-like. "Homo Erectus is Latin for *upright man.* These are the forms of ape-like humans that had elevated beyond tree climbing and were adapting to life on the ground. The Homo Erectus started to travel beyond Africa and began to migrate to other continents." Professor D.L. Ridge pointed his lecture stick to the image of life on the screen. "They also were the first to make and control fire. Yet, who can tell me who Homo Sapiens were?" He turned back to the class and allowed his eyes to scan the crowd. "How about you?" He pointed his stick and it took me a second to realize he was speaking to me! Luckily, I was enlightened and had read Charles Darwins, *On the Origin of Species* and his other book, *The Descent of Man*.

"Homo Sapiens is Latin for *wise man,* and evolved 250,000 years ago in Africa. They were hunters and gatherers, and their brains were much larger than the former three Homo humans." I opened my mind and to save anyone else the trouble, I pointed at the other two examples on the screen. "Those are Homo Neanderthals who were not only larger than current humans, but their brains were bigger. Around 30,000 B.C. they died off with no apparent cause." I smiled as the professor stared at me in shock. I pointed at the last depiction. "And that's Homo Sapiens Sapiens, who lived as far back as 300,000 years ago and were spread across Europe. They were known as Cro Magnons which are almost just like modern humans today."

The professor's round of applause caused me to blush.

"You are a very studious girl, and I appreciate your help," he acknowledged before looking at the class. "My point is, if civilization *began in Africa* and it's said that the first people evolved from apes, then how can a black person be a monkey, but a white person not be one? Isn't this a nigger perspective? An ignorant mindset that's just as ignorant as the man that concluded that we evolved from apes in the first place?"

***

Ghetto

When I made it to the front of the line, there was someone already standing before a judge of some sort. Behind them was a twelve-foot golden gate, and when my eyes took in the man who judged, I realized it was none other than God-my reflection! On both sides of him stood security that brandished military-type weapons and the two soldiers had no nonsense etched into their scowls. Each wore black and white camouflage, and both had a majestic pair of glossy feathered, black wings.

"Hell, you mean, God, man, look, that dude was asking for it! If I didn't step on him first, I would've been a victim; one of us had to go!" The man standing before them pleaded his case as God licked the tips of his fingers. He began flipping the pages of a humongous book until he found what he was looking for.

"I believe that, son, but what about the other four people you killed? The little girl and her mother didn't deserve that." he acknowledged while tracing his finger down the page; nodding.

"Yes, you gave a few dollars to the poor, and yes, you even went to church a few times, but your stealing, lies, and murders outweighs the good you've done." God's eyes lifted to capture the man.

"But, God, I tried to—"

"No!" God cut him off. "You didn't rock with me while you lived, so I'm not rocking with you now that your time has expired. Guards!" he suddenly demanded, and the two soldier angels snapped into motion. The condemned man fought and cursed as they drug him off, and as I watched, the ground cracked open at their feet and though I couldn't see into it, something dark called from it and the condemned man was snatched in before the ground snapped back shut.

"Next," God called and before an elderly black woman who'd been waiting could step forward, I cut her off.

"Hey, mothafucka, you wait one damn minute! I've been waiting here in this line for months and I—" she was saying as I stepped up to the judge's bench.

"And who are—" God began, but paused when his vision lifted to me.

"Ghetto, I don't believe it's your turn, sun, you need—"

"Naw!" I eighty-sixed that shit. "You need to quit playing with my life and let's get it done wit." I was tired of the waiting game, and God or not, playboy had me fucked up. Me and my reflection had a stare off and I'm assuming the two toy soldiers wasn't feeling my 'boldness cause they stepped toward me as if a real nigga would tuck his tail. I smirked with gangsterisms playing within me. I ain't have a tail to tuck, but I do have a set of gorilla nuts that had been dragging the concrete since I'd come off the porch.

"He's okay," God's words paused the clowns and their eyes shot to him before they looked at each other in surprise. When their visions returned to me, I chuckled. God knows his creations, prey, and predator alike.

"Let me have a quick word with you, sun." God beckoned to me. I looked both of the soldiers up and down before making my way over to him.

"Wud up?" I nodded when it was nothing but the judges' bench between us. God glanced down at what I assume was the record of sins, but for some strange reason, he did not consult the book. His vision returned to me and in that moment, an unexpected coldness eased into my chest.

"Ghetto, I've tried and tried to get you to see beyond the abnormal perspective the streets has birthed in you, but it seems as though you're content with being a broken creature." His tone was cryptic, but his eyes held a sadness that bothered me; I shrugged indifferently, "he's" the one that designed my story.

"I ain't ask to be born a street nigga. Niggas ain't make you nor ask you to create poverty and let it rain on the ghetto. "So—" I frowned before lifting my hands. "What's next?" I asked. God leaned forward, his eyes suddenly turning as dark as a demon's heart.

"You know I keep it real, sun." His eyes fell to the book of sins before recapturing me. "You didn't make the cut, sun, I'm sorry."

"Huh? Fuck you mean I didn't make the"—

"Guards!" God cut me off.

"Say, wha-what! Naw, y'all get the hell off me!" I demanded when the angel soldiers seized my arms. I fought and struggled but those cats had an unnatural strength that made my attempts seem feeble.

"Yea, um hmm, that's what yo funky ass gets! The good lawd don't likes no ugly!" The old hag I'd cut in line laughed as the sounds of the ground cracking open echoed throughout the land.

"Naw, what kinda bidness you on. God, you never gave me a chance! You never!" I shouted but when I was flung down the hole in the ground, I cried out in fear of the unknown. I cursed God as I

fell from the heavens, plummeted through clouds, tumbled passed the sun, dived through blue skies, and finally; with a bone-crushing impact, I crashed through the earth!

***

Heaven

By the time I exited the lecture hall, the sun had vanished from the sky and the breeze that flowed through Ft. Worth Texas was welcomed. I was on my way to my car when my phone rang, and rummaging through my purse for it, I wondered what the hell I was gonna do about Ghetto's situation. There was no one I could turn to because only two other people knew he was still breathing. Catrina, and I'd vowed Egypt to silence. Both my girls believed I should pull the plug on my heart, but they could kiss my ass right along with Doctor Thorton, cause that wasn't even an option! I smiled when I saw it was my sis calling; *speaking of the devil!* I thought as I answered.

"Hey, girl."

"Damn, bihh, you got too fancy to check in with ya girls?" Egypt was always extra, but I loved her.

"Don't start, I just talked to you two days ago, slut, stop being extra extra."

"Whatev-errr!" She mimicked a white girl. "So what's on the agenda? Chick, are you working at that lame ass club where the men's dicks are skinny and they like their women even skinnier?" She giggled. "Or are you spending time with Mr. Tyler, that sexy ass lawyer?"

I rolled my eyes—"First off, Skeezer, Cocktails is called a *gentleman's* club for a reason. Where nikkas ain't groping you like you're some tramp, and if you didn't have dick on the brain, you would be more concerned with filling your purse. Brandon?" I considered my words, Mr. Brandon Tyler was a beautiful creature that to be truthful, had slipped under my skin. The man was a fire that I had to keep at a distance. Fire is an element that has too much power, and if not tamed before it becomes wild, it has the power to consume all that it touches. "Brandon is cool, but there can never be anything between us, Egypt, I'm spoken for." I drew the line, but even as the words slipped from my lips, my lower self-declared war against my fidelity.

"Umph!" Egypt sucked her teeth and I could picture her rolling her eyes at the phone. "Look, sis, you know I love me some Ghetto, but sis—" her voice trailed.

"Don't start, Egypt," I warned before glancing up at the sky. It was predicted to storm.

"No chick, you need *to start!* It's been a year, baby, Ghetto is not waking up."

"He will!" I spat, my eyes instantly watering, "and I'm sick of y'all and all the negative energy. Ghetto is gonna wake up, and until he does, I'm gonna be waiting. Period!" She must've detected the finality in my tone 'cause silence became the third wheel. I sniffled before wiping the wetness from my eyes before the river could drip down my face. Egypt exhaled.

"I love you, sis, we've flirted with, twerked on, and worked niggas together. Heaven, all I'm saying is, wait as long as you like, but know that good men are rare these days, and Brandon Tyler is as good as it gets. Besides," she giggled, "I know that little cootie cat been purring to be pipped. Ghetto put that grown man on ya ass, and I know once a bitch gets that D, she ain't concerned with *E, F, or G!*" she sang into the phone. Though a storm of conflict raged through me, I smiled.

"Lame, heffa, *E, F, or G?* Really, Egypt?" I rolled my eyes, but paused when I saw a sense of danger leaning against my car.

"Girl, yes! E for eventually, F for friends or family, and G for God! When a bitch getting some good dick, she's not concerned with what may *eventually* happen, she's not concerned with what her *family or friends* thinks, and *the D* will make us so not concerned with what *God* may think." She was laughing at her own craziness when I disconnected the call without a goodbye. I dropped the phone back into my Chanel bag and discreetly slipped my hand around the can of mace I kept for moments like this. *Damn, I wish I had my baby!* I thought of the gun I'd forsaken for a better life. I didn't know what it was about the man that leaned against my car; smiling at me as he exhaled a cloud of kush smoke, but I'd never liked him. His vibe was just snakish! Stick Talk tossed the stub of the blunt as his eyes fell to the notion of my hand still inside my purse.

He chuckled. "So, that's how family greets family now, Hey?" He nodded at my purse and when my vision fell to the bulge on his waist, I knew the can of mace would be of little help if the man wanted to do me harm. So, when I pulled my hand out, I smiled before holding up the tube of lip gloss I'd traded for the frivolous weapon.

"Well," I began before applying some to my lips and making them pop.

"I'm not sure, but I do know that you're not *my* family, you're my man's people." I drew the line.

"*Was* your man's people; rest his soul." He smirked and I could've sworn his pupils became slits like a snake, but when I blinked and refocused, they'd regained their shape. "See you and my gal ain't as close as y'all used to be." He spoke the obvious. I wasn't fucking with Empress as I used to; sis was just too much! Always with negative energy, yet my love for her was unquestionable! Even before she'd become a woman, when she was still Preston; the little boy that helped me and Catrina after school that day, I respected sis. People change though, and as my vision took in dude, I wondered if he was the cause of the change in my girl? I'd never really vibrated with him. A woman knows a snake, and he was one. I shrugged.

"That's between me and sis, but you can tell me why you're here?" I was done with the small talk. Stick Talk rubbed a hand over his wavy hair and my blood froze in my veins as my mind boomeranged me back to the strange experience I'd had with Genevieve at the hospital. *Kill the enemies! Murder! Kill the perpetrator! Kill the one with the tattoo! My* eyes become slits as I remembered the chants of the strange voices. *Jah must find the killer, gal, trust de cards, Jea.* Genevieve's words played in my mind as my eyes captured the obviously new ink. The scar on my chest that the evil bitch Genevieve carved into my flesh began to itch when Stick Talk noticed my fascination with the tattoo. He held out his forearm to reveal the depiction of half the face of a roaring lion with the words, *by any means*, inked above it. When my eyes lifted to him, his pupils had blinked into slits again, and I shook my head vigorously, shock and fear becoming lovers within me.

"I'm here to tell you who killed Ghetto." He turned my world upside down.

Chapter Eleven

The Forecast

Ghetto

After crashing through the earth, I fell through a darkness so black that it defied the definition of darkness. I fell and fell until- "Poof!" I smashed into solid darkness, unconscious! Don't know how long I'd been out, but when my eyes snapped back open, I went into an instant panic attack! Claustrophobia! I could barely move, like I was trapped inside a box! The darkness inside whatever I was locked within wasn't absolute, more of a dimness, and it was within that dimness that I recognized my surroundings! The silk padding- the smell, I was in a casket! "Hisss!" I froze as the serpentine hissing of a man's greatest enemy filled the small confines. Loud! That's when my body began to slither! Fuck?! It felt as if I were laying upon a bed of moving noodles, and when I went to move, shit got crazy! "Hssss! Quissss! Pssss!" A multitude of different kinds of snakes hissed threateningly. I trembled though I was paralyzed by fear. I glanced down into the darkness to find hundreds of slick snakes slithering over my body! Green, yellow, strange purples-oil black, the serpent's twisted around and over my body as if they were mating.

"Qsisss!"

"Hssss"-Their hisses made my skin crawl.

"AHHHHHHH! AHHHH!" I was hysterical! Going mad! Then-an oil black cobra slithered up my chest, its forked tongue flickering as it tasted the air. Its "s" shaped crawl was slow, and as the snake's cold tongue danced over my neck, the head of the snake slid over my chin, its tongue rapidly slipping in and out of its mouth as we came face to face. I shouted at the top of my lungs and in the darkness, the snake reared its ugly head back, its flaps spreading wide before it flashed an impressive gleam of vampire-like teeth- "Quissss!" It hissed and just as it went to strike, I pushed up with all I had—click! The lid of the casket flew open and I shot upright.

"Ahhhhrr! Helllp mee!" I cried out, of my mind with distress. In a mad attempt to escape the snake pit, I rocked it sideways and me and the casket crashed into rocky ground. Hundreds of snakes spilled out and I flailed my arms wildly. The reptiles slithered in all directions and still screaming, I fought to my feet. "Arrrahhhhh! AHHHH!" I cried until—

"Ummmm, fuck! Fuck! Fuck, babyyy!" Erotic cries merged in the dark until they became a symphony of contradictions. I slapped my hands down my body, and freaked out while someone got their freak on. And only after I was sure nothing serpentine slipped below my clothes, did I pause for the cause. Glancing down at my attire, I was surprised to see the all black designer threads.

"Daddy, youuu-u—u, suckkkking the shit out this-sss-pussy!" a woman cried in ecstasy. I frowned as my eyes took in my predicament, and only then did I realize how hot it was. I found myself in a dark cave and glancing up, I spotted thousands of sleeping bats! Fuck I'm at? I thought as I searched for an exit. Steam hovered in the air and fed the heat.

"It's hot as a motha—" I began, but paused.

"Yes! Yesss!" the sounds of pleasure cut me off. Curiosity is a double-edged sword, it can either lead one to something beautiful or to something ugly, and as I followed the sounds of fucking, I prayed that I didn't get cut by the wrong edge of its blade.

"I'm-I-mmma al-most-there, bae, keep-e-eating thisss-pus-sssy!" the woman cried and as I rounded the corner, my jaw dropped. The cave was naturally formed by jagged, ash-black stone that opened up into a wide space, and there-in the middle of it, I spotted a large sleigh bed covered in red silk sheets. Black sheer curtains hung from the high bed posts, but it was the exotic feline that lay spread eagle in the middle of it that had my undivided. Her back was propped against a pile of pillows, her long thick legs were in a V-shape, and her toes looked to be throwing up gang signs as a light-skinned cat sucked her pussy as if he were attempting to suck her soul from her vagina. "Fuck!" the lady cried before reaching back and gripping the headboard with one hand and the back of the man's head with the other. Her legs trembled, and as if the world

had become one with her orgasm, a full-blown earthquake shook the ground and walls. I had to fight to keep my footing as lady's eyes lifted and bore into mine, it was as if she wanted me to share within her euphoria. She was a siren that had so much allure within her energy that even earth, wind, and fire bowed to her. Grinding her nature back and forth over the man's face, her juices flowed so freely that at any moment, I knew she'd drown him in her cum.

"Ohh-myy-fuc–kinggg-fuckking goddd!" She screamed at the top of her lungs and her escape was an explosion! Thick! Powerful! The seductress's climax caused wind to swirl throughout the cave, and as her tremors subsided, so did the quaking of the earth. The man between her legs continued to lick at her honey pot as if he wanted to fill himself with her.

"Come here, daddy," she called to him and like an entranced puppet, he obeyed! Crawling up her body until he came face to face with beauty, the lady pulled him down for a hungry tongue kiss. "Mmmauh!" She moaned as their tongues danced. I was speechless, dick on steroids and erotically, queens hand trailed over her boy toys ass, up his back, trailed off the back of his neck, and paused on both sides of his head. She wrapped her thick thighs around his waist and with unnatural strength, the woman twisted the man's head to the left. My eyes widened in shock, my dick deflated, and I jumped when the crack of his neck echoed throughout the cave.

"Fuck?" I couldn't believe the bitch had snapped his neck, and as she pushed the corpse off her, and slipped off the bed, a wicked smile curved her full lips. She was perfection. Poetry in motion as her hips swayed with each step she took. At five foot nine, the lady was the hue of butter, with fire-red, wavy hair flowing from her head, and everything below her navel was waxed. Her titties were the size of small watermelons, with large chocolate areolae surrounding her hard nipples. Her face? Damn! She resembled a thick version of a young Vanessa Williams, same exotic eyes, but fuller lips. Her walk was feline-like Aaliyah in the movie, Queen of the Damned, and once the sexy mu'fucka paused before me with merely

*a foot of space between us, she allowed her tongue to brush her lips
freakishly.*

*"I've been waiting on you, Ghetto, "we've" been waiting on
you," she smiled seductively. When her eyes fell to my attire, so did
mine, and to my surprise, the black over black outfit was exclusive,
and was a complement to the matching loafers, but it was my RNO
Cuban link that added some spazz to my class. VS2's were pretty
beneath soft lights, but special when captured within the gaze of a
boss bitch!*

*"Oh yea?" I responded as our vision lifted and had a head-on
collision. "And who might you be? Who is us?" I inquired, and
lady's laughter began low before rising in timbre as she tossed her
head back. When she returned her eyes to me, I flinched before taking a step back in alarm.*

*"What the—" I spat. Her irises became dancing flames as she
smiled wickedly.*

*"Me?" she purred seductively, and before my eyes, her beauty
melted away like hot wax from a candle. Lady melted into a creamy
puddle and as I stared with my mouth open wide, the puddle rose
and began to take form! An albino beast with a set of wicked ram
horns sprouting from his head appeared, and with a snap of his fingers, everything went black! I couldn't see shit besides a pair of eyes
so red they glowed in the darkness. "Me?" he asked. "Some call me
Satan, some even confuse me with Lucifer, but all know me as"—
He paused and the moment became demonic! Fire exploded from
the ground, scorching everything in its path, burning hot! Yet, before me, not touched by it, but illuminated by the flames stood the
evilest mothafucka I'd ever set eyes upon! His ivory skin was the
color of piano keys and his eyes were as red as blood, but in spite
of his strange features, dude was a playa! He smiled, revealing
thirty two gold-capped teeth. "The Devil!" he whispered before
dusting lint from his black tailored suit. The creature wore diamond
rings on every finger and the flooded diamond choker around his
neck was magical! His long dreads were freaky as he pointed out at
the flames, the creature began to laugh. "And us is them."*

"Help me!"

"Rrrraaah!"

"Waterrrr! Pleeeease!"

"Ghetto, help us!" a multitude of cries merged as one as my eyes shot to the flames. There were men and women alike, cooking! Some writhing in agony. Others literally pawing at their skin as their flesh melted away, but it was when I recognized grandma Genevieve, Kiest, and a few of my other niggas frying that caused me to throw up. The devil laughed, I couldn't understand how my grandmother got there. Why?*

"What's the bidness, gangsta, welcome to my humble abode," Satan smiled.

***

Heaven

Three Hours Later

"Wha-what?" I stumbled over my words, wondering if I'd heard him correctly. Stick Talk chuckled bitterly with a shake of his head as if he couldn't believe it himself.

"Shit crazy, Heaven, ain't no loyalty no more. Niggas out here spinning on their own family for the love of money." The man spat on the asphalt in disgust. *"I warned bruh! I told Ghetto that bitch wasn't right!"* He spewed vehemently. I frowned as my heart began to pound against my chest, and steering closer to him, Stick Talk knew he'd awaken that deadly part of me.

"Bitch? Warned him? Nigga, quit tip-toeing around what you're trying to say and spit that shit out!" I lost patience, and my trigger finger began to itch. Stick Talk's eyes became downcast as a crestfallen expression blanketed his facial.

"The only reason I'm telling you this shit is cause "I" can't take her down, there's rules of RNO and the table forbids one to speak ill of another piece of our flesh without "physical" proof." He again shook his head sadly. Our eyes connected and I thirsted for his next words.

"Tell me, Nigga!"

"Ghetto was still fucking Red Diamond, and her girl, Kitty, found out, and Kitty is ruthless, Heaven." Though he was still talking, the shattering of my heart was so loud that he sounded muffled. Tears baptized my vision.

"Kitty killed Ghetto, and Red Diamond, out of love for her, kept the secret," he revealed, but his words sounded distant. Like I was hearing him from beneath water. I stared at him, but honestly, I wasn't seeing him, and after a moment, he came to that exact conclusion. I remember him giving one last shake of his head before leaving me standing there with a rainstorm rolling from my eyelids.

"She's nuts, Sarah, look at her!" The sound of their voices pulled me from the fog of memory, and snatched me back into the present. I blinked at my reflection staring back at me from the mirror I sat before and that's when I remembered where I was. After the unexpected visit from Stick Talk, I'd driven to cocktails, a *white man's* gentleman's club I'd began to work. It was a far cry from what I was used to, *but* it added to my purse *and* I didn't have to worry about the untamable disrespect of nikkas that feel like, just 'cause a bitch dances naked for them that she's a thot. Staring in the mirror, I found the reflection of the two white girls behind me at another vanity mirror. Trish and Sarah were twig thin and their like for me was even thinner.

"Yes, I am nuts, Trish, you may wanna consider that when bumping your gums, skinny mini." I smiled. Trish was the loudmouth of the two and I'd been tempted to lay hands on the racist bitch. Fear blossomed within Sarah's eyes as she hurriedly gathered her things.

"We're not looking for trouble, come on, Trish." She spoke over her shoulder as she headed for the door, but Trish glared at me.

"I'm not scared of you," she *lied.* "Why don't you go back to wherever you came from, we don't do your kind around here." She *finally* shed her skin before placing a hand on her bony hip. I laughed slightly *God, fix it!* I thought while sliding from my seat. The girl was dopefiend skinny and as we faced off, I knew if I tore into that, the bitch would press charges.

Make it make sense, God! I thought as my eyelids drifted shut and I began to massage my temples. "Bitch?" I spat, my right leg bouncing as the black girl in me merged with the Dominican me. "You won't believe the type of day I've had and I promise, I-promise-you, I will beat-yo-dopefiend-asss!" I spat through clenched teeth before my eyelids fluttered back open. "You may not like me, but you will respect me, by choice or by force, skank! It's not my fault your pale ass men have a taste for—" I paused as my eyes fell to my thickness before reclaiming her. "A little darker meat. Hell, your kind. As you say, should be used to it by now. Thy massa been sneaking out to get a taste of well-done pussy since the beginning of time." I laughed when Trish began gathering her things.

"What-the-fuck-ever!" she spat.

"What, you ain't know, baby?" I taunted. "Girl, yassss! That ole cracka man loves him some sweet-tasty, nigga girl pussy. Bihh, why you think white women getting thick now? Ass shots, silicone in the titties, all that was made for white women, so they can get their shape thick, just like *my kind.*" I was balled over in laughter when the lady gave me the finger before following her friend right out the door. *How's that for black history month!*

***

Ghetto

Fire engulfed me-hot and hungry. It hurt, it burned so bad that my words were lost. I opened my mouth to scream, but no sound came forth. I was on fire, and as I slapped at the flames, the devil laughed.

"This is one form of pain, my "G", but there's deeper form," *he said with a smile; the flames somehow not bothering him. My body jerked into a wicked dance of pure agony, I'd never experienced that level of pain, and as the flames ate at my flesh, it beckoned my tears forth. Yet as soon as they fell down my face they'd evaporate. All around us, people cried for mercy, a mercy that wouldn't come. The devil studied me curiously as I burned and out*

of the flames; a screaming woman, naked and ablaze stumbled by. The devil took her by the wrist, pulled her to him, and there within the purge of fire, began to dance with her. The woman screamed in pain as the devil spun her in a circle.

"Come, Ghetto, take a walk with the king of darkness and let me show you the difference between love and pain…Real and fake." He smirked evilly before waving a hand through the fire. *The scene tore like the page of a book and before I could wrap my mind around what was happening, he and I were transported into another world. One without fire, but alive with soothing drops of rain.*

"Ahhhhrrugh! AAH!" I was still growling in agony.

"Shut yo weak ass up, nigga, that shit ain't hurting you no more, it's a mind thing!" The devil laughed and to my surprise, the burn was gone. The wind blew with soft power and as I took in the night, my mouth fell open. The sky was black as rain cried from heaven, but spread out before us…Hundreds of feet below, the city of Dallas, Texas was aglow with different colored lights. I couldn't understand how we had such a majestic view until I glanced down.

"Mann!" The word slipped from my lips in awe at what I saw. We stood atop of Reunion tower, five hundred and sixty feet above the slick streets below. The big ball of the skyscraper is the pride of the triple D just as much as the Dallas Cowboys football team is, and as the decorative lights surrounding it glowed beneath our feet, I became trapped within the moment.

"Ghetto" The devil waved his hand out toward the crooked city. "I once took Jesus high upon a mountain after he had fasted for forty days and forty nights, and I offered the sucka all the kingdoms of the world and their splendor—" He paused to glance out at the city. From that height, we were able to see Nawf Ghanistan, sunny South Dallas, the stiff cliff, and even the wicked west. If it wouldn't have been raining, we'd even be able to see the outline of murda worth. "And you know what that corn ball ass dude did?" The creature shook his head in amazement. "He refused! the man chose crucifixion over being a boss, now tell me, my guy, what type of mutha—"

He paused to set his red gaze upon me. "Naw, "Why" would a mu'fucka that can see the future, sacrifice it all for people he knows don't give a fuck bout him? I'll tell you"— *He laughed as the rain fell upon us.* "Because he is a genius! Bruh, that boy Jesus refused me because he had his own agenda! The nigga created a cult! Now, he's the epitome of immortality. The church considers themselves "Christians" and partake of communion. Only cannibals and cultists find it religious to eat of a man's body, or drink of his blood. Think about that shit!" *he laughed. Rain water fell upon me as I gazed out at the metroplex, wondering if I'd ever see the city lights again? I wondered of what I'd give to walk, talk, love, and be loved again, and that's when it hit me.*

"Maybe Jesus didn't accept your offer because he truly believes in his sacrifice, or maybe because he wanted to make his "own" way?"

"Fam," *the devil tapped my arm,* "Jesus's sacrifice doesn't change shit! Who made it law that a mu'fucak has to go through him to get to God? Why ain't no other religion saying the only way to get to the OG is through anotha person? You can't be that lame, Ghetto, I offered dude the kingdoms!"

"Yea under the condition that he bowed to you"

"Nigga fuck you think "I" got kicked out of heaven for? I didn't wanna bow to no angels-no humans! I wanted my own shit, and since I was being ambitious, God's sucka ass disdained my G and exiled me." *Dude spat. I shrugged.*

"I feel you, playboy, we live and die for the shit we want or love."

"The fuck!" *The demon scoffed.* "You don't even know what love is, dude!"

"You can't tell me what I do or don't know!" *I spat, eyes locking wit' his. The devil chuckled.* "Oh, so now you're a gangsta, but where was all that G shit just a moment ago when yo black ass was being turnt into a Kentucky fried negro? Huh? You were on ya—"

"Pleeeease make it stop! It burns...Plesssse, ahh wan wan wan!" *The creature mocked the female voice. I shivered at the thought, and the devil smirked in recognition.*

"Okay, toughy." He smirked. "Let's see how deep your love runs." He spoke cryptically. I frowned. "Huh?"

The devil laughed before proving his wickedness—he pushed me off the building.

"Ahhha! Rahhh!" I screamed as I fell five hundred and sixty feet towards the concrete.

***

Heaven

"You boys behave yourselves and make sure to give a warm welcome to our newest girl—*Heavenly!*" I almost laughed, even the DJ at the establishment was corny! Yet, I had a show to put on. Ginuwine's, *My Pony,* single blared through the sound system and I stepped out onto the stage in nothing but a nude, colored thong that blended so well with my skin that I appeared pantiless, and a pair of peach-hued, knee-high boots that went perfectly with the same colored Stetson Cowboy hat on my head. The crowd went wild, as I straddled midair and imitated riding a bull. It didn't take much to get a rise from a mostly white audience, and though dollars fluttered in the air, my mind was a thousand miles away.

Ghetto was still fuckin Red Diamond and her girl, Kitty, found out, and Kitty is ruthless, Heaven! Stick Talk's revelation played within my head. *Kitty killed Ghetto!* I tried to fight back the words, but they were relentless enemies that attacked my thoughts with all they had. Spinning and putting my back to the crowd, I put my hands on my knees and like Megan thee Stallion said, *shook my ass like a thot thot!* Yet, the entire time dollar bills rained on stage, I was thinking of me and Ms. Red Diamond's encounter at the mock funeral- *The rain fell horizontally, the sky was as gray as ash, and when I made it down to the river bank where she stood gazing out at the dying flames of the casket, Red Diamond's bloodied gaze shifted to me. Studying me for only a moment to gauge my intent, the bitch had the nerve to roll those ugly ass contact lens-covered eyes before returning her attention to the simmering embers the coffin had become.*

"Who are you to Ghetto?" I wasted no time with formalities. The rain soaked us as I awaited an answer, and just when I thought I'd have to become a bit more forceful with my questioning, sista girl turned to face me.

"I'm the bitch whose place you took." She said it as if it were a known fact.

"Sooo"— I began before reaching down to take off my heels; the earth had become too soggy for them. "You're the ex or the side bitch?" I snickered with the question, and sis's gaze fell to my bare feet as if she thought I'd relieved myself of the heels preparing for a fight. When her eyes returned up top, I took the hat and veil off so she could see it in my eyes that I didn't give no fucks; we could do it her way. Red Diamond's smile was a flash of rose gold capped fanged teeth.

"Ex?" she laughed as the wind danced around us. A flash of lightning struck across the gray havens as she wiped a strand of wet hair away from her face. "Wrong bitch, sis, and the side bitch slug?" she shook her head as if to say; shame on you. "I'm a boss bitch, sweetie, neither of those titles fits my class of woman, but"— Her eyes trailed to the still smoking casket. "Out of respect for "our" man?" When her vision returned to me, the bitch had a smug smirk on her face. "I'll keep it real with you. Ghetto loves you, even while I loved him unconditionally, still do and always will love him without conditions, yet, he made his choice. What he and I had or has is none of your business." Her truths were exactly that, but it was her smugness that had me ready to bust her in the mouth.

"Heaven?" His voice froze me as the memory melted away and I fell back into the present. "Heaven, is that you?"

I spun, and found Brandon Tyler standing at the edge of the stage, surrounded by his colleagues. I stared horrified at him seeing me there.

"Let her be, man!" Someone shouted before waving a handful of dollar bills in the air.

"Shake it, honey, shake it for papa!"

"Tyler, isn't that your"—was the last thing I heard before I rushed off the stage. I'd never been so embarrassed in my life! What a fucking day!

***

The sea was turbulent beneath the gray skies, it's waves waging war against nature. It was a civil war that caused the waters to rise and fall within a motion of beautiful dangerousness as God sat oblivious to the chaos around him. The deity's mood was somber as he gazed down at the chess piece, still glowing with a piece of Ghetto's story within it, but it was the vision within the King's piece that showed him what was transpiring in the present. Shriirp! A ripping sound emitted just before a dark hole appeared in midair, but God never took his eyes from the chess piece. A muscular angel with skin as white as milk stepped out of the gash, and once he stood before the Lord, he stood at attention like the soldier he was. His massive white feathered wings spread out in all their magnificence as he saluted God, and only then did the OG's vision lift to behold him— "Peace, Michael, what's the science?" He greeted Michael the archangel at ease.

"The science is understanding, Lord, which is to see with the third eye. The mind. Understanding is also the manifestation of its father, knowledge, and its mother, wisdom. It's the best portion of living mathematics because without understanding, one can't possess true peace, which is what keeps sun, moon, and their stars within the natural order of man, woman, and child." The celestial creature built. God nodded.

"That's 120 degrees, now tell me, what brings you here?" He acknowledged.

The angel glanced back at the hole he'd stepped out of before his vision returned to the almighty.

"Well, Lord, we caught someone trying to break into heaven."

God frowned- "Who is it, and why "you" couldn't handle it?" He lifted a brow.

"Well, she"—Michael began, but there was no need.

214

"Cause, I wasn't hearing it, Jea. Now why don't ya tell an old lady why ya let my boys' soul go to the devil?" Genevieve was no nonsense when she stepped through the hole. God smirked, he'd been expecting her; He'd been the one to crack the hole in the wall of hell so she'd be able to escape.

"Genevieve, a pleasure, Earth, how have you—"

"Don't Genevieve me, Lord, the science is knowledge, plus wisdom, which births understanding"— She held up three fingers. *"The science, I'm earth, the third planet from the sun, so I'm always within the third eye of God. So, tell me, God, how does the devil—"* her words trailed off as her orbs fell to the chess set, and when they lifted to God, a knowing smirk curved her lips. God glanced to Michael who shrugged as if to say: I can't help you.

"Give us a moment," the Lord dismissed him. The angel nodded before stepping back into the tear in the air, and as soon as the rip mended, God waved toward the seat across from him. *"Have a seat, moon."*

"The moon orbits the earth in twenty-nine days, 12 hours, and 44 minutes to keep the natural order of the earth. If the moon is truly the force behind the rising and falling of tides, then you can see—" she nodded toward the thrashing waves of the Caribbean sea. *"Then you can see that I'm not too happy with your little"—* she gazed down at the chess pieces; aglow with wisps of Ghetto's spirit trapped within their belly. *"Games,"* she added, and God ran a hand through his dreads before exhaling a frustrated whoosh of air.

"He won."

"The devil won?" Genevieve asked in disbelief. God nodded.

"Yes, the devil won fair and square; merely because I'm God doesn't mean I can't lose."

"Well, I suggest you prepare to win, 'cause ya wrong, ya hear? Ghetto deserves better from you! He doesn't belong where you sent him, nor does he belong here. So, for once, Lord, for once in de boys life; intervene. Give him a chance." Genevieve pleaded, her eyes saturating as she studied him. God leaned back in his seat, conflicted.

"You made deals with the devil before, Ms. Genevieve, and"—

"And for that, I'll regret for all time, but for your help, I'll burn down there in hell; happily! Save Ghetto, God, many lives depend on it!"

***

Heaven

Thirty Minutes Later

It took me thirtyfive minutes to leave the club, navigate through the pouring rain, and make it to my apartment complex. Brandon had tried to talk to me back at the club, but shame was real and wouldn't allow me to explain, so I ignored him. Yet, the man wouldn't be denied, he'd jumped into his Vette and followed me through the rain. When I found my parking spot, so did he, and killing the ignition, I knew an explanation was inevitable. Rolling my eyes, I just sat there, listening to the rain fall while gripping the steering wheel as if it were my anchor to sanity. Rainwater fell so powerfully that as it washed down the windshield, it put me in the mind of when I pull through one of those drive-through car washes. I truly couldn't understand *why* after so much time stripping, it bothered me for that man to see me like that. I sat there for ten minutes, and so did he. I guess we were both waiting on the other to make a move. I blew a soft breath before pushing the car door open and hurriedly climbing out. Brandon did the same, and as the rain soaked through my clothes, I wondered if he was there to tell me I was fired. I didn't have long to wonder cause about three feet away from my apartment building, Brandon grabbed my wrist.

"Will you just stop for a second!" he demanded and just as lightning struck across the heavens, I spun to face him.

"What you want form me, nigga, damn!" I exploded before snatching my arm free. Heavens tears fell upon us in fat drops as we stood beneath its shower. It bathed Brandon's face and only added to his handsomeness. It only took seconds for his dress shirt and slacks to become drenched, but wiping the water from his face, he seemed not to care about much more.

"Your heart, Heaven, that's what I want from you." There it was. *The moment of truth!* Thunder rolled, sounding like an angry bear, and I eyed the man that I'd known had been playing for my heart all along.

"Brandon, I—"

"Naw, Hev, kill all that." He cut me off before stepping into my personal space. With rain water rolling down our faces, our eyes searched each other as if we'd found hidden treasures within a gaze.

"You're not married, sweet heart, and there's no man in the service."

"I—I" tried, but the man placed a finger to my lips.

"No more lies. I know you're scared, but I promise not to hurt you, baby." The man wrapped his arms around my waist and pulled me into his body. A drop of rain rolled down his nose as he gazed at me, and maybe it was because I felt vulnerable after hearing Ghetto had betrayed our love? Maybe it was after going a year plus without being touched? I just wanted to feel *wanted? Appreciated?* I don't know, but at that moment, a second storm arrived. Tears leaked over the rim of my eyelids and merged with the water already pouring down my face.

"You don't want me, Brandon, you *shouldn't* want me. I'm damaged goods." I confessed, but Brandon Tyler wanted what he wanted. He kissed my forehead, and cupping my face with his cool hands, he grasped a vibe.

"I care nothin about the damaged part, Heaven, let me mend you, Boo. You're crazy...Muah!"

"You're sexy..." Muah! "You're cool." Muah!

"You're dangerous...*muah!* And I think I'm falling in love with you."

"Muah!" With every word he planted a soft kiss in a different place on my face. My temple...My cheek...My nose...My eyes. *Muah!Muah!* Our eyes danced a wicked waltz, mine moving to the beat of uncertainty, and his stepping with confidence. The rain fell in cold drops against our hot skin, and when another flash of lightning struck across the sky, followed by a roar of thunder, I wondered if God was in agreement with our intimacy, or warning me that when unleashed, passion could become a dangerous conquest. Then Brandon Tyler kissed my lips! Softly. Surely. Then I accepted his tongue. A sin. A sin that was too sweet to not partake of.

Chapter Twelve

Love

Ghetto

"Arrrugh! Ahhh!" I shouted all the way down. The pavement was close, and I was about to smash against it at soul-snatching speeds. "Ahhhh!" I cried, and just when I was about to crash into it—
"Say, weenie ass dude, stop screaming like a lil' bitch, you're fuckin up the vibe!" The devil demanded, and when I opened my eyes, I was frantic! I patted my body to ensure everything was intact.
"Say, fool, don't ever, ever, ever, do no shit like that, I"— I began until I heard the melody of soft moaning and wet kisses. I glanced around curiously, hearing the fall of rain against the window pane. The room was dark, the only light source being the gray-washed glow the midnight sky emitted. We'd materialized inside someone's apartment and it seemed as if we'd arrived in the middle of a couple getting their freak on. My eyes cut to Satan questioningly, only to find the nigga sitting on those people's couch eating popcorn with an amused smirk on his face as he observed their passion. Fuck he get popcorn? I thought as he nodded at the couple.
"Watch this shit, bruh, it's bout to get real nasty up in this piece!" He chuckled. That's when I tuned in. The man had just pulled the lady's shirt up and over her head before she ripped his button up shirt open. The pearl buttons flew everywhere!
"Damn, Heaven!" he growled, and my heartbeat sped up. Heaven? I didn't want to believe it, but when her bikini top slipped away and his head lowered to her breast, shit couldn't get more real. The ecstasy on her face was a familiarity I once treasured selfishly, and my heart cracked.
"Fuck!" I spat
"Fu-Fukkkk!" Heaven moaned.
"Fuckin right!" Satan cheered, and as Brandon's lips wrapped around her right nipple, I lost it. I ran over and punched his fool ass in the back of the head! Over and over, and over again. When I

219

was tired of beating his ass, I reached up to wrap my fingers around Heaven's throat; I planned to choke life out of her treasonous ass, but that's when it hit me! I wasn't hurting anyone but myself! Sweating and tired, I stumbled back and put my hands on my knees to catch my breath. I was a spirit, they couldn't feel me or hear me, but I could see and feel them! In the worst way-In my heart!

"Bran-donn!" Heaven moaned as he suckled her nipple and rolled the other one between his thumb and pointer finger. "We-we have to-to stoppp!"

"No," the one word was an entire sentence spoken around a mouthful of titties, but it was when he began to shimmy her shorts down her thick thighs that I knew my heart would never be the same. In moments, they'd undressed each other and though Heaven continued to whisper that they needed to stop, she willingly allowed the clown to pull her down to the floor. Slipping on top of her, he gazed down into her eyes.

"I need your heart, Heaven, I'll take care of it," he vowed.

Tears sprang to her eyes "My heart is taken, Pa, and the one that holds it"—

"Doesn't exist." He cut her off. Heaven nodded "yes"

"Yes, Brandon, he does. I'm not who you think I am, I'm a-ohhmmm!"

Her words became a moan when he stroked up into her. "Brandon, no-nooo," she cried, but her legs spread as wide as a butterfly's wings in mid-flight. Tears filled my eyes—where were the doves when a gangsta needed them to cry for me?

***

Heaven

Before I could protest, he'd entered me! The pain was a strange mixture of pleasure, but my heart was hurting. I felt low, like—like a snake!

I wanted to stop him, but my mind kept replaying visions of Ghetto giving what he'd promised to me to Red Diamond, and at that moment, revenge was sweet!

"Damn, Hev-you feel-soooo-motha-fucking-so-good!" Brandon growled as he explored me.

"We-we can't catch-ch-feelings, Brandon, no feelings!" I moaned as my eyes drifted closed. Warm tears ran down the sides of my face; not because of the pleasure, but 'cause my heart cried for Ghetto! Even while another man was currently reigning over his kingdom. My mind rebelled against my body as Ghetto invaded it. *"Heaven, what you know 'bout being crossed by a mu'fucka you'd kill for, huh? You know what it feels like to wanna love somebody, "anybody", but you've been hurt so much that your heart just doesn't know how to no more?"*

His words spoken on the night we'd stood out in the rain caused my eyes to snap open. Brandon stared down upon me as if he'd awaken into a dream. My vision was blurry from the oceans they'd become.

"I-I love you," he gifted me as he stroked.

"Don't" I shook my head against his gift. "Don't love me, Brandon."

"It's to-too late," his pace quickened; his nature touching somewhere deep inside of me.

"Huhhhh" my lips parted.

"Damn!" he growled.

Tears fell harder. "Love is a natural disast-errr," I moaned.

"That's what it is!" I spoke as my climax rose like a dangerous wave any surfer would love to crest. I felt Brandon throbbing. His dick had a pulse!

"Don't-don't nut inside me, pul-pull out"—

He nodded his understanding but pleasure is often stronger than will, and the man exploded! *Inside me!* I pushed with all I had; no release for me.

"Get-off me!" I was fuming as he slipped out and stared at me with an innocence that would've been funny under different circumstances, but at the moment, I was contemplating blowing his face off.

***

Ghetto

"You need to leave," Heaven demanded. I sat on my knees, tears staining my face while gritting my teeth against the betrayal. I wanted to look away, but naw-I needed to feel every stab of the knife she drove into my back. "Fuck Love!" my heart cried.

"Heaven, I-I'm sor—"

"Leave!" Heaven demanded before gathering her clothes and rushing to the back room. Brandon shook his head bewildered at how passion had evolved into the lack of. Dressing, the man cursed himself for losing control, and moments later, Heaven entered the room. In dry shorts, shirt, and a towel twisted around her damp hair, she crossed her arms over her breast

"Brandon."

"Heaven." They spoke at the same time. Brandon chuckled, Heaven didn't. He nodded to her. "You go first."

Heaven studied him before making her way to him- "You are a beautiful man." She whispered while running a finger down the side of his face.

"But love?" Her finger trailed pasT his chin, down his neck, and over the pecks of his bare stomach. "Love is an irrational emotion that can evolve into a tornado. A tornado that will pick you up, spin you round and round, and then toss you somewhere far off, without concern of where you land! And that's what you're doing to me; becoming that tornado, threatening to pick me up into your irrational storm and swallow me inside your forecast. That can't happen, Pa."

"Why?" Brandon captured her hands and began to kiss her fingertips.

That's when I stood up and glared at them.

"Ole weak ass nigga, look at you!" the Devil taunted with a chuckle. My blood shots cut to him with that gangsta shit on full display, but the evil creature merely laughed.

"See what I'm talmbout, my dude? You "cant" love this bitch!"

I stepped towards him, the threat evident. "Aiiight, my fault, this"— He paused to consider his words. "Lady." He smirked before nodding to the man and woman. "Ghetto, you've been on ice for a year plus, my nigga, not in jail-not in the Navy or some shit, but shut down co'ner! You expect this bi—" He caught himself before calling Heaven out her name, and slipping from his seat, the albino popped a few kernels of popcorn in his mouth. "Bruh, you can't expect this woman to be anything more than what God intended her to be, and all women were created sixty percent initiative, and forty percent vulnerable. Lady's just in her forty percent right now, at least you ain't got the type of bitch that's fuckin just cause her pussy is stronger than her loyalty."

"Nigga, fuck what you kickin,"I spat. "Let's go!" I glared at him. The devil chuckled before nodding. Cool as a spring breeze, the creature made his way over to where Heaven and Brandon stood, and he smiled as the man kissed Heaven.

"The bible, in Corinthians 13, gives an example of love, Pimp. How can you say you love this woman if you want her to suffer? Spend her days weak and in tears? How can you claim to love her, but fault her for doing exactly what you'd be doing under the same circumstances?" He shrugged. "Nobody said love don't fuck up, fam." the devil revealed. I frowned, surprised that he could be so compassionate, but it was short lived.

"That's why yo' weenie ass shouldn't have fell in love, now look at you, you should've been trying to whoop this bitch's ass instead of swinging on this playa. He didn't steal the pussy, she gave it to 'em!" He laughed, and when I lunged at him, the sucka disappeared!

"Hoe ass, dude!" I spat, and by the time I turned to glare at Heaven's punk ass, Brandon had made his exit. I watched her lock the door before making her way to the back, and I had some shit on

223

my chest, so I followed. She wound up in the bathroom, adjusting the water before stripping down and stepping into the shower. I was so crushed, that I stepped in right behind her, not even bothering to undress. Steam filled the small bathroom in seconds as Heaven stopped beneath the showers spray, and it took me a second to re-alize she was crying.

"I'm sorry, baby, I'm so-sooo sor-ryy," she cried before wrap-ping her arms around her midsection. Lady cried like a big baby, her ears blending with the shower water and slipping down the drain. I shook my head.

"Heaven, see"—I began before my own eyes watered. I was fucked up, Flesh, so much so, that I took a seat in that tub and al-lowed the water to splash all over me. Her pain became mine, that Devil was right!

Ma, this why I never believed in love, I know most people's love is based off of the type of shit the bible described in Corinthians 13, but "I've never" believed in that kinda shit" I whispered as she cried.

"I fucked, up Ghetto, soo bad, I-I-mann!" she balled before fall-ing to her knees, and burying her face in her hands while rocking back and forth. Tears leaked from my sights as I watched her pain becoming mine. Just beyond my crushed pride, I knew love loved me, but I also knew that merely because love loved didn't make love exempt from proving that love could hurt. So, just as humans do, love fails sometimes. *"Corinthians says that love is patient?"* I vibed. *"But if love was so patient, there wouldn't be such a thing as betrayal because love would wait! It says love is kind? But how, mama, if love is "pain?"* I climbed to my knees and slid behind her. *"When a nigga that's never believed in love or never trusted it, he contradicts the bible's words of love not being boastful or arrogant. Shid, why wouldn't a nigga be boastful or arrogant when he finds the type of bitch worthy of that type of claim? I want the world to know about it!*

"I swear it meant nothing to me, Papi, I was just-so mad at you." Heaven cried and rocked before shaking her head against what she was about to say. "No, baby, I won't make an excuse, there is none. Forgive me? Please?" She was an emotional thunderstorm.

"Corinthians say love isn't irritable, rude or self-seeking, but mine is, Queen. My love can become irritable and rude if handled too roughly." I said. Heaven quietly rocked while she held herself. I slipped my arms around her waist. *"My love, Heaven, is always self-seeking, cause it's self that's seeking what only your love can give me. Most importantly, they say love isn't selfish but "mine" is when it comes to you, Earth, that's why your betrayal hurts so bad."* I placed my head against her back and allowed my tears to bathee her.

"I love and miss you," Queen whispered, and if I didn't know how bad false hope hurt, I would've thought she'd heard all I'd said. "Sooo much, pa!" she cried and I nodded, allowing her to have my diamonds.

"I saw what you and Brandon did, you told him y'all couldn't catch feelings, but, Heaven, there's no such thing as fucking; giving your pussy to another nigga and not catching feelings. When he enters you, that's a feeling within itself. A woman's emotions are connected to her pussy, no matter how many men she gives it to, and no matter how much you deny it, every time you see a nigga you gave your womanhood to, y'all will remember the connection." I kissed the back of her neck before my spirit melted and merged with the water as I slipped down the drain.

Renta

Chapter Thirteen

Papi

12:30 a.m.

The hospital room was dark, save for the Christmas colored LED lights that glowed from the respirator, EKG machine, and other life-cheating robots that monitored Ghetto's status. He lay almost peacefully within the chill of the room, and as the door quietly opened to allow an intruder to enter, the peacefulness was kidnapped by their negative energy. Dressed in doctor's scrubs, hat, and wearing a surgical mask over the bottom half of their face, the intruder had snuck into the hospital easily. They smiled behind the mask as their crooked intent fed th-ir mind.

Now, let's see if sneaking his ass up outta here will be as easy! The intruder thought before glancing down at their watch. "Where is he?" The intruder wondered about their accomplice's whereabouts, and when the intruder's vision settled upon Ghetto, the stranger shook their head. "With the help or without it, your ass leaving up out of here. Tonight!" the intruder whispered.

***

Heaven

The moon was full and high, the sky as black as a monster's heart at that late hour, and as my headlights illuminated the black snaking backstreet, I cursed my GPS! I'd tried to take a short cut home, and this funky navigational system had lead me down this dark ass street, that's lined on both sides with tall ass wheat fields. The scene looked like something straight out the movie, "Jeepers Kreepers." A black night on a deserted road. It was eerie and as I drove, nodding to Queen Naija newest jam, "Hate Our Love", the strangest thing happened. "The fuck?" I frowned when the song suddenly changed to some type of folksy Zydeco music. The weird kind that you usually hear in deep Louisiana. "Strange!" I thought, I mean, how does Pandora do that!

To make matters worse, no matter what I did to change it, fix or merely cut it off, the damn stereo was not trying to hear it! My frown deepened into one of confusion until the chime of my phone alerted me to an incoming text. "Ugh!" I rolled my eyes before retrieving my iPhone 13. Tapping the icon, I read the message: "Believe the cards of fate?" I read aloud before glancing at the strange number. "Who the—" I was mumbling when glancing up to see if I'd made it back to civilization, and that's when I saw her. An elderly woman in a black dress.

"Ahhhh!" she screamed as her eyes grew wide.

"Oh my God!" I cried just as I hit her head-on. She flew backwards just as I stomped down onto the brakes. From the light of my headlights, I watched horrified as she fell to the asphalt with a sickening plop. I stared, mouth ajar in a silent scream as the strange music played. I killed her! Why was she way out here on this lonely road in the wee hours of the night? My mind was plagued with questions as I threw the car in park and hopped out. Rushing over to her, I prayed that I hadn't killed the woman. "Can you hear me, lady? Are you okay!" I panicked as I fell to my knees beside her. She'd landed on her side, with her back to me, and as I looked her over, the smell of smoke assaulted my nostrils. Was she out there burning something in those fields? I wondered as I took in the oversized black dress she wore. Yet, it was when my vision landed on the black veil that a feeling more than worry oozed into my energy. Hell? "Can you talk?" I asked her. Nothing! Her skin was pale against the darkness. Placing my fingers to see if I found a pulse, I couldn't shake the nagging feeling that I needed to run as fast and far as I could from that woman that wore funeral clothes and wandered back roads in the height of night. My heart had evolved from its darker version, and as I began to turn the woman onto her back, I realized that it felt good to care.

"Hhhehehe!" A strange sound came from the lady and I jumped in surprise when I realized she was laughing. It sounded like a demented cackle, and before I could react, everything happened in a

blur. *The woman was as quick as the blink of an eye when she rolled over and plunged something into my stomach.*

"Huuhhh," I inhaled a breath infused with pain. My eyes fell to find the handle of some sort of knife jutting out of my belly; the blade was buried inside me and it seemed as if she'd held it over a burning flame before stabbing me with it. "Why?" I mumbled while gripping my stomach, blood slicking by hands as it flowed forth, and when my vision lifted to recapture the woman, she was gone! Just—vanished! I sat on my knees, my life oozing from my wound as I stared in horror. How could she have just disappeared? I wondered, and as if things hadn't been crazy enough, the headlights of my car blinked out! The strange circus-like music still played, and my mind seemed to be filling with oil when— A crack of lightning flashed and my eyes shot up to find that old woman a few yards from me, somehow slowly rocking in a familiar rocking chair! The chair! My mind cried as the hem of her black dress flattered when a strong gust of wind suddenly blew. The tall grass on both sides of the road began to sway, and a dark energy swam in the air surrounding us. I stared, mouth agape in terror at her pretty face that was barely visible behind the sheer veil—Genevieve! It dawned on me.

"Trust de cards gal, they won't lie. You and my boy are in danger, open your eyes, Jea." Her southern voice was thick with her Cajun. "Ghetto is in trouble, save him! You're in trouble; he must save you!"

"Wha-what are you talking about? Why'd you stab me, bitch!" I cried as tears dripped from my eyes. "Why are we in—"

"Listen, I don't have much time!" she demanded as she rocked. "Love isn't pain, but pain can become love if shared with the right person. Be careful whom you share yours with." She spoke cryptically before things got crazy. The wind picked up and the woman's rocking chair became so fast it seemed inhuman.

"You must find de devil and kill him. Ghetto's soul is calling for you. Only you can save him and only he can save you!"

"You're crazy, lady, what the—"

"*Ya must go to my house, she's waiting for you, Heaven, she will tell ya how to find de devil, Jea!*" she told me as the wind picked up and the veil on her head began to whip to the west.

"*What the hell are you talking about, Genevieve! The devil? Ghetto is in A—*"

"*Go to Opelousas, she's waiting for ya, girl! De answers will be given.*"

"*The fuck! Who is she? Answer me damn it!*" I demanded and that's when my jaw dropped further, Genevieve began to laugh wickedly before—Whoosh! She exploded. There was a brief ball of fire before the flames became a flock of ravens. They screeched threateningly as they took flight, and that's when another gust of strong wind raged, parting the tall grass to my left.

"*Oh my!*" I began when I saw the scarecrow that was nailed to a tall wooden cross, crucified as it stared at me with bloodied, empty eye sockets.

"*Trust de cards!*" It screamed. "*Kill the lion! Beware of the wolf!*" It roared menacingly. "*666! Murder!*" he roared, and a rustle of grass to my right snatched my attention just in time to see a lion step from the tall grass. Its eyes glowed in the night and when it roared, the ground trembled! The beast flashed its sharp teeth and without further delay, it charged!

"Ahhh! Ahhhh!" I screamed at the top of my lungs as I shot up in bed, swinging wildly. "Nooo!" I cried as my eyes shot open to find dull sunshine pouring in through the cracked drapes of my window.

"Heaven? Girl!" Catrina's voice trembled.

"It was just a—" I was saying until my eyes found her. The expression of horror on her face made my skin crawl, and my eyes slowly fell to where hers focused. I screamed with all I had. I'd fallen asleep naked, and it was there-across the left side of my chest that the carved, Red Rum 666 had been reopened. It bled fresh and was the evidence that what had just happened was more than a dream.

"Heaven?" Catrina called to me, her voice shaky.

My eyes rose to recapture her. "Catrina, Genevieve is haunting me in my dreams, and she won't stop cutting me!" I cried as I trembled. Blood leaked down my left breast, cresting over my nipple before dripping onto my white sheets. "I have to go to Louisiana to see her."

***

The Florida Keys—
Cannon Royal Dr., Shark Key

9:10 a.m.

The sun seemed to have paused in the middle of the Heavens, showering the islands with its glare, and on the Shark Key Island, the four thousand five hundred and seventy-three square foot, aged Mediterranean oceanfront masterpiece sat beautifully upon five acres of lush gardens. The facade of the house was red clay designed with the entire front half of the house made of large plates of special glass. The large, red and white tiled, diamond-shaped drive hosted a beautiful water fountain with a naked woman of stone spitting water ten foot high, yet, though beautiful, it was the interior of the home that captured the heart. Peach and Strawberry decor; the ash gray marble floors breathed life into the opulence, but it was just up the butterfly staircase, where one could reach the second landing by either set of floating staircases, right down the owl's feathers gray carpeted hallway and just through the masters suite, is where a view of splendor could be beheld. Four men stood out on the ocean's view balcony; two heavily tattooed Salvadorians stood guard, brandishing assault rifles. Both men's faces promoted the MS 13 gang insignia. Fat Dawg stood in the middle of the gallery, looking unsure as he stared at the back of the man that stood at the railing of the balcony; gazing out at the rolling waves of the Gulf of Mexico. His skin was sun baked and his bald head glistened beneath the shine of the massive yellow ball that brightened the skies. The tropical themed short set he wore had pink flamingos imprint variously upon its linen material, and matched perfectly with the peach loafers on his feet. From behind a large pair of designer eyewear, he appreciated the view of aqua waters while he took slow pulls from a wood tipped *black and mild.*

"So—" He exhaled a slow cloud of cigar smoke. "You have a little problem back home, huh?" He chuckled. He was privy to all he was connected to and knew his cousin had been robbed numerous times for large quantities of Fentanyl, and even more; the man had allowed his enemies to terminate his people! Even his mother!

"I've told you that four times, Iceberg, damn, dawg, what else you—" Fat Dawg's words faltered when Iceberg spun on his heels.

"Nigga, don't ever use that *dawg* shit in my presence, *cuz*!" his temper flared, very much still in tune with his Crip roots. Fat Dawg glared, but didn't tempt fate.

"All I'm saying is these RNO niggas are savages that ain't respecting the game, Kin Folk, they"—

"Ain't no more respect in the game, Homie, everybody cut throat out there in them streets, and if you and your squad wasn't ready for the ways of the jungle, you shouldn't have put on no apes suits pretending to be King Kong when you're really just a curious George!" Iceberg's tone was deadly. Shaking his head in disappointment, he glared from behind the tinted lenses of the Dolce frames. "You let them niggas kill auntie Janice, and nigga, that brought tears to my mama's eyes." He paused to take a pull from his cigar. "And for that, I'm sending a squad to Dallas/Ft. Worth to eradicate them pussy ass RNO niggas!" he spat above a lungful of smoke. "You just go and sit tight and await the next shipment." Ice-Berg instructed before spreading his arms wide for a hug. Fat dawg exhaled the breath he'd been holding; he knew how irrational his cousin could get. Stepping into the embrace, he smiled.

"Preciate that, family, you and Kinfolk Nutz always come through," he acknowledged as they parted. "Where is my nigga anyway?" Fat Dawg asked. Iceberg's eyes lifted to stare at something behind the fat man.

"Cuz right there." He nodded and Fat Dawg turned in time to see a man clad in all-black designer apparel, with a black and white pair of Retros on his feet, wheel himself out onto the balcony. Nuts had grown dreadlocks, and somehow the man's drip gave the custom wheelchair he was confined to an air of playarism.

"Kinfolk!" Fat Dawg smiled while spreading his arms wide.

"What's crackin, loc?" Nuts smirked, and just as Fat Dawg stepped forward to embrace his beloved older cousin— *Boca!* The explosion of the gun was the last thing he heard as the ball of lead punched a small hole in the back of his dome, but knocked a sizable chunk out his forehead.

"Damn, Berg, nigga, fuck you couldn't wait till I was ready, cuz!" Nutz raged before using the back of his hand to wipe blood from his forehead. Iceberg laughed while tucking the .44 back onto his waist.

"My fault, lil' bruh, I was just tired of hearing that weak ass nigga's voice. He got our bloodline looking real weak up there on the soil," he revealed before pulling his iPhone from his pocket.

"So what's next?" Nutz asked as his vision fell to his slain relative.

"We're gonna send a death squad to the metroplex and step on them fuck boys bloodline!" Iceberg seethed before speed dialing a number.

"Who we sending?"

"You, and—" He paused when the call was answered.

***

Heaven

"What the hell do you mean he's gone! How? What are you saying, dude? That a man that was just in a coma a few hours ago just upped and walked out. Huh? Talk to me damn it!" I was beside myself with anger, and felt as if I was going mad! Doctor Thorton merely stared bewilderingly while his mouth moved as if he were trying to speak, but no words sufficed. Just a lot of confused head shakes, and before I could tame the urge— Smack! I'd slapped the fuck out of him. The nurse in the room moved as if she wanted to intervene, and I was happy to oblige.

"Bitch," I turned to her. "I'll drag your poor ass all around this room, try me!" I promised but Doctor Thorton stepped in between us.

"It's okay, Douglas, she's right." He calmed her while rubbing a hand over the spot I'd slapped. Looking to me, he again, shook his head sadly.

"I don't know what happened, Ms. Domingo. When the nurse came in to check his vitals, they found—" His words trailed off as all our eyes drifted to the empty bed Ghetto had spent the last year in. I turned and left the room before I caught a murder charge.

***

Brussels, Belgium

Belgium is a country in Northwest Europe and sits on the North Sea, and Brussels, its capital is a beautiful city, and has earned itself a moniker that makes it a paradise for crooks. La Forged identification card industry! Which is exactly why Papi, a black Greek, found himself sitting at the kitchen table of one of his many victims. Papi was a contract killer who had many homes around the world and in spite of his refined mannerisms and easy smile, the man was a spawn of the devil! He was a killer that was addicted to the taste of human flesh. A cannibal!

"You know something, Englishman?" He smiled before pushing his fork down into the squishy flesh of the boiled white and red veined egg on his plate. "I love the eyes so much because though people are taken with the expression of them being the windows to the soul, they couldn't be more wrong." He chuckled, his dialect impregnated with a strong combination of Greek to broken English. Dressed impeccably in a black dress shirt and charcoal hued slacks, the man looked as if he belonged on the cover of a GQ magazine. He was having an intellectual conversations with the man he'd been hired to expire. The black trench coat and leather gloves kept him warm for the chill of the snow covered night, but it was the thrill of the kill that heated the blood flowing to his dick. "The soul has no features, only a presence that's immured to the body." He smirked before using the steak knife to cut through the egg. "Very tough," he whispered while cutting a thick layer from it. "Though the eyeball appears to be soft, it's actually composed of dense and fibrous tissues. See—" he skewered the severed piece of flesh onto the end of the fork. "Every time one takes a look at something, an image is created on the retina of the eye—a light sensitive layer at the back of the orb. It has photoreceptors that send visual info to the brain via optic nerve." He smiled broadly before sucking the morsel off the fork and chewing. "Mmm!" he moaned appreciatively as his eyes drifted shut in relish, "Absolutely delectable!'" he gushed with a jab of his fork toward his captive. Across from him at the small dinette table, a short, potbellied man with a terribly receding hairline, sat bound to a chair. He stared with one eye, that was wide open in horror, but his other socket was an empty red mass of bloodied tissues. Papi had professionally popped the eye out and it was the very egg-like cuisine he was partaking of. A thick trail of blood oozed from the empty right socket and as he took in Papi with his remaining orb, the horrified man registered from Papi's expression, that the killer was an aphrodisiac for the taste of fear. Papi drank in the man's trepidation with apt fascination, "I'm sure you're not interested with the functions of something so trivial, so—" he began before sucking eye juice from the fork.

"Let me ask again." He smiled wickedly. The captive's name was Scott Wilmes, better known as The Forger to the underworld of crime, and it was said that he was one of the best in all of Europe.

Not only the Belgian police, but authorities all over Europe was privy to his unlawful expertise but the man was as slippery as sewage scum. Yet at the moment, Scott Wilmes didn't feel so elusive. He perspired heavily as he trembled in his seat, eyeing the strange man before him with dark skin that contradicted his Greek roots, and long curly hair that was passed down from his Portuguese mother. The man was a paragon.

"Where's the copies of the passports you forged for Donte Frey?" Papi's tone was neutral.

"I-I've told you, Monsieur, I know nothing of the name you speak of. I'm a poor bartender at a dive bar just off the Rue Neuve." Just then the ringing of Papi's cellular sounded. The killer held up a finger; he'd been expecting the call.

"One second please." He paused before retrieving the advice from the pocket of his long coat. "Yes?" He answered and from there he listened as Iceberg called upon his services. After he was finished, Papi disconnected the call without refusing or confirming if he'd take the job. All that solicited his services knew that if he didn't want the job, he'd told them they'd had the wrong number before hanging up, but a silent disconnection meant he'd appear like an apparition in the night. Replacing the phone he'd soon dispose of, Papi's dark eyes found his victim.

"You're lying Scott, but," he smirked before sliding a silencer-equipped .357 Sig auto from inside his coat. "At least you, the devil, and the grave will be the only ones to have the secret," he whispered while taking aim.

"Nooo! Please!" Scott's screams echoed throughout the house before—*Peww!* The first slug punched through his Adams apple. Blood shot forth as Papi stepped around the table, his eyes radiating lust as he basked within the heat of the kill. The fear of death reflected from Scott's only eye as blood squirt from his throat.

"Bonjour, Monsieur," Papi bade him farewell. *Pewww!* The second slug rocked Scott's head back, knocking a splash of brain matter out the back of his cranium. Papi leaned down and pressed his lips against the neat little hole in the center of the man's forehead and planted a soft kiss there before turning to depart. Yet, he paused by his breakfast, considering it. He lifted the remaining piece of flesh and popped it into his mouth, and chewing feverishly, he could already feel the power of its sight merge with the hundreds of others he'd fed upon. *The vision of his future!*

Chapter Fourteen

Children's Laughter

Heaven

I'd arrived at the old house in Opelousas, Louisiana, at a quarter to midnight, and just as before, I could feel the dark energy surrounding it. I sat inside that car for close to thirty minutes, gripping the steering wheel for dear life. *What if I'm losing my mind! What am I supposed to say to the woman? Hey, I've been having nightmares of you, and each time I've awakened with mysterious cuts on my body?* I thought before absently rubbing a hand over the bandage covering the carvings on my chest. The night was alive with nature, the chirping of crickets filled the air, and I could've sworn that I'd heard an animal roar in the distance. The woods surrounding the aged house were dark and gave off the impression that they were breathing! My skin crawled as I gazed out into the darkness. The weeping willow trees with these cascading branches and dripping leaves felt as if they concealed a watching pair of eyes. I took my purse from the passenger seat, taking a bit of comfort from the pistol inside. "Forgive me, baby," I whispered. I know I'd promised Ghetto I'd lay my gun down but too much had happened and it was time to get back in the field. Slipping from the car, I hurriedly secured it before racing up the shaky steps leading up the porch. The house was so old that it didn't have a doorbell, so I knocked before glancing behind me. I swear I felt someone or *something* watching me! I knocked a bit harder before sticking my hand down into my Chanel bag and grabbing the handle of the Bersa Thunder .380 I'd just bought. *Lion, tiger, or bear, they'll be dead before sunrise if they try me! I ain't in the mood!* I thought just as the door cracked open, and to my surprise, it wasn't Genevieve. I frowned at the older woman's shock of snow-white hair, and her green eyes ran deep with dark secrets.

"I-I'm looking for Genevieve, is she home?" I asked, and the woman gave me a peculiar look, studying me as if she wanted to know if I was joking. She drew the door open and warmth flowed out the dark house. She wore an old-fashioned dress, with a brown shawl draped over her shoulders, and for some strange reason, my body seemed to just relax in her presence. I mean, it felt as if she were hypnotizing me and putting me in a soft trance-like relaxation! The lady smiled sadly and then, she rocked my world!

"I'm sorry, suga, my sista Genevieve has passed onto the next plain, yea, she's been dead for a year and a half, chile, but—" Her dialect was heavy with Louisiana's Cajun sound, and as my jaw dropped in shock, she stepped to the side. "Come on in, Heaven, I've been waiting on you."

***

Empress

Stick Talk was at the club doing his do, and I was hurriedly packing my bags. *Time for part two of my plan!* I thought. I'd forwarded the entire conversation between Stick Talk and Ghetto, the one front the night Stick Talk's dumb ass killed his man. I sent it to the DM of the bitch Red Diamond; sis is a savage and I knew she'd do what's necessary! Stick Talk was a lame; he was so pussy whooped that he never realized that I never gave a damn about him. Yes! That dick was good, but my heart belongs to Heaven's skank ass, but now that her days were numbered, it was time to make waves somewhere far away from the metroplex. I was thinking maybe a bitch like me could really get paid up there with them get money niggas in New York? Cali? Maybe even Miami? I didn't know, but I could figure that part out later! At that moment, I was rushing through our new apartment and heading to the bed we shared. As soon as I reached it, I fell to my knees and reached under the box spring. "Come on!" I mumbled while feeling around for what I'd hidden there. *Bingo!* I thought when I felt it. I yanked the tape away before pulling the first package down; the K-Pack of pills were just as pretty as they were the night we'd taken down Stick Talk and Ghetto for them. Before long, I'd had all six packs of a thousand pills stacked atop each other and when I went climbing back to my feet, I froze as the cold kiss of a barrel pecked the back of my neck. My eyes grew wide as I gazed straight ahead, my mind racing beyond the speed limit as I tried to envision the face of the monster that held my life in his hands. He chuckled and I knew my tombstone was guaranteed!

"So, now it makes sense!" Stick Talk growled, his eyes no doubt falling to the packs of pills me and my girls had taken him for. "Heaven, you, and who was the third one? Huh? Catrina's bitch ass? Egypt's hatin' ass, huh, bitch!" He'd shouted so loud I trembled; there was no making it out of this one. The evidence was the truth that would set me free! Set *my spirit* free from my body, that is.

"Stick Tal—" I began.

Boca!

***

Heaven

The house was pitch-black, save for the flickering flame of the candle that sat in the middle of the dining room table we sat at. She'd introduced herself as Erzulie Bousard, Genevieve's eldest sister, and the woman had a mysterious air about her that I couldn't quite put my finger on. "The spirits told me you'd come, chile," she smiled from across the table and a chill ran down my spine.

"Spirits?"

"Ummm," she nodded. Her skin was the color of oats and shadowed by the darkness, it almost glowed. "The spirit tells me plenty, daughter, even that you have the power of providence; Is that so chile?" Her old voice was lightly raspy, like an old slave grandmother. I glanced around, and for the fifth time since I'd entered that house, my eyes froze on the large china cabinet filled with black slave figurines. Some had hardened faces from toil, others danced, and others were naked, whip marks tainting the small bodies.

"I've been having nightmares," I revealed before slowly returning my eyes to her. Erzulie merely studied me, the shadow of the dancing flame flickering across her face as she awaited me to continue. "Of Genevieve, she keeps cutting me!" I spat. Erzulie nodded before slipping from her seat and making her way over to the China cabinet. Opening it, she pulled something out as she studded the dolls inside.

"In these dreams," she spoke over her shoulder, "does she seem to warn you of any danger?" She asked, and I flinched. How'd she know that!

"Yes."

Erzulie nodded her understanding before making her way back to her seat, and in her hand she held a velvet pouch. My eyes fell to it suspiciously as she took her seat.

"When she cuts you, she's using your blood to pay the gatekeeper to allow her to enter this realm and warn you. She's—"

"But," I cut her off before reaching down and pulling my shirt over my head, "what the hell kinda warning is that!" I didn't mean to yell while jabbing a finger at the strange scar, but I wasn't about to let her downplay the crazy shit I'd been going through. *To pay the gatekeeper! Really though?* I slowly peeled the bandage away to reveal the Red Rum-666 and Erzulie flinched. I saw fear blossom within her gaze but disappear as quickly as it arrived. "What does this mean!" I demanded.

Erzulie's eyes fell to the bag as she pulled a tiny string holding it closed. "It means that for you to obtain your greatest wish, you will have to murder someone and send their souls to the devil or—" her voice trailed off as she poured the contents of the bag onto the table. Whatever it was, was hard and numerous, and beneath the candle's glow, I recognized them! Bones!

"Or what!" I spat when my eyes lifted to recapture her.

"Or Ghetto dies and you'll follow with your son behind him." She smiled sadly as my mouth fell open in shock. "You've been marked by the sign of the beast."

"What!" I began, but Erzulie's eyes drifted shut.

"I understand you have questions?" she cut me off as she scooped the bones into her hands. My mouth moved, but no words came out. "The bones know the answers," She whispered before she shook them in her cupped hands. *Go to Opelousas, the answers will be given. She is waiting on you, gal!* Genevieve's words from the dream played within my mind. I frowned skeptically, surely this old hag and the rolling of chicken bones couldn't give me the answers to all my problems? Yet, what else did I have? So, I tried it.

"Who killed—" I bit my lip. "I mean, who tried to kill Ghetto? What does Genevieve mean by the lion? The wolf? How can I kill the devil! I—"

"Shiish," she shushed me and cast the bones onto the table. The strange pieces tumbled in many directions and as they came to a stop, things got weird! "You must not fear, gal, don't move! Don't fear the spirits!" The woman moaned eerily.

"Shiish!" something other than me or Erzulie whispered as a cold breeze drifted through the room out of nowhere. The flame of the candle swayed dangerously sideways as if it would fall off its wick.

"Murder," something dark whispered.

"Betrayal!

"Demon est Deus inversus!"

"The Devil is God invented!

"Queen Marie Laveau-awaketh!

"Blood."

"Thirst!" Numerous voices merged into growls as Erzulie's lids fluttered open to reveal the whites of her eyes. The woman's hands lifted and she held them poised over the scattered bones.

"The lion," she whispered. "Is a two-headed dragon, man, and woman! You will know them only when they're together. "That's who shot Ghetto." Her words came out in a hiss and as if shit wasn't scary enough, there came a voice—

"Darkness!" a demonic voice spat, and the flame of the candle blinked out. A snaking tendril of smoke rose from the scorched wick, and though the room was bathed in darkness, from the soft glow of the moon that oozed through the living room window, Erzulie's light skin glowed. A thin layer of sweat glistened on her face as her eyes continued to fade to the back of her head as her hovering hands began to tremble.

"The wolf is a lover in your world that seeks to bring destruction."

"*Kill him!*"

"*Kill the wolf!*" a child's voice cried in fear. My heart pounded against my chest as I sat there in shock. Erzulies hands shook terribly.

"De gates has been open, gal, and the father of the dark has risen. You can only kill him by killing yourself!" she hissed.

"Kill yourself!" the voice of a little girl cried, I frowned.

"Don't fear death, gal, it is only the highest elevation of life! Live!" Erzulies cried loudly.

"Live!" the sound of a little boy shouted. I shot from my seat so fast that the chair fell over, and all I could think of was to get to my gun.

Boooom! The sound of thunder roared across the sky just before a flash of lightning flashed and briefly illuminated the room.

"Lady?" I began just as a downpour of rain fell upon the house as if a lake had opened up in the Heavens. Erzulie's eyes rolled back to the front and focused on me. The woman looked haunted!

"The smell of betrayal is upon your flesh, gal, you've broken your faithfulness to de boy."

Though her words were not accusative, I stumbled backwards in shock—

Hell she know that? I wondered. I shook my head in amazement before turning and rushing for my purse; I was getting the hell out of there. Damn my shirt and all! As soon as I reached my bag, I snatched it up and was at the door in record time. I pushed it open and rushed out onto the sagging porch only to step into a raging downpour! There's nothing like a storm in Louisiana, they're like God turning his rage on that state with all the water he has. The rain was falling so hard that I could barely see, it was maddening! I stared in horror as the sharp pellets of rain poured, and a warm fog lifted from the earth. There was no way I could drive through it. Then I frowned. I blinked rapidly as the rain began to soak through my clothes, but I was still frozen. Genevieve had appeared out in the storm, the black veil and dress waterlogged as she stared at me. It was hard to see her but the strange sound of her cackle was unmistakable. My mouth fell open as I took a step back, my hand instinctively going for the gun in my bag.

"Come on back in, gal, let the Lord have his way with the earth, Jea, there won't be any driving through his tears." Erzulie's voice, so close, made me flinch before I spun to face her. She'd moved and was now sitting in Genevieve's old rocking chair, with the shawl pulled tight around her shoulders. She'd relit the candle and though the sky's gray hue had darkened to a dusk's greeting, the dark energy felt more powerful than ever.

"Genevieve," I whispered before glazing back, only to find that the old woman had vanished! This wasn't a dream though, I'd actually seen her! Erzulie Bousard began to hum some kind of old slave hymn. "Close de door, Jea, Genevive is a protector. Now, ya can use Ghetto's old room to rest, ya look tired," she said before returning to her hum, but I'd be damned if I fell asleep in that house. I'd shoot her and every spirit floating around there before I did.

***

2 a.m.

Fort Worth, Texas

The night was cool in the city and at that hour of the night, Brandon Tyler was in a foul mood! He eased his car into the parking space in Walmart's large parking lot before killing his engine. "this is some bullshit man!" he spat before exiting the car and hopping into the back seat of the black SUV parked next to it. "Man, this couldn't wait until the morning?"

He wasted no time once the door was closed to the chill.

243

"Well, happy to see you too, sweet cakes." The man in the passenger seat chuckled with his sarcasm. The man in the driver's seat smiled as he met Brandon's agitated gaze in the rearview mirror.

"It's fucking two o'clock in the morning, Crosby, and you dickheads wake me and my wife out of our sleep!" Brandon huffed.

"The higher-ups want to know your progress in the case, we're only minions, Tyler," Agent Crosby responded.

Brandon exhaled a strong whoosh of breath before rubbing a hand over his stubbed chin. "Man, I'm close. Heaven is getting more comfortable with me," he revealed.

Agent Joseph shrugged. "And?"

"And I need a little more time in the field with her."

"Bullshit!" Joseph exploded. "It's been eight months, agent, eight months since you went under deep cover as esquire Brandon Tyler. Yet, I'm starting to think you're losing yourself to your character."

"I don't give two fucks what you believe, Joseph, you're not my superior!" Brandon had had enough. "I'll talk to Bryant myself," He spat before pushing the truck door open.

"Tyler," Crosby called to him. Brandon glared, and the other agent held up a calming hand. "We're all a bit up tight here, but we're all on the same team. All my partner is saying is, we know the psychological effects going under deep cover can have on a person, no matter how strong you may be."

"Well, that's not *me*!" Brandon cut him off. Their eyes danced in the rearview mirror as Crosby remembered the day their superior brought in the younger agent in the guise of Lawyer Brandon Tyler. After he'd whisked Heaven out of that interrogation room, Crosby had turned to their senior officer only to be told they'd brought Brandon in to kill two birds with one stone.

Crosby nodded, "We need to find where the guy, Ghetto, is hiding and you have to get Heaven to admit to her deadly team."

"I know what my job is, Crosby." Brandon was irate and craved nothing more than his California king. He pushed the door open and slid a foot out the truck before Joseph called to him; Brandon blew a hot breath before turning to glare at him.

"What's up, man?"

"No sex, with the target, that will shoot the case to shit."

"As I said," Brandon spoke over his shoulder before slipping from the truck. "I know my job. Night, fellas." He wished them well before hopping back into his car. The SUV departed first, and Brandon Tyler slammed a fist into the steering wheel before resting his head against it. "Damn," he declared. He knew he'd become a victim of his make believe character, and though in the beginning he was determined to take Heaven and Ghetto down, somewhere along the blurred line, he'd not only made love to the woman he was ordered to build a case against, but he'd also been an adulterer in the process. *He was falling for the black widow!* He thought before heading back home to his wife.

***

The house was dark and as quiet as a grave. The red candle in the center of the table had melted down to a hot mountain and just as the flame burnt down the wick, and licked at the liquid wax, it extinguished. A tendril of black smoke snaked into the air and from somewhere deep in that house, that strange circus-like zydeco music began to play softly. The rain had slowed down to a soft drizzle and as the pitter patter of its drops intermingled with the strange music, the unbelievable happened. Tiny laughter came from the darkness-HEHEHe! Lightning flashed just as the glass door of the china cabinet creaked open and something leapt down from one of the many shelves. The dark-skinned nappy headed slave doll's eyes were as black as coals as it studied the room. The tiny being wore slave clothes made from a rough material, and though the dingy pants he wore flooded, the barefoot thing had one thing on his mind—revenge! In seconds, at least sixty little evil dolls were standing on the china cabinet's edge. Some held pitch forks, others gripped field hoes, and some even clutched tiny, but razor-sharp machetes. All the tools they'd used in the hot fields they'd worked for massa, were now tools to commit murder! The lead and first doll to come to life began to whisper in a tiny voice that couldn't be heard by human ears, but his minions understood completely! Murder! "Heheheehe!" They laughed giddily before one by one leaping from the ledge onto the ground.

The sound of soft rain beat against the window as the strange music played in the distance, and when a light-skinned slave woman stepped forward, face hardened by toil, she screamed a war cry! Pointing a sharp little butcher's knife toward the back of the house, she was the signal to charge, and all sixty little dolls took off into the night!

***

Erzulie had seen it all from her rocking chair. She hadn't moved since earlier that night, and as she he hummed along with her zydeco, rocking softly in the chair, she stared into the darkness. "De spirits test the fate of the gifted, chile, from the dark waters of the deep, the spirit queen hungers," she whispered before her eyes fell to the ragdoll she'd filled with a scoop of the earth from Marie Laveau's grave at St. Louis Cemetery number one.

***

Heaven

"Wake up, gal, evil is in de house!" The harsh whisper penetrated my sleep and my eyes shot open as wide as a bug's. Genevieve! I registered the voice. I lay still, eyes focused on the ceiling as I listened to the soft fall of the rain. Was I dreaming? Did I really hear her? I wondered while waiting to see if she'd say more. Nothing! I shook my head in disgust. "This has to stop!" I whispered before cursing myself for falling asleep in the creepy ass house. Sliding my gun from beside me, I sat up in the bed. "I need to get—
"

HEHEHEEHEEH! What sounded like tiny children's laughter cut me off. I frowned at the evilest child's laugh I've ever heard! I slid one foot onto the floor, I'd slept in my clothes.

"Heaven is hell" a child's voice whispered. *Fuck!*

"Hell is heaven!" a little girl cried.

"HEHEEHEH!" A multitude of laughter caused my blood to freeze in my veins.

"Who's there!" I shouted.

"HEHEHEEHEH!"

"HEHEHEHEEHEH!" The strange laughter filled the room. I hurriedly scurried out of the bed and just as I took a step, something stabbed me in the leg!

"Shit!" I cried and before I could understand what the hell was transpiring, they were upon me! "AHHHHHH!" I cried out at the top of my lungs just as I was snatched to the floor!

To Be Continued...
Heaven Got a Ghetto 3
Coming Soon

Renta

Lock Down Publications and Ca$h Presents assisted
publishing packages.

BASIC PACKAGE $499
Editing
Cover Design
Formatting

UPGRADED PACKAGE $800
Typing
Editing
Cover Design
Formatting

ADVANCE PACKAGE $1,200
Typing
Editing
Cover Design
Formatting
Copyright registration
Proofreading
Upload book to Amazon

LDP SUPREME PACKAGE $1,500
Typing
Editing
Cover Design
Formatting
Copyright registration
Proofreading
Set up Amazon account
Upload book to Amazon
Advertise on LDP Amazon and Facebook page

***Other services available upon request. Additional charges may apply
Lock Down Publications
P.O. Box 944
Stockbridge, GA 30281-9998
Phone # 470 303-9761

Submission Guideline

Submit the first three chapters of your completed manuscript to ldpsubmissions@gmail.com, subject line: Your book's title. The manuscript must be in a .doc file and sent as an attachment. Document should be in Times New Roman, double spaced and in size 12 font. Also, provide your synopsis and full contact information. If sending multiple submissions, they must each be in a separate email.

Have a story but no way to send it electronically? You can still submit to LDP/Ca$h Presents. Send in the first three chapters, written or typed, of your completed manuscript to:

LDP: Submissions Dept
Po Box 944
Stockbridge, Ga 30281

DO NOT send original manuscript. Must be a duplicate.

Provide your synopsis and a cover letter containing your full contact information.

Thanks for considering LDP and Ca$h Presents.

NEW RELEASES

THE COCAINE PRINCESS 7 by KING RIO

GRIMEY WAYS 3 by RAY VINCI

HEAVEN GOT A GHETTO by RENTA

Renta

STRAIGHT BEAST MODE III
De'Kari
KINGPIN KILLAZ IV
STREET KINGS III
PAID IN BLOOD III
CARTEL KILLAZ IV
DOPE GODS III
Hood Rich
SINS OF A HUSTLA II
ASAD
YAYO V
Bred In The Game 2
S. Allen
THE STREETS WILL TALK II
By Yolanda Moore
SON OF A DOPE FIEND III
HEAVEN GOT A GHETTO III
SKI MASK MONEY II
By Renta
LOYALTY AIN'T PROMISED III
By Keith Williams
I'M NOTHING WITHOUT HIS LOVE II
SINS OF A THUG II
TO THE THUG I LOVED BEFORE II
IN A HUSTLER I TRUST II
By Monet Dragun
QUIET MONEY IV
EXTENDED CLIP III
THUG LIFE IV
By **Trai'Quan**

THE STREETS MADE ME IV

By **Larry D. Wright**

IF YOU CROSS ME ONCE III

ANGEL V

By **Anthony Fields**

THE STREETS WILL NEVER CLOSE IV

By **K'ajji**

HARD AND RUTHLESS III

KILLA KOUNTY IV

By **Khufu**

MONEY GAME III

By **Smoove Dolla**

JACK BOYS VS DOPE BOYS IV

A GANGSTA'S QUR'AN V

COKE GIRLZ II

COKE BOYS II

LIFE OF A SAVAGE V

CHI'RAQ GANGSTAS V

SOSA GANG II

BRONX SAVAGES II

BODYMORE KINGPINS II

By **Romell Tukes**

MURDA WAS THE CASE III

Elijah R. Freeman

AN UNFORESEEN LOVE IV

BABY, I'M WINTERTIME COLD III

By **Meesha**

QUEEN OF THE ZOO III

By **Black Migo**

CONFESSIONS OF A JACKBOY III

By Nicholas Lock

KING KILLA II

By Vincent "Vitto" Holloway

BETRAYAL OF A THUG III

By Fre$h

THE MURDER QUEENS III

By Michael Gallon

THE BIRTH OF A GANGSTER III

By Delmont Player

TREAL LOVE II

By Le'Monica Jackson

FOR THE LOVE OF BLOOD III

By Jamel Mitchell

RAN OFF ON DA PLUG II

By Paper Boi Rari

HOOD CONSIGLIERE III

By Keese

PRETTY GIRLS DO NASTY THINGS II

By Nicole Goosby

PROTÉGÉ OF A LEGEND III

LOVE IN THE TRENCHES II

By Corey Robinson

IT'S JUST ME AND YOU II

By Ah'Million

BORN IN THE GRAVE III

By Self Made Tay

FOREVER GANGSTA III

By Adrian Dulan

GORILLAZ IN THE TRENCHES II

Renta

By SayNoMore

THE COCAINE PRINCESS VIII

By King Rio

CRIME BOSS II

Playa Ray

LOYALTY IS EVERYTHING III

Molotti

HERE TODAY GONE TOMORROW II

By Fly Rock

REAL G'S MOVE IN SILENCE II

By Von Diesel

GRIMEY WAYS IV

By Ray Vinci

Available Now

RESTRAINING ORDER **I & II**

By **CA$H & Coffee**

LOVE KNOWS NO BOUNDARIES **I II & III**

By **Coffee**

RAISED AS A GOON I, II, III & IV

BRED BY THE SLUMS I, II, III

BLAST FOR ME I & II

ROTTEN TO THE CORE I II III

A BRONX TALE I, II, III

DUFFLE BAG CARTEL I II III IV V VI

HEARTLESS GOON I II III IV V

A SAVAGE DOPEBOY I II

DRUG LORDS I II III

CUTTHROAT MAFIA I II

KING OF THE TRENCHES

By **Ghost**

LAY IT DOWN **I & II**

LAST OF A DYING BREED I II

BLOOD STAINS OF A SHOTTA I & II III

By **Jamaica**

LOYAL TO THE GAME I II III

LIFE OF SIN I, II III

By **TJ & Jelissa**

BLOODY COMMAS I & II

SKI MASK CARTEL I II & III

KING OF NEW YORK I II,III IV V

RISE TO POWER I II III

COKE KINGS I II III IV V

BORN HEARTLESS I II III IV

KING OF THE TRAP I II

By **T.J. Edwards**

IF LOVING HIM IS WRONG…I & II

LOVE ME EVEN WHEN IT HURTS I II III

By **Jelissa**

WHEN THE STREETS CLAP BACK I & II III

THE HEART OF A SAVAGE I II III IV

MONEY MAFIA I II

LOYAL TO THE SOIL I II III

By **Jibril Williams**

A DISTINGUISHED THUG STOLE MY HEART I II & III

Renta

LOVE SHOULDN'T HURT I II III IV
RENEGADE BOYS I II III IV
PAID IN KARMA I II III
SAVAGE STORMS I II III
AN UNFORESEEN LOVE I II III
BABY, I'M WINTERTIME COLD I II
By **Meesha**
A GANGSTER'S CODE I &, II III
A GANGSTER'S SYN I II III
THE SAVAGE LIFE I II III
CHAINED TO THE STREETS I II III
BLOOD ON THE MONEY I II III
A GANGSTA'S PAIN I II III
By J-Blunt
PUSH IT TO THE LIMIT
By **Bre' Hayes**
BLOOD OF A BOSS **I, II, III, IV, V**
SHADOWS OF THE GAME
TRAP BASTARD
By **Askari**
THE STREETS BLEED MURDER **I, II & III**
THE HEART OF A GANGSTA I II& III
By **Jerry Jackson**
CUM FOR ME I II III IV V VI VII VIII
An **LDP Erotica Collaboration**
BRIDE OF A HUSTLA **I II & II**
THE FETTI GIRLS **I, II& III**
CORRUPTED BY A GANGSTA I, II III, IV
BLINDED BY HIS LOVE
THE PRICE YOU PAY FOR LOVE I, II ,III

Heaven Got a Ghetto 2

DOPE GIRL MAGIC I II III
By **Destiny Skai**
WHEN A GOOD GIRL GOES BAD
By **Adrienne**
THE COST OF LOYALTY I II III
By Kweli
A GANGSTER'S REVENGE **I II III & IV**
THE BOSS MAN'S DAUGHTERS I II III IV V
A SAVAGE LOVE **I & II**
BAE BELONGS TO ME I II
A HUSTLER'S DECEIT I, II, III
WHAT BAD BITCHES DO I, II, III
SOUL OF A MONSTER I II III
KILL ZONE
A DOPE BOY'S QUEEN I II III
TIL DEATH
By **Aryanna**
A KINGPIN'S AMBITON
A KINGPIN'S AMBITION **II**
I MURDER FOR THE DOUGH
By **Ambitious**
TRUE SAVAGE I II III IV V VI VII
DOPE BOY MAGIC I, II, III
MIDNIGHT CARTEL I II III
CITY OF KINGZ I II
NIGHTMARE ON SILENT AVE
THE PLUG OF LIL MEXICO II
CLASSIC CITY
By **Chris Green**
A DOPEBOY'S PRAYER

Renta

By **Eddie "Wolf" Lee**

THE KING CARTEL **I, II & III**

By **Frank Gresham**

THESE NIGGAS AIN'T LOYAL **I, II & III**

By **Nikki Tee**

GANGSTA SHYT **I II &III**

By **CATO**

THE ULTIMATE BETRAYAL

By **Phoenix**

BOSS'N UP **I , II & III**

By **Royal Nicole**

I LOVE YOU TO DEATH

By **Destiny J**

I RIDE FOR MY HITTA

I STILL RIDE FOR MY HITTA

By **Misty Holt**

LOVE & CHASIN' PAPER

By **Qay Crockett**

TO DIE IN VAIN

SINS OF A HUSTLA

By **ASAD**

BROOKLYN HUSTLAZ

By **Boogsy Morina**

BROOKLYN ON LOCK I & II

By **Sonovia**

GANGSTA CITY

By **Teddy Duke**

A DRUG KING AND HIS DIAMOND I & II III

A DOPEMAN'S RICHES

HER MAN, MINE'S TOO I, II

Heaven Got a Ghetto 2

CASH MONEY HO'S

THE WIFEY I USED TO BE I II

PRETTY GIRLS DO NASTY THINGS

By Nicole Goosby

TRAPHOUSE KING **I II & III**

KINGPIN KILLAZ I II III

STREET KINGS I II

PAID IN BLOOD **I II**

CARTEL KILLAZ I II III

DOPE GODS I II

By **Hood Rich**

LIPSTICK KILLAH **I, II, III**

CRIME OF PASSION I II & III

FRIEND OR FOE I II III

By **Mimi**

STEADY MOBBN' **I, II, III**

THE STREETS STAINED MY SOUL I II III

By **Marcellus Allen**

WHO SHOT YA **I, II, III**

SON OF A DOPE FIEND I II

HEAVEN GOT A GHETTO I II

SKI MASK MONEY

Renta

GORILLAZ IN THE BAY **I II III IV**

TEARS OF A GANGSTA I II

3X KRAZY I II

STRAIGHT BEAST MODE I II

DE'KARI

TRIGGADALE I II III

MURDAROBER WAS THE CASE I II

261

Renta

BRED IN THE GAME

By S. Allen

TRAP GOD I II III

RICH $AVAGE I II III

MONEY IN THE GRAVE I II III

By Martell Troublesome Bolden

FOREVER GANGSTA I II

GLOCKS ON SATIN SHEETS I II

By Adrian Dulan

TOE TAGZ I II III IV

LEVELS TO THIS SHYT I II

IT'S JUST ME AND YOU

By Ah'Million

KINGPIN DREAMS I II III

RAN OFF ON DA PLUG

By Paper Boi Rari

CONFESSIONS OF A GANGSTA I II III IV

CONFESSIONS OF A JACKBOY I II

By Nicholas Lock

I'M NOTHING WITHOUT HIS LOVE

SINS OF A THUG

TO THE THUG I LOVED BEFORE

A GANGSTA SAVED XMAS

IN A HUSTLER I TRUST

By Monet Dragun

CAUGHT UP IN THE LIFE I II III

THE STREETS NEVER LET GO I II III

By Robert Baptiste

NEW TO THE GAME I II III

MONEY, MURDER & MEMORIES I II III

Renta

Heaven Got a Ghetto 2

By **Anthony Fields**
THE LIFE OF A HOOD STAR
By **Ca$h & Rashia Wilson**
THE STREETS WILL NEVER CLOSE I II III
By **K'ajji**
CREAM I II III
THE STREETS WILL TALK
By **Yolanda Moore**
NIGHTMARES OF A HUSTLA I II III
By **King Dream**
CONCRETE KILLA I II III
VICIOUS LOYALTY I II III
By **Kingpen**
HARD AND RUTHLESS I II
MOB TOWN 251
THE BILLIONAIRE BENTLEYS I II III
REAL G'S MOVE IN SILENCE
By **Von Diesel**
GHOST MOB
Stilloan Robinson
MOB TIES I II III IV V VI
SOUL OF A HUSTLER, HEART OF A KILLER I II
GORILLAZ IN THE TRENCHES
By **SayNoMore**
BODYMORE MURDERLAND I II III
THE BIRTH OF A GANGSTER I II
By **Delmont Player**
FOR THE LOVE OF A BOSS
By **C. D. Blue**
MOBBED UP I II III IV

265

THE BRICK MAN I II III IV V
THE COCAINE PRINCESS I II III IV V VI VII
By King Rio
KILLA KOUNTY I II III IV
By Khufu
MONEY GAME I II
By Smoove Dolla
A GANGSTA'S KARMA I II III
By FLAME
KING OF THE TRENCHES I II III
by **GHOST & TRANAY ADAMS**
QUEEN OF THE ZOO I II
By **Black Migo**
GRIMEY WAYS I II III
By Ray Vinci
XMAS WITH AN ATL SHOOTER
By Ca$h & Destiny Skai
KING KILLA
By Vincent "Vitto" Holloway
BETRAYAL OF A THUG I II
By Fre$h
THE MURDER QUEENS I II
By Michael Gallon
TREAL LOVE
By Le'Monica Jackson
FOR THE LOVE OF BLOOD I II
By Jamel Mitchell
HOOD CONSIGLIERE I II
By Keese
PROTÉGÉ OF A LEGEND I II

LOVE IN THE TRENCHES

By Corey Robinson

BORN IN THE GRAVE I II

By Self Made Tay

MOAN IN MY MOUTH

By XTASY

TORN BETWEEN A GANGSTER AND A GENTLEMAN

By J-BLUNT & Miss Kim

LOYALTY IS EVERYTHING I II

Molotti

HERE TODAY GONE TOMORROW

By Fly Rock

PILLOW PRINCESS

By S. Hawkins

<u>BOOKS BY LDP'S CEO, CA$H</u>

TRUST IN NO MAN

TRUST IN NO MAN 2

TRUST IN NO MAN 3

BONDED BY BLOOD

SHORTY GOT A THUG

THUGS CRY

THUGS CRY 2

THUGS CRY 3

TRUST NO BITCH

TRUST NO BITCH 2

TRUST NO BITCH 3

TIL MY CASKET DROPS

RESTRAINING ORDER

RESTRAINING ORDER 2

IN LOVE WITH A CONVICT

LIFE OF A HOOD STAR

XMAS WITH AN ATL SHOOTER

Heaven Got a Ghetto 2

www.ingramcontent.com/pod-product-compliance
Lightning Source LLC
Chambersburg PA
CBHW071131260626
47162CB00003B/752